THE GREAT JEW PIRATE

DAVID NOBYL

THE GREAT JEW PIRATE

Copyright © 2025 by David Nobyl

All rights reserved. No part of this book may be reproduced, stored in a retrieval system, or transmitted in any form or by any means—electronic, mechanical, photocopying, recording, or otherwise—without prior written permission of the publisher, except in the case of brief quotations embodied in critical articles or reviews.

First Edition: 2025

Published by Nobyl Books Publishing [CA, USA]

ISBN: 979-8-26-228958-5

This is a work of fiction. Names, characters, places, and incidents are either products of the author's imagination or used fictitiously. Any resemblance to actual persons, living or dead, or actual events is purely coincidental.

Cover design by David Nobyl

Interior design by Candice Nobyl

Printed in the United States of America

10 9 8 7 6 5 4 3 2 1

Past

Chapter Two begins here.

1504: Sinan and Dr. Badoz diagnose the dying Queen Isabella.

1506: Sinan and his companions are captured by Diego and taken aboard the slave ship, The Cavalleria.

1514: Sinan becomes Chief Physician of Djerba. He and Rahel get married.

1492: Ferdinand & Isabella order Jews to convert, flee, or die.

Dr. Badoz is tortured in Toledo. Sinan learns his fate from the mystical dybbuk, Zequiel.

1507: Barbarossa brothers free Sinan, Rahel, and Dr. Badoz. In Djerba, Sinan cares for Rahel.

Present

1515: Andrea Doria attacks Tunis, capturing Rahel and gravely injuring Sinan.

Chapter One begins here

Sinan and Sayyida free enslaved children on the Isle Ischia

Sinan retrieves the Sword of Solomon from the Green Grotto.

The Pirate Queen, Sayyida Al-Hurra, finds Sinan as a drifter on the open sea.

Sinan fights in the a gladiator arena against the Spirit of Vengeance.

The Spanish Inquisition invades North Africa, and Sinan unleashes the power of the Sword of Solomon.

Dedicated to the two most important women in my life. To my wife, Candice, and my mom.

Prelude

The year 1492 is remembered in schoolbooks for Christopher Columbus and the "discovery" of a New World. Yet for the Jews of Spain, it was remembered as the end of their world.

For centuries, Jewish life in Iberia had flourished despite hardship. Jews served as physicians, scholars, poets, and financiers—indispensable to kings who borrowed their wealth and their counsel. King Ferdinand of Aragon and Queen Isabella of Castile were no exception. To finance their long war to reclaim Granada, the last Muslim stronghold, they borrowed heavily from Jewish bankers. When victory finally came, so too did betrayal. With zealotry inflamed and debts conveniently erased, the monarchs turned against the very people who had sustained their throne.

In March of that year, the Edict of Expulsion was signed. All Jews were given four months to leave Spain, convert to Christianity, or face death. More than two hundred thousand were driven from their homes—families who had lived in Iberia since Roman times were reduced to beggars and exiles overnight. Those who stayed under forced conversion, called Marranos (pigs in Spanish; now referred to as crypto-Jews), lived in constant fear of the Inquisition, where even a candle lit on Friday night could be enough to condemn an entire household.

This was not only a matter of faith, but of inheritance. Ferdinand and Isabella taught their children, and their children's children, that Jewish survival itself was an error of history. Their grandson, Charles V—who would grow to be the most powerful monarch in Christendom, ruling Spain and the Holy Roman Empire—was raised to despise Jews before he had ever known one. Thus was born generational antisemitism: hatred passed like a birthright, poisoning the minds of rulers yet unborn.

Antisemitism in this age took many forms. It was generational, bred in courts and homes where children were taught to hate by inheritance. It was bystander, when neighbors who had once shared bread and markets turned their eyes away as Jews were stripped of dignity, property, and life. And it was societal, woven into laws and decrees that punished Jews simply for existing, elevating those who persecuted and silencing those who resisted.

The deepest wound was not only in the violence suffered, but in the helplessness imposed. The Jews of the fifteenth and sixteenth centuries had no homeland, no sovereign flag, no army to call their own. They were wanderers, reliant always on the mercy of others—and mercy, more often than not, was denied. To be Jewish in this world was to live at the edge of the sword, forever vulnerable to the next decree, the next pogrom, the next expulsion.

Yet from this crucible of fire, new paths emerged. Some found refuge in the Ottoman Empire, where Sultan Bayezid II welcomed the exiles as artisans, scholars, and merchants. Others survived as conversos, outwardly Christian but secretly loyal to the religion of their ancestors. And some, stripped of land and law, turned to the sea—where no crown could command them and no Inquisition could bind them.

The Mediterranean of this era was a world of shifting empires and fractured loyalties. Venice and Genoa clung to their fading wealth, Spain and Portugal cast long shadows with their fleets, and the rising Ottomans pressed westward into North Africa. Amid this struggle for dominance, the sea itself became both weapon and refuge. Corsairs and privateers—some sanctioned by crowns, others beholden to none—turned the balance of power with cannon and sail.

Among them rose men and women whose names would echo through history. The Barbarossa brothers, Oruc and Hizir, began as outlaws along the Aegean coast before forging an empire of the sea, first as pirates and later as admirals of the Ottoman fleet. Sayyida al-Hurra, the last queen of Tétouan, ruled her city with iron resolve, defying Spain and Portugal alike as both monarch and corsair commander. And Sinan Reis, known as "the Great Jew Pirate," was a Jewish refugee from Iberia who rose from exile to become one of the most feared navigators of his age.

Their exact stories blur the line between history and legend, but what remains certain is this: they lived at the crossroads of oppression and freedom, wielding the sea as their battleground. For Jewish exiles like Sinan, piracy was not merely plunder. It was reclamation. Deprived of a homeland, stripped of agency, and hounded by the Inquisition, Jewish corsairs claimed on the waves what was denied to them on land—liberty, vengeance, and a voice in a world that sought their silence.

This was not rebellion for its own sake. It was survival, born from values as ancient as Sinai itself: that no people is free unless they can live without fear; that dignity cannot be granted by kings, only claimed by those determined to keep it; and that sovereignty—over body, over faith, over destiny—is worth any risk. These truths, hammered into a people through exile and endurance, became the wind in Sinan's sails.

Thus the tale you are about to enter is both history and myth. Its events may be fantastical, its details imagined, but its heart beats with what is real: the Jewish struggle for freedom in a world that denied them home, and the eternal longing for a sovereignty no expulsion, no decree, no empire could extinguish.

Table of Contents

1: Drifter and the Pirate Queen 1

2: Marranos in the Palace 11

3: Markey Riot 21

4: Deadly Foxglove 29

5: The Inquisition of Dr. Badoz 37

6: Sinan the Sailor 43

7: The Dybbuk Zequiel 51

8: Tales of Iberia 57

9: Lone Auroch 67

10: The Pirate's Physian 73

11: Sayyida's Solemn Vow 81

12: Catalonian Conversos 91

13: Valencia's Hidden Kingdom 99

14: Fates Converge 107

15: Into the Void 113

16: Slaves and Survivors 121

17: Shards of Truth 129

18: Barbarossa Brothers Attack 135

19: Slave Children of Isle Ischia 143

20: Wrath of Asmodeus 149

21: Sayyida's Suffering 155

22: Storm at Sea 163

23: Tempest on the Horizon 171

24: Dead or alive 179

25: The Demon King 185

26: The Holy Roman Emperor 191

27: Forgotten Kabbalah Library 197

28: Mast of the Scimitar 205

29: The Boy & The Lynx 215

30: Djidjelli Desert Raiders 227

31: King Sāllim's Gladiator Arena 239

32: Spirit of Vengeance 247

33: Jews of Djerba 255

34: Seven Years 263

35: Crimson Sails 275

36: Man with the Silver Arm 283

37: Revelry & Revelations 291

38: Plague Doctors Ambush 299

39: The Grim Sultan 309

40: Mirror to the Soul 319

41: Green Grotto 327

42: Sword of Solomon	335
43: Sea of Fire	343
44: Nexus Realm	351
45: Within the Void	357
46: Millennia A Deux	365
47: Sunset Sonata	371
48: Epilogue	379

1

Drifter and the Pirate Queen

It was a cool December night on the Mediterranean Sea, the year 1515. Moonlight caressed the turbulent ocean waters. A dense mist hung low until a great vessel parted the fog—its crimson sails giving it away. It could only belong to the fearsome Pirate Queen, Sayyida al-Hurra.

She stood on the prow, a dark silhouette against the star-pierced sky. Her eyes scanned the horizon, but her mind drifted farther. Nights like this could either soothe or scald her tormented soul. The universe itself seemed to question her resolve. Dead ends had plagued her search. Tonight, the weight of every failure pressed upon her.

She inhaled deeply. Giving up was never in her nature. But forward momentum was hard to summon with nothing but dead leads. Her missing son remained a phantom. One final trail remained—uncertain, like every one before—but it was all she had. Hope, thin as a strand of rope, kept her from tumbling into the abyss of regret.

Wind tugged at her traditional Moroccan bangles, and her intricate gold necklace shimmered faintly in the moonlight. She tried recalling the warmth of palace life, but after years at sea, the ship's sway had become her comfort. It was what reminded her she wasn't alone.

Samson, her loyal first mate, paced beside her, his ashen frame looming in the moonlight. He was hunched, hands behind his back—unlike himself. His unease was obvious. So was hers.

They waited for Braman, their second-in-command, to return in the scout ship. He'd gone ahead to spy on the Spanish galleons they'd followed through the fog.

Sayyida ran through battle scenarios in her mind: sword, cannon, scimitar, pistol. She liked her odds. All was accounted for—except one unknown.

"Captain, he's back!" Samson called. A rope was thrown; Braman hoisted his craft aboard with practiced ease.

"How does it look?" Sayyida asked as Braman landed on the deck.

"Not great," Braman replied, tying a knot. "It's not Spanish after all."

"What is it?"

"Genoese."

"Doria?"

"No insignia, but it might be."

Sayyida paused. Attack Admiral Doria? The same man who destroyed the Barbarossa fleet weeks ago and turned Tunisia to ash? Her one ship wouldn't stand a chance. She hated that fact—no matter how she turned it.

"There's one more thing," Braman added. "A drifter. He was aboard."

Sayyida raised an eyebrow. "A drifter?"

"Yes, Captain. Floating on debris. Still alive."

She smiled. "Then let's meet him."

The ship slowed with precision. Samson cast a rope toward the wreckage. A man clung to a plank, barely breathing. He was hauled aboard like a sack of grain, landing with a sick thud on the deck.

Samson coughed as he flung the soaked figure down. Braman grinned around the reed dangling from his mouth.

Sayyida, meanwhile, pored over a map weathered by salt and time. Calligraphy and mythic beasts adorned its fading surface. It was more legend than guide. But she loved it. It stirred something fierce in her.

In 1515, adventure was no gentle thing. The Christian north and Islamic south of the Mediterranean warred endlessly. Sayyida served no king or caliph. She served herself.

Sayyida eyed the drifter: soaked, scorched, half-dead. "Who are you?"

"I'm nobody," he said, but his voice shook.

Sayyida smiled, drawing her ivory pistol. "Well, Nobody... you just became somebody very interesting."

Samson coughed again—worse this time. Sayyida frowned. "See that it's looked at. I need a living first mate."

"I'm fit, Captain," he muttered, hiding blood-streaked fingers behind his back.

"Good."

The drifter barely clung to consciousness. His skin was burned, traced with lightning-shaped scars.

"He didn't call out," Samson said.

"Refused rescue," Braman added.

Sayyida knelt beside the man, who murmured verses in a foreign tongue, rocking in a steady rhythm.

A kippah atop his curly hair caught her eye. A man of faith.

No place for that here.

She kicked him flat and pinned him with her boot. "Where are you from—north or south?"

He didn't flinch. The prayers continued.

Sayyida's patience snapped. She raised her pistol. "Speak. Or die."

The man's eyes opened. He lunged, grabbing the pistol, pressing it to his forehead.

"Shoot," he cried in perfect Moroccan Arabic. "Please. Shoot!"

Sayyida froze. He begged for death. That intrigued her more than anything.

She wrenched the gun back. "Why?"

"My faith forbids suicide. But I want release."

"Who are you?"

"Set me free, Hakimat Titwan."

Sayyida's breath caught. "How do you know that name?"

"I knew you. Once. You were the Queen of Morocco."

Her blood chilled. That life was ash. Her family murdered. That name buried.

"You lie."

"I remember you," he whispered. "You fought for justice."

She turned away. Rain drizzled from the clouds. She had no time for ghosts.

"Take him to the hold," she ordered. "Let him beg the demons below."

The crew seized him. "Please!" he screamed. "Let me see my wife! My brothers! Let me die!"

Sayyida turned her back. "That man's fate is his own."

THE GREAT JEW PIRATE

Samson approached. "You're hard, Captain."

"I didn't survive by being soft."

"Still... don't you miss who you were?"

Sayyida's eyes narrowed. "That name means nothing now."

"Understood."

Samson helped haul the drifter away, but a terrible coughing fit gripped him. He collapsed, vomiting blood.

"Demon!" someone shouted. "He cursed us! Drown him!"

Crewmen dragged the drifter toward the sea.

"Wait!" he cried. "I can save him!"

Sayyida raised a hand. "Let him try."

The drifter dropped beside Samson and listened to his chest.

"Right midaxillary line, fourth rib," he muttered. "Lay him on his side."

The crew obeyed.

He worked fast, focused, precise.

Sayyida watched in stunned silence. The man who wanted death now fought to preserve life. A contradiction. A mystery.

And Sayyida al-Hurra had always loved a mystery.

"All right, perfect!" the drifter exclaimed, surveying the men around him. "Now, all I need is a knife."

He was met with confused glances, a few grunts, and even some chuckles. Clearly, these sailors weren't eager to entertain his urgent request.

"Do you want your friend to breathe or not?" he snapped. "If so, then give me a—"

A blade sliced through the rain and buried itself in the wood just before his knee. The drifter stared, wide-eyed.

The crew turned to see the Pirate Queen, arm still outstretched from her throw.

"He said he needs a knife," she said coldly. Then, to the drifter, "Well? Are you going to stand there, or save him?"

Without hesitation, the drifter yanked the dagger from the deck. He snatched a bottle of rum from a protesting crew member, grabbed Braman's reed from his mouth, and got to work.

He eyed the spot carefully. "Between the fourth and fifth ribs, best to avoid the neurovascular bundle."

He plunged the dagger into Samson's chest at a precise angle and depth, then poured the rum into the wound. The hiss of the disinfectant mingled with the sound of rainfall.

A brass object rolled out of the drifter's rags while he worked. Sayyida noticed. She filed it away in her memory.

The drifter broke the reed's ends and plunged it into the incision, through muscle and into the space around Samson's lungs.

He held it steady. A gasp of air burst from the wound, followed by a gush of blood. Then Samson's chest rose—and he breathed.

"Blood had filled in the space around his lungs," the drifter explained calmly. "A hemothorax. Now that it's drained, he can breathe again."

Confused silence.

"He's breathing," the drifter clarified.

Relief swept the deck. The crew cheered. Sayyida let out a soft breath.

Still focused, the drifter removed the black linen from his arm and used it to secure the reed, adjusting the pressure just right.

He stared at the blood-stained blade in his hand.

THE GREAT JEW PIRATE

"I'll take that back now," Sayyida said, smirking as Samson stirred, breathing in raspy, musical gasps.

The drifter hesitated, blade in hand. The temptation was clear in his eyes—but it passed. He handed the dagger over and lowered his head.

"Please, Queen Sayyida," he murmured, "grant this wretched drifter his final wish. Grant me freedom from this cruel world."

Sayyida studied him. "What's your name?"

"Sinan."

"Well, Sinan, why me? Why not do it yourself?"

He hesitated. "I am a Jew. Our faith forbids suicide. If I end my life, I cannot reunite with my family in the afterlife."

Sayyida leaned in. "Do you fear death?"

"Why fear the inevitable?" he replied. "People spend their lives preparing for it."

"So, you are mad," she mused, smiling. "You're saying that letting you live is a greater torment than killing you?"

"Wait, no! I fear death! Truly! Killing me would be torture!" he stammered.

Sayyida chuckled. "Flattery won't get you anywhere. Let that be your first lesson."

She turned. "Take him below. Feed him. Dress him. And give him the pickles—they're pure agony."

The crew laughed as they dragged a protesting Sinan below.

"Oh, and Sinan," Sayyida called after him. "Call me Captain Sayyida."

With Sinan gone, she helped Samson to his feet.

"What happened?" he wheezed, breath whistling.

"Our new guest decided a dagger and a reed would do the trick," Sayyida said with a grin.

"And our plans?"

"We stay the course," she replied, unfurling her map. "We're a few weeks out, and the lives of enslaved children depend on us."

"What if it's too late?" Samson murmured.

"We try. Some things are worse than death," she said, her eyes flicking toward the stairwell.

"And the drifter?"

"He's coming with us. He needs us as much as we need him."

"Why exactly do we need him?"

"He fears nothing. Not even death."

"You sure that's not madness?"

"Either way, he's useful. Just... keep sharp things away from him."

She spotted something glinting on the deck. It was the brass case that had fallen earlier. Opening it, her expression changed.

Inside lay an ancient bronze astrolabe, etched with Hebrew script. Its surface shimmered silver in the rain.

"Seems our drifter might be more than he appears," she murmured.

Samson nodded, wheezing. "So, we're no longer doomed, just... strategically disadvantaged?"

Sayyida snapped the case shut and grinned.

"Oh hush, you... human harmonica."

David Nobyl

2

Marranos in the Palace

Sayyida al-Hurra sat alone in her cabin, the stormy hum of the sea just beyond her walls. She cracked open Sinan's brass case once more, drawn to the object inside. The bronze astrolabe shimmered faintly, then began to glow.

Wisps of silver light spilled upward, swirling and coalescing into a mirror-like oval suspended in the air. But it was no mere reflection. She recognized the magic—an ancient portal into memory. A living mirror.

She narrowed her eyes and leaned in.

The image clarified. Not her memory—but his.

She exhaled sharply. If this was what she thought it was, it could not only reveal the drifter's past, but also the knowledge of what surrounded that moment in time. Perhaps... perhaps even the thread that led to her lost son.

Cracking her neck, she allowed the light to flood her senses.

David Nobyl

***

It was 1504. Queen Isabella of Castile lay gravely ill. Her palace, El Medina del Campo Alcázar Real—just outside Toledo—was a fortress of Moorish stone and Christian wealth. Vibrant mosaic tiles framed golden halls. Tapestries hung on either side of the queen's bed, depicting her victories over the Moors of Granada and Seville.

Yet no triumph shielded her now.

The queen sweated through silks, her breath ragged. A beaked plague doctor leaned in to examine her heart. His gloved hand paused.

A murmur. That sound could mean only one thing.

He rolled up her sleeve, revealing a ragged-edged rash. Erythema marginatum. Her trembling hand and jerky movements sealed it: Sydenham chorea.

"Please, doctor," Isabella rasped. "Help me..."

The doctor bowed wordlessly, then turned and left the room.

Outside the chamber, he was met by a squat, crimson-faced man—King Ferdinand II.

"Well? Will she live?" he barked.

The plague doctor said nothing.

Ferdinand's rage flared. He seized the mask—ripping it off. He stumbled back.

Beneath the robes was only shadow.

Then, from under the cloak, a boy scrambled out. No older than thirteen.

"I'm sorry! It's not fully functional! The suit can't speak yet!" the boy cried.

"What is this?! Where is Doctor Lorenzo Badoz?!"

THE GREAT JEW PIRATE

"Here," came a calm voice.

A tall, elegant man stepped forward. Dr. Badoz—sharp mustache, sharp eyes, and a necklace bearing a heavy key.

He bowed to the king, then turned to the boy.

"Findings?"

The boy—Sinan—fumbled, then stood straighter.

"The queen presents with joint pain, fatigue, jerky movements, rash, and heart murmur."

"Diagnosis?"

"Congestive heart failure secondary to rheumatic heart disease," Sinan answered, his voice gaining strength.

Dr. Badoz nodded.

"Treatment?"

Sinan paused, then blurted: "Foxglove. Digitalis. Five milligrams every four hours, dissolved in alcohol ether to maintain potency for up to 48 hours."

Even the king blinked in surprise.

Dr. Badoz smiled slightly. "It was in there."

To the king, he added, "The boy speaks true. I saw her this morning. This is the only path forward."

The king lowered his head. "How long does she have?"

"Not long. Perhaps days, a week at best," Dr. Badoz replied solemnly. "She's had her morning dose of foxglove extract, but if we don't secure more from the market before nightfall, missing her evening dose could prove fatal."

"Well, then," the king snapped, face red with frustration, "what are you converso fools still standing here for? Go find her some fox-blood or whatever it is!"

Dr. Badoz and Sinan bowed deeply and turned to leave.

"And take your infernal contraption with you!" the king shouted after them.

Sinan quickly scooped up the plague doctor mask and hurried after Dr. Badoz, pushing the wheeled apparatus down the corridor. "Uncle, wait!"

They crossed the royal courtyard, the echo of their footsteps skimming across polished tile. A mosaic frieze caught Sinan's eye—reliefs of the monarchs and their grandson, young Charles V. In less than two decades, that boy would become the Holy Roman Emperor and command more of the world than any Christian since the Roman Empire.

Sinan shivered. That cruel, pompous child was always destined to rule an empire. But how many would suffer?

They descended marble stairs, passed towering Corinthian columns, and skirted a courtyard crowded with peacocks.

"Vile creatures," Sinan muttered as one lunged at his cloak. He swatted at it. The bird shrieked, feathers flaring like a royal banner in a storm.

"Converso?" Sinan asked once he caught up. "Why does he say it like that—like it's filth?"

"Because to him, it is," Dr. Badoz replied curtly. "He despises conversos, and even more so, Marranos."

"What's the difference?"

"Marranos are Jews who were forced to convert, but still practice Judaism in secret. Conversos is a broader term—some practice, some don't. To the king, it doesn't matter. We are all the same to him."

Sinan nodded solemnly. "I'm grateful to be a pure-blooded Christian, then... but how can that be if you're my uncle?"

Dr. Badoz rolled his eyes. "By marriage, not blood. And if anyone asks—you're not a Jew. You're not a Marrano. You're not even a converso. Understood?"

THE GREAT JEW PIRATE

"Understood," Sinan replied.

They turned a corner into the assistants' courtyard—less ornate than the royal halls, its wooden floors creaked underfoot. As they passed a nearby door, Dr. Badoz quickened his pace, trying to avoid attention.

Too late.

The door flung open. A smiling man blocked their path, clean-shaven and handsome in the pristine style of a Spanish inquisitor.

"Permit me to introduce my guest to the famed physician," the man said loudly.

Dr. Badoz halted, clearly irritated.

"Dr. Badoz, meet Admiral Andrea Doria," the inquisitor declared with theatrical flair. Doria stepped forward, his military garb stiff and immaculate. A subtle but unnerving smile played on his lips.

Sinan stiffened under Doria's gaze.

Dr. Badoz quickly stepped between them and bowed. "Welcome to Medina del Campo, Admiral. To what do we owe the pleasure?"

"That's Sebastián de Olmedo, thank you very much," the inquisitor snapped.

Dr. Badoz didn't miss a beat. "Yes, of course. Strange how people insist on a family name even when no one calls them by it. Perhaps it's their only way to climb the royal ladder."

Sebastián glared, but Doria chuckled.

Dr. Badoz turned back to the admiral. "You were saying, sir?"

Doria took a long drink of sangria, then limped forward, looming. His voice dropped low.

"Have you heard of the Barbarossa Brothers? Barbary pirates, preying on Spanish cargo."

Dr. Badoz said nothing.

"The King wants me to command Aragon's fortress in Ischia," Doria continued. "Whoever controls Ischia controls the Mediterranean trade routes... and holds the key to North Africa."

Dr. Badoz's brow furrowed. "I wasn't aware the Crown's ambitions had expanded so far."

"They have," Doria said. "And we need a physician on board. Someone discreet. Someone like you."

Dr. Badoz bowed lightly, hand over heart. "I serve Queen Isabella. I must decline."

Doria nodded once, eyes narrowing. He exchanged a look with Sebastián—something wordless passed between them. Then he turned and limped down the corridor, leaving the air tense and still.

Moments later, a donkey brayed from the outer courtyard.

"It's Luís!" Sinan called out, darting away.

A creaking wagon rumbled into view, flattening rosebushes as it turned into the garden. Dr. Badoz followed, pointedly ignoring Sebastián.

"You made it!" Sinan beamed, catching a peacock just before it could peck at the donkey's legs.

"Three months across Spain," Luís said, jumping down awkwardly. He wore too many layers for the Andalusian heat. His long hair clung to his face.

"Where's your mother?" Dr. Badoz asked.

Luís gestured to the back of the wagon. A woman slowly stepped down, regal despite travel-weariness.

"Welcome, Blanquina," Dr. Badoz said with a bow.

"Spare me the curtsies," she smiled. "We're old friends."

"How is he?" the doctor asked.

"Declining," she said softly. "But that's not why I came."

THE GREAT JEW PIRATE

She reached into her coat pocket.

"I brought what you asked for."

Dr. Badoz's eyes flicked toward Sebastián's window. Two glinting eyes watched from within.

"Come inside," he whispered. "Now."

They climbed the wooden steps to his private quarters. Blanquina touched the wall as she walked, eyes tracing the worn patterns.

"You've done well," she remarked. "Chief physician to the Queen. Deliverer of her children."

"You have no idea the suffering," he muttered.

Sinan and Luís entered behind them. Just before closing the door, Dr. Badoz spotted Sebastián peering through the crack of his own.

With deliberate calm, he closed his door—and locked all five iron bolts into place.

David Nobyl

David Nobyl

3

Market Riot

Dr. Badoz's living quarters were a feast for the eyes, adorned with vibrant cuerda seca tiles. Though more affordable than their lusterware counterparts, their intricate brush-painted designs paid homage to Christian Gothic traditions and Moorish precision.

Out on the shaded patio beneath orange groves, Sinan and Luís set up a chessboard made of stained glass. The clatter of wooden pieces echoed softly as they played. Meanwhile, inside, Dr. Badoz led Blanquina to the dining area—a cozy space that doubled as a kitchen.

Blanquina's gaze lingered on the marble table and the ceramic tableware, their glaze catching the light like moonlit seas. Though she said nothing, Dr. Badoz noticed.

"A golden cage, nothing more," he muttered.

"I never—"

He raised a hand to silence her. "Please. The letter."

Blanquina sat, producing a long, narrow envelope. The wax seal bore the Medici crest. Dr. Badoz cracked it open with practiced fingers, devouring the contents with his eyes. A slow smile spread across his face.

"What did he say?" Blanquina asked.

"Sinan!" Dr. Badoz called. The boy appeared in a heartbeat.

"Take this vial to the city market. Refill it with foxglove extract—forty-five percent alcohol ether, no more. Take Luís with you."

Sinan nodded, seized the vial, and vanished with Luís in tow.

As the door shut, Blanquina leaned forward. "It's not fair to keep him in the dark. He deserves the truth."

"The less he knows, the better," Dr. Badoz replied, folding the letter and slipping it into his coat. He closed the shutters and lowered his voice.

"Piero di Medici wants me in Venice. He's offering protection. But Queen Isabella has less than a week. Once she dies, King Ferdinand will give Diego de Deza full authority over the converso purge. And then... he'll come for me."

Blanquina's expression darkened.

"We leave tonight," he said quietly. "All of us. Back to Valencia."

***

Outside, Sinan and Luís descended the stone steps. A chorus of indignant peacocks greeted them.

"I'd kill for a pet tiger," Sinan muttered, batting away a peacock lunging at his tunic. He accidentally snagged a bright turquoise feather. The peacock shrieked and charged.

"What do we do?!" Luís cried, dodging behind him.

"There!" Sinan pointed to a nearby bush and dashed toward it, disappearing.

"It's a dead-end, you idiot!" Luís yelled, but followed anyway. A shriek, a slap of feathers against marble—and Luís found himself in total darkness.

"Bless you," came a voice.

"Who's there?!" Luís stammered, sneezing again.

A spark flared. Sinan lit a stubby candle. His face flickered like a ghost's.

"What's with the sneezing, Luís?"

"I sneeze when I'm nervous. Okay?!"

Sinan grinned. "Come on. This way."

The tunnel was narrow and ancient—grutesco in design, blending raw stone with decaying architecture.

"How'd you find this?" Luís asked, hand on his dagger.

"It was built for a king's mistress," Sinan replied. "Forgotten for centuries. Princess Catherine and I stumbled on it a few months back."

"You know Princess Catherine?!" Luís blinked. "I love her."

"You're twelve. She's sixteen," Sinan scoffed. "Also... she's a princess. You're a—"

"Converso?" Luís cut in.

"You said it, not me."

Luís scowled, brushing cobwebs aside as they continued. "Do you know what you want to study? A trade?"

"I'll do a Grand Tour of Europe's great cities," Sinan mused. "Then maybe study medicine. Maybe flee the crown. Or become a pirate, just to spite my uncle."

Luís chuckled, then winced as his knee struck something soft and heavy.

"What was that?!"

"Just leftover supplies from Columbus's first voyage," Sinan said, lifting the candle. The flame revealed crates of timber, grains—and sealed cannon barrels.

"They say he made a secret deal with the King—for a Jewish homeland," Luís whispered.

"Or land for himself," Sinan countered, eyes dancing with mischief. "Tómato, tomáto. Too bad his body's not buried down here. Now that would be spooky."

He laughed and opened a wooden hatch. Blinding light poured in.

Little did Sinan know Columbus would die in 1506—and his bones would travel farther than he ever did alive.

***

They emerged into a pavilion outside the castle, a tribute to the future union of Prince Charles V and Isabella of Portugal. The architecture fused Mudejar domes with Renaissance symmetry.

Beyond the pavilion, the bustling market roared.

The boys arrived just as a crowd formed. An old man with torn clothes and bloodied face was being pelted with stones.

"Behold—a converso!" bellowed a man in red-and-black robes. "He prays with us by day and wears a yarmulke by night! This heresy ends now. I am Diego de Deza, Chief Inquisitor! Cleanse the towns! Purge the filth!"

Sinan and Luís ducked away—but another group approached. Soldiers.

"You've gone too far!" shouted one. "You cleanse Jews, Muslims, Gypsies—and now good Christians?"

"Name yourself," the Inquisitor hissed.

THE GREAT JEW PIRATE

The officer stepped forward. "I am Don Diego de Córdoba, General of the King's armies. Governor of Oran. And I've had enough."

He drew his sword. His men followed.

Deza paled. He bowed slightly, turned, and disappeared into the dispersing crowd.

***

Sinan and Luís slipped into a tucked-away herb shop, the scent of crushed leaves thick in the air. Wild plants sprawled across wooden shelves. Golden Loza Dorada plates shimmered among them, more art than dishware.

"Foxglove extract, 45% alcohol ether," Sinan said, offering gold coins stamped with the Queen's profile.

The shopkeeper, a small woman with silver-streaked hair, smiled gently.

"Ah. Digitalis purpurea. The 'fox's glove.' They say foxes wore the flowers on their paws to silence their steps."

"Yes, great, thank you," Sinan replied dryly.

"You don't want to know the side effects?"

"No."

"Tremors. Seizures. And hallucinations. Yellow halos. It's the only herb that causes xanthopsia."

"I said no."

Luís, of course, leaned in. "What do they see?"

"Light like honey. Everything tinged with gold."

The woman ground the flower calmly—then stopped, looking out the window.

Soldiers argued with citizens. Tensions boiled.

"It's happening again," she murmured.

"What is?" Luís asked.

"You're too young to remember. The night the Alhambra Decree was signed in 1492... Thousands died."

"My mother told me," Luís said softly.

"That's because you're a converso," Sinan snapped.

Luís looked down, hurt.

The woman leaned in. "It's good she told you."

"Why?" Sinan asked, impatient.

"Because the people who tell stories will die. But the stories of those who saved us—those survive."

She handed them the vial.

Then pulled a second, smaller one from behind the counter.

"The antidote. Free of charge. In case... you ever need it."

Sinan took it in silence.

Then, glancing at the street, he asked, "The man out there. Do you know him?"

Her lips trembled.

"That is my husband," she said, closing her eyes.

David Nobyl

4

Deadly Foxglove

By the time Luís and Sinan returned to Dr. Badoz's living quarters, night had already fallen. Moonlight bathed the castle's exterior, while flickering candles cast dancing shadows across the tiled walls within. They found Dr. Badoz packing with swift, practiced hands, his movements sharp with urgency.

"Are we going somewhere?" Sinan asked.

"No time to explain," Dr. Badoz snapped. "Give the queen her nightly foxglove dose, then return. We're leaving."

Stunned, Sinan nodded and rushed off. As he navigated the dimly lit corridors, resentment swirled in his chest. How could Dr. Badoz uproot their lives with no warning?

He rounded a corner and froze. The queen's bedroom door stood ajar—a clear breach of protocol. Only he and Dr. Badoz were permitted entry.

Sinan stepped into the darkness. Wind howled outside. Moonlight poured in through the window, casting pale streaks across the queen's ornate bedframe. He crept forward, eyes flicking to every shadow, and reached for the foxglove vial.

Then he saw it. The morning's vial—uncapped. He was sure he had sealed it.

A rustle behind him. He whirled around.

A figure stood in the shadows, wearing the black plague doctor mask from his old contraption. The figure bolted for the window and vanished into the night.

Heart hammering, Sinan turned back to the queen. She stirred as he approached.

"Your medicine, Majesty," he whispered, counting twelve drops into her mouth. He recapped the vial, turned to leave—

—but a horrible gurgling noise made him stop.

Queen Isabella convulsed violently. Foam bubbled at her lips. Her scream shattered the night.

Chaos exploded.

Princess Joanna burst into the room, wild-eyed. "What have you done?!"

Her sisters, Maria and Catherine, hovered behind her. King Ferdinand pushed through the doorway, voice thunderous. "Explain this treachery, boy!"

"I gave her the foxglove," Sinan stammered. "Only the required dosage—"

"Y-Yellow," the queen gasped. "Yellow spots... everywhere."

Sinan paled. Yellow halos—xanthopsia. Classic sign of foxglove overdose.

"She's been poisoned!" he cried, reaching for the antidote.

"Seize him!" Joanna shrieked.

Armored guards slammed into the room. Sinan tried to administer the antidote, but Joanna yanked him away.

"Witchcraft!" she spat. "Just like your uncle!"

"Joanna, stop!" Catherine cried. "You're scaring Charles!"

Joanna spun, grabbing her young son by the collar. Her voice turned venomous.

"You are to be Emperor! You will show no mercy! Do you hear me?!"

Charles, wide-eyed, nodded silently.

Sinan took the opportunity and dashed to the queen's side. But Joanna screamed again, and he was tackled to the ground.

He struggled, but froze as the queen exhaled her last breath. Her eyes stared vacantly at the ceiling.

Everything stopped.

Even Joanna fell silent.

Maria's face lost its smugness. Catherine broke into sobs.

King Ferdinand stared at Sinan with cold fury. "You will join Badoz at the stake."

"She was poisoned," Sinan pleaded. "I saw the real killer—"

"Silence him."

Boots crashed into his ribs. Sinan collapsed, choking on blood.

Then—

A scream.

Catherine collapsed, convulsing. Foaming. Screaming.

Joanna shrieked for help. Guards rushed in. They laid Catherine beside her mother.

In the chaos, no one noticed Sinan crawl beneath the bed.

By the time the guards looked for him, he was gone. Only blood remained.

Joanna screamed in rage.

King Ferdinand stepped forward. "Find the boy. Arrest Badoz. And Joanna—"

He looked at his wife's lifeless body.

"—you are now Queen."

Joanna's expression twisted with triumph—then suspicion. She leaned down to whisper into Catherine's ear.

"If you helped him escape, I'll make sure you join your dead husband."

Not more than a few minutes later, there was a knock at Dr. Badoz's door.

"What do you want, Sebastian de Olmedo?" Badoz called.

"Oh, just reflecting on the late Torquemada," came the oily reply. "A hero of Spain, wouldn't you agree?"

Dr. Badoz motioned for Blanquina and Luís to flee through the back.

"Still upset I disproved your libelous accusations in court?"

"No, no," Sebastian cooed. "But today... I bring tragic news."

Dr. Badoz opened the door—and stepped back.

A dozen guards stood behind Sebastian.

"Seems I can't bring it up with the queen anymore," Sebastian said, leering. "She's dead."

Dr. Badoz's heart pounded.

"The king would like a word."

The guards cuffed him and marched him to the royal dining hall. Sebastian lingered, then began ransacking the doctor's quarters. From a hidden compartment in the stone wall, he retrieved a curved, ancient key.

Grinning, he slipped away.

THE GREAT JEW PIRATE

Dr. Badoz was shoved into the dining hall. King Ferdinand sat alone, carving into roasted meats.

"Your kind—you crypto-Jews," he said, not looking up, "is a poison. You pretend to be like us. But you never let go of the past."

"Your Majesty—"

A guard punched Badoz across the face.

Unbothered, Ferdinand dabbed his mouth with a napkin. "Isabella insisted you were irreplaceable. That you could do what no other physician could. And yet... she died."

Badoz tried to speak again but was knocked to the floor.

Sebastian entered with Chief Inquisitor Diego de Deza.

"Let him be made an example," the king said.

"With your decree, he will," De Deza replied. He extended a document. Ferdinand signed it.

"Take him," the king ordered.

The guards dragged Badoz away. Sebastian followed, nearly skipping.

Elsewhere, Sinan emerged through the secret trapdoor beneath the queen's bed. Limping and bloodied, he crept through the castle's hidden tunnels, heart set on warning his uncle.

He reached their quarters—ransacked.

Gone.

His breath caught.

Then, he heard voices.

Outside in the gardens, he found Blanquina and Luís, pale and shaken.

"He's been taken," Luís whispered.

Sinan's eyes burned. "We have to save him. We have to prove the truth."

Blanquina nodded. "Then we run. Tonight. Before it's too late."

And together, the three disappeared into the tunnels, beneath the castle.

David Nobyl

5

The Inquisition of Dr. Badoz

Sayyida watched as the astrolabe mirror sped forward in time, revealing Dr. Badoz being dragged like a sack of potatoes to Toledo, the heart of Spain's capital. The medieval fortress perched atop a hill overlooking the winding Tagus River was quite the sight—but it wasn't the view that caught his attention. It was the looming presence of the Spanish Inquisition's headquarters that awaited him.

As they neared the bustling city, the sting of chains cut through Dr. Badoz's wrists and ankles, grounding him in the horrific reality of what was to come. Jeering crowds and murmured curses filled the air. His heart pounded.

At last, they arrived at the grand Plaza de Zocodover, where the infamous auto-da-fé was to be held. A shiver ran down Dr. Badoz's spine as he took in the scene. Thousands packed the square, eyes gleaming with excitement and cruelty. The scent of charred flesh mixed with sweat and incense, turning his stomach.

Sebastian and Chief Inquisitor Diego de Deza stood at the center, reading aloud the King's decree that granted expanded powers to the Inquisition. Any protest would result in the loss of land, title, and citizenship. Sebastian paused over one name on the list—Diego de Córdoba. The very same general who had challenged the Inquisition weeks prior.

That evening, in the shadowed corridors of Toledo's darker quarters—far from the marzipan vendors and swordsmiths—Dr. Badoz endured unspeakable torture. Whips lashed. The rack stretched his limbs until tendons screamed. Then came the Cat's Paw, the Spiked Chair, the Knee Splitters.

Still, he didn't speak.

"You've known pain, Doctor," said the Chief Inquisitor, almost casually. "But not like this."

Dr. Badoz was forced into the Head Crusher. Metal bore down against his skull.

"Your teeth will break first," De Deza explained calmly. "Then your skull. Eventually, your brain will... well, you'll see."

Dr. Badoz spat blood. "Pain is just a cobblestone on the road to my grave."

The machine stopped.

"Alas," De Deza said, "you've not heard the news. Your nephew, Sinan... he's dead."

Dr. Badoz didn't speak. A single tear ran down his bruised face.

The Grand Inquisitor continued, "Tell us... was Sinan's mother a Jew?"

No response. The machine creaked to life again.

"Was. She. A. Jew?"

"Yes!" Dr. Badoz screamed, his jaw cracking. One inquisitor behind Sebastian gasped.

"There you have it," De Deza smiled. "He's confessed to the Queen's murder—and to raising a Jew."

"He's hiding something," Sebastian sneered, slamming a familiar curved key on the table. "Time for the Judas Cradle."

The Grand Inquisitor gave a solemn nod.

"Have you heard of it, Doctor?" he asked. "We hoist you up, then lower you slowly onto this pike. It purifies the soul."

"Or purees it," one hooded inquisitor muttered.

De Deza narrowed his eyes but said nothing. "Fasten him. We'll return shortly."

As Dr. Badoz was dragged to the contraption, one of the inquisitors sneezed. Then again. His robes shifted awkwardly.

"Careful, Luís!" the other hissed. "We've come too far."

"¡Lo siento, Sinan!" Luís whispered.

Together, they supported Dr. Badoz's broken frame and made for a hidden hatch in the dungeon wall. Sinan, dressed in a lesser inquisitor's robe, opened it with swift precision. They slipped through the stone passage, resealing it behind them.

When Sebastian returned and found the prisoner gone, he searched his robe pocket and froze.

"The key," he growled. "It's gone."

His fury erupted. "Lock down the city! Burn the streets if you must! Find them!"

***

David Nobyl

Back in Sayyida's cabin, the astrolabe's mirror began to blur. She closed the device with a quiet hum.

"So," she murmured, "they escaped. But at what cost?"

Her gaze lingered on the brass case before she tucked it away.

The storm outside began to lift.

David Nobyl

6

Sinan the Sailor

The sun rose on Captain Sayyida's ship, casting warm light over the glistening sea. Samson believed he was the only one awake—until he noticed Sinan, cross-legged in the shadows of his barrack, staring into the distance.

"You seem to be the only one who knows how to keep me breathing," Samson said reverently. Sinan didn't respond. He was chained to the floorboards, his emaciated body clad in fresh clothes, though his spirit remained untethered.

"I don't take your actions lightly," Samson continued, unlocking the chains. "My debt to you will be repaid."

"If you spoke the truth," Sinan muttered, hair falling over his eyes, "you would've already granted my last request."

"Maybe there's another way to bring you peace," Samson said gently. "A way that doesn't defy the captain's orders. She wants to see you this morning."

"I hope she's not taken with me," Sinan smirked. "I'm still mourning the loss of my wife."

"Dark humor is good," Samson said seriously. "It protects the soul, especially one that's long sought death."

They made their way to the captain's cabin. Sayyida reclined in her chair, peering into a flickering memory window projected from Sinan's astrolabe. As their footsteps approached, she swiftly shut the artifact and tucked it into her coat.

Sinan was distracted by the lavishly decorated room: maps draped across the ceiling, Moroccan rugs layered underfoot, curved swords and ancient relics adorning the walls.

"I see you're still alive," Sayyida said, lowering her feet from the table.

"Glad to bring someone joy," Sinan said with a shrug.

"Let's lighten the mood, shall we?" Sayyida replied.

"You could always throw me overboard," Sinan offered innocently.

"Are you a jester or a physician?" Sayyida asked. "I only need one."

"Which one earns a faster trip to the sea?" he grinned.

Sayyida leaned back in her chair, her dark eyes narrowing. She studied him in silence before speaking.

"I control my men through greed or fear," she said. "But that won't work on you. You have neither desire for wealth nor fear of death."

"For my own life," Sinan added bitterly.

"For your own life," she echoed, slower this time.

"I heard you the first time," Sinan replied, voice cracking just slightly beneath the weight of his pain.

Sayyida tilted her head, watching him. "Does the name Andrea Doria mean anything to you?" she asked.

Sinan's demeanor changed instantly. His rage simmered beneath the surface like magma, yet he

THE GREAT JEW PIRATE

remained still. His hand, still blackened and charred, trembled as he clenched his fist.

"He laid siege to my home," Sayyida continued. "Where I was once queen. He slaughtered thousands—Moriscos, Muslims, families. He allies with the Inquisition now. He wants our kind erased."

"Our kind?" Sinan growled. "What do you know of our kind?"

Sayyida pulled out the astrolabe and set it on the table. "My kind were expelled from Spain, hunted across Morocco. Yours are the Hebrews and Marranos of Iberia. You were forced to flee, convert, or die. But even after conversion—did the persecution end?"

Sinan's fists unclenched. A wave of memory surged through him like a storm tide, and he stumbled. Samson steadied him. When the wave passed, Sinan stood tall again and met Sayyida's eyes.

"You're not just some castaway," Sayyida said, voice firm. "You're educated. Trained. But more than that—you think differently. That's something that can't be taught. It's a gift."

"What do you want from me?" Sinan asked quietly.

She tossed him the artifact. "Tell me about this."

The moment it touched his hand, the ship trembled violently. A piercing blue light surged from the artifact, illuminating the entire room. The sailors on deck stumbled, and crewmates shouted in alarm. But Sinan stood still, his eyes shut.

The blue glow burned through the blackened flesh of his hand, revealing ancient Hebrew sigils etched into his skin like molten brands. His knees buckled.

Memories returned in a violent flood: capture, betrayal, family, loss. Loneliness so profound it hollowed him out. And worst of all—divine abandonment.

When the storm passed, the blue faded, and his hand returned to its charred state.

"What was that?" Samson breathed.

"A mystic astrolabe," Sinan murmured, his voice hollow. "An ancient Kabbalistic compass. It's supposed to guide us."

"To what?" Sayyida asked.

"I don't know," Sinan admitted. "I've never gotten it to show more than memories—mine, or others'. I thought it would protect my family... but it didn't. It failed them."

Sayyida leaned forward. "Maybe it didn't fail you. Maybe you missed something."

"I've searched every memory," Sinan said. "Begged for answers. Nothing came."

Sayyida's voice softened. "Sinan, I know you don't want to live. But is there any part of you left that would live for others?"

He stared at her, unsure.

"Because in two weeks," she said, "we reach the Isle of Ischia. We believe Andrea Doria runs a prison there—children are being experimented on. Slaves. Survivors of Djerba's massacre. Maybe even people you knew."

Sinan closed his eyes. The pain was unbearable.

"You don't have to kill to fight," she added. "There are other ways to set people free."

"Not against Doria," he whispered. "Not against the Inquisition."

"I don't wish to prolong your pain," Sayyida said. "If you truly want to reunite with your family, I will help you.

THE GREAT JEW PIRATE

That's a promise—not from a captain, but from a mother who's lost her own child and husband to Doria."

Sinan was silent for a long time. Finally, he nodded.

"Let me consider your offer—without pressure."

"Take your time," Sayyida said. "But know this: your home, Djerba, may still hold survivors."

Sinan's eyes flickered briefly.

"You're welcome here," Sayyida concluded. "If you accept, you'll serve as ship's physician. Go rest."

Sinan bowed and departed. The door shut quietly behind him.

"Do you think he'll choose life?" Samson asked.

"You can't tame the wind," Sayyida said, gazing out the window. "You can't fight the thunder. But if there's even a spark of hope—just a spark—you can ignite the will of anyone."

Below deck, Sinan found a hammock and collapsed into it. He withdrew the artifact from his coat and opened it. It glowed again, its quiet hiss announcing the memory portal.

A memory flickered before him: the escape from the Inquisition, the rescue of Dr. Badoz. But Sinan wasn't focused on nostalgia.

He scoured the memory for anything he had missed—something useful.

He had told Sayyida he needed time. But he already knew.

If he was to defeat Andrea Doria...

He needed a plan.

And the astrolabe was ready to show him where to begin.

David Nobyl

David Nobyl

7

The Dybbuk Zequiel

The young Sinan awoke from his nightmare, panting heavily. He picked himself up off the floor and washed the sweat from his face in a small fountain. The lukewarm, brown water offered little relief, but it was enough to ground him. As he looked up into the cracked mirror above the basin, he met the gaze of a boy he hardly recognized—haunted, hollow-eyed, broken.

A few days had passed since he and Luís had accomplished the impossible—rescuing Dr. Badoz. But something inside him had shifted. He had crossed an invisible line. He was no longer a good Christian boy of the court. He was a marked heretic. A Jew. A Marrano. A target.

The shame and terror pressed down on him like iron weights. The torture devices he'd seen were no longer just implements of pain for others—they were threats meant for him, his mother, and everyone like them. In the mirror, he saw a filthy, damned creature with devilish eyes. He shut them tightly and wept in silence.

They had not left Toledo. Not really. Their small band of fugitives—Dr. Badoz, Luís, Blanquina, and Sinan—had found refuge in the catacombs beneath Santa María la Blanca, once a synagogue, now a church. The irony stung deeper each day. They were hidden by Cláro, a secret converso priest who owed Dr. Badoz a great debt. He asked for no payment, only discretion. He had sheltered many Jews in his lifetime. He knew what was at stake.

When Sebastian and his Inquisition men came searching, Cláro told them he had seen no travelers. The lie was enough. Sebastian eventually left the city, chasing phantoms across the countryside.

But the group's situation was dire. They had to reach Valencia—a 370-kilometer journey—if they hoped to escape Spain. Passage to Venice awaited there. But Dr. Badoz's condition worsened by the hour. Sinan did all he could: binding wounds, cleaning infections, administering herbs, praying to a God he wasn't sure was listening. Yet the wounds festered. The fever burned. The man who had once commanded royal courts now drifted between seizures and coma.

Then Luís burst into the chamber. "He's here!" he shouted. "Master Alfonso of Rome, the Moorish mystic—and his protégé, Eugene Torralva! They've come!"

Sinan barely had time to wipe his hands before sprinting after Luís. In the flickering candlelight, the two mystics stood over Dr. Badoz, cloaked in wet robes and shadow. Cláro hovered in the background, reluctant to step closer.

Master Alfonso's deep-set eyes contrasted with Torralva's vivid green irises. One bore a long gray beard, the other a short, tight mustache. They moved swiftly, already diagnosing, assessing.

"Sepsis. Kidneys, lungs, heart," Torralva murmured.

"Bleed him," said Alfonso.

"He's lost too much blood," Sinan argued.

But the master did not respond. Instead, he produced a small pouch of black powder and handed it to Torralva, who mixed it with a mysterious liquid. Alfonso sanitized a needle with fire and rum, then inserted it into a vein on Dr. Badoz's arm. Slowly, the black mixture entered his bloodstream. The convulsions lessened.

Sinan watched, stunned.

"Fungal ash from the Far East," Alfonso explained. "The Ottomans have used it for generations."

Sinan could only nod.

But then, Dr. Badoz seized again—violently. Torralva struggled to hold him down.

"He's too far gone!" he cried.

"Call him!" Alfonso ordered.

"I cannot!"

"NOW!"

With visible reluctance, Torralva raised his arms and invoked, "Spirit of Zequiel, come to our aid!"

The candle extinguished.

When it flared back to life, a small, black-eyed child stood beside it—teeth sharp like a predator. His voice was impossibly deep.

"Doctor Lorenzo Badoz is destined to die tonight," said Zequiel. "Why fight fate?"

"Please," Torralva begged, "help us save him."

"I'll need a soul in exchange." The child grinned, licking his fangs. "Any volunteers?"

"Yes," said Sinan, stepping forward. The silence that followed was complete.

The spirit tilted his head. "A life so young, yet already spent? You seek redemption?"

"My soul is already condemned," Sinan said flatly. "Let me trade it."

Zequiel's laugh echoed like thunder. "Even if I wished to, I cannot. There are laws older than me."

"Why?"

"Because your death would doom millions. Your destiny is too... significant."

Sinan scoffed. "I'm just one dirty Jew."

The spirit's grin widened. "You seek purpose, not death, Sinan Reis." He reached out, seized a nearby rat, and snapped its neck. From its mouth flowed a thin, spectral mist that drifted into Dr. Badoz's lips.

Sinan gasped. "Is my family alive?"

"You won't find them. But they will find you. Your path is pain—but not without meaning."

The candle flickered. The spirit vanished.

Dr. Badoz's breathing evened. Color returned to his face. The worst had passed.

Master Alfonso and Torralva turned to Sinan, eyes wide.

"Reis," they said, bowing their heads.

"What does that mean?"

"Ottoman," replied Alfonso. "It means 'king of the sea.'"

David Nobyl

8

Tales of Iberia

The mirror through which the aged Sinan watched the memory became hazy, and the image changed. It now showed a disheveled man approaching the medieval city of Toledo. This was not Sinan's own memory—it belonged to someone else. He leaned in, eyes narrowed. Perhaps the mirror was revealing a key to defeating Andrea Doria—the man who had cost him everything.

The figure was none other than Diego de Córdoba, the once-venerated governor of Oran, stripped of title and sword after protesting the Spanish Inquisition in Medina del Campo. With nothing left to lose and the fire of a desperate man, Diego crossed the Bridge of San Martín, his ragged clothes whipping in the wind, eyes set on the Inquisition's grim headquarters.

"I seek Sebastian de Olmedo," he declared at the gate.

The guards answered with violence. They hurled him headfirst into the cobbled street.

Staggering upright, Diego wandered into Toledo's famed blacksmith district, drawn by the sound of hammer on steel. He stepped into a forge and faced a broad-shouldered man at work.

"I need a sword," Diego rasped. "Old friend."

The blacksmith laughed bitterly. "You think I don't know what happened to you? All of Spain knows."

Diego's eyes drifted to a half-forged Tizona dagger gleaming on the bench. Its handle and scabbard were of classic black and gold Damasquino design—oxidized copper and inlaid gold, shimmering like firelight in the forge.

"Walk away," the blacksmith warned.

But Diego slammed his scarred fists on the counter. "Or else what?"

The blacksmith shouted for the guards. A dozen armored men appeared, and they beat Diego down until his limbs were numb and his pride shattered. Bleeding, he dragged himself into a filthy alley, where he found a skeletal greyhound curled near death. He pulled the creature to his chest and named her Ester—for a woman he once loved.

The next day, Diego begged for work. None would have him. He turned to pickpocketing, stealing scraps of jamón and marzipan from crowded tapas stalls. What little he stole, he shared with Ester. And there, among broken tiles and rotting bread, a dangerous idea took root.

That night, he returned to the blacksmith. As the shop closed, Diego crept inside and ambushed the man. His fists pounded bone until the blacksmith collapsed, limp and groaning. Diego seized the Tizona dagger and fled into the night, Ester bounding close behind, both chasing the blood-red trail of the setting sun.

THE GREAT JEW PIRATE

He traveled southward. Past sun-cracked fields and plague-stricken villages, through wind and rain and silence, until months later he arrived in his birthplace: Córdoba.

Through the Arc of Triumph, he walked like a ghost. Ester padded loyally beside him.

Diego made his way to the Mosque-Cathedral, the Mezquita. Marble floors echoed beneath his worn boots. He passed the great forest of arches—the red and white voussoirs, the jasper columns—and wandered beneath them like a soul in purgatory.

At the end of the nave, he entered a confessional and knelt, hiding his weathered face.

When Mass ended, the Archbishop arrived. "What brings you here?"

"Father," Diego said, voice breaking, "I've disgraced us. I seek forgiveness."

"God forgives with penance," the Archbishop replied coldly. "But your parents' disappointment is eternal."

"Please, Father."

"Walk with me."

They strolled the periphery of the Mezquita.

"You protested the Inquisition and lost everything—your command, your city, your honor. One son disgraces me. The other changes his name to climb the ladder."

"What does Mother say?"

"She wishes it had been you who changed your name."

Diego trembled. "My fiancée is gone. My brother's ashamed. My name is mud. Please—show mercy."

The Archbishop handed him a candle. "When the Christians reclaimed Córdoba, they turned this mosque into a cathedral to pray. It's time you did the same. Pray. Only God may forgive you."

Diego stared at the flame. Then, with deliberate defiance, he crushed it in his palm. The wick hissed. He dropped the candle to the floor.

He left his father behind forever.

At the city's main tavern, Diego found old comrades—soldiers, spies, assassins—men he had once led in North Africa. Their faces bore the same tired grief.

Fernando, his best friend, raised a glass. His title lost, his wife mad, his parents dead.

They drank sangria and forced laughter into the smoky air. Then outside, Ester barked.

A mutt lunged at her. The street filled with snarls and blood. Diego leapt forward—but too late. The dog had already torn into her neck. He pulled his dagger and buried it in the mutt's skull.

He knelt beside Ester, trembling. Her eyes, once bright, now dulled.

With shaking hands, he whispered, "Forgive me," and drove the dagger through her throat.

He rose, covered in her blood. His comrades stood behind him in silence.

"We must find our way back," Diego panted. "We must reclaim what we've lost... by any means necessary."

***

The wispy, floating mirror before the older Sinan changed once more and now it showed him a view of King Ferdinand II and his grandson Charles making their way through the Alcázar, the royal fortress in Seville. The boy was no older than eight years old, Sinan guessed.

King Ferdinand wasted no time in instilling certain "truths" into the young boy's mind.

THE GREAT JEW PIRATE

"You have a birthright, Charles," the King declared. "One that will be the greatest in history since Roman times. With your future betrothed, you will unite the Habsburg Kingdom with the kingdoms of Castile and Aragon, as well as our captured territories in Naples and North Africa. One day, you will be crowned the first Holy Roman Emperor."

Charles, for his part, was understandably nervous.

"This shall be no easy task," Ferdinand continued, "but do not fear, for I shall teach you the secrets of ruling such a vast empire."

The young prince looked up at his grandfather, eager to learn.

"Grandpapa?" Charles asked. "What happened to the Judíos in Spain?"

Ferdinand paused, noting that the boy was far more perceptive than most children his age.

"The Jews were eliminated from our lands, or converted, for the greater good of the country," he said carefully, leading Charles around a crystal-blue pool bordered by green fronds and alabaster columns.

"In 1492, we had just conquered Granada, the last Muslim stronghold in Spain, and we needed to rally our people. We chose the Jews as the source of their misfortune because—what could they do? They had no home, no army, no soil to root themselves in."

The young prince absorbed his grandfather's words, seeds of hatred quietly germinating.

"Now, we face a new problem. Conversos threaten our way of life," King Ferdinand said, his voice growing cold. "Swear to me, Charles, that when you become Holy Roman Emperor, you will always put our people first—by whatever means necessary."

"Yes, Grandpapa," Charles replied reverently, his voice soft but sure.

They exited into the Alcázar Gardens, walking among orange trees, fountains, and the brilliant plumage of royal peacocks. King Ferdinand inhaled deeply, savoring the citrus air as his eyes rested on La Giralda, the former Moorish minaret turned Christian bell tower.

"This is where your grandmother and I discussed many key matters, including the Spanish Inquisition," he said, smiling at the memory. "We gave them power—for economic reasons. You, too, will face such monumental choices. Remember, human life is fleeting. But dynastic power? That is eternal."

Charles nodded again, wide-eyed.

They stopped at a marble fountain, where a tall, dark-cloaked naval officer awaited them. The man's face bore the weathered signs of age, but his black beard remained thick and disciplined.

"Admiral Andrea Doria," Ferdinand announced proudly, "may I introduce to you my grandson, Charles—soon to be the Holy Roman Emperor."

Doria bowed and shook the boy's hand with the reserved grace of a lifelong mercenary. "The pleasure is mine, young prince. I trust we'll have a fruitful relationship in the years to come. The survival of my kingdom of Genoa depends on it."

"Not survival," Ferdinand corrected, accepting a glass of vino de naranja from a passing servant. "Prosperity."

Doria dipped his head in acknowledgement but showed no sign of agreement. He was a tactician, loyal only to the tide of fortune.

"So, how have our trade routes been faring? Any disturbances?" the king asked.

THE GREAT JEW PIRATE

"None, sire," Doria replied smoothly. "Our informants have been reliable. They've led us to the sites of every planned pirate ambush. We've eliminated them all."

"Excellent," Ferdinand said. "Now, Admiral, tell Charles about the three pillars of dynastic power."

Doria knelt—his joints audibly creaking—to meet the boy at eye level. "Political power, religious power, and economic power," he said, raising three fingers. "Political power comes from military force. Economic power funds your rule. Religious power? That's how you bend the will of the people when the sword or the coin fail."

They walked on, talking amidst the soothing sounds of water and birdsong.

Young Charles listened with the attention of one who knew that greatness—and cruelty—were expected of him.

Little did he know that the "truths" imparted that day would be the roots of countless atrocities yet to come.

From behind the memory mirror, the older Sinan clenched his jaw, his eyes burning with the quiet rage of history remembered all too well.

David Nobyl

David Nobyl

9

Lone Auroch

The wispy, floating mirror before the older Sinan changed once more and now it showed him a view of his younger self again—this time crammed in a small wagon with Dr. Badoz, Blanquina, and Luís on the outskirts of Valencia.

Weeks had passed since his fateful encounter with the dybbuk, Zequiel, and only now had Dr. Badoz healed enough to travel. The group, wary of Spanish patrols, avoided main roads, sticking to narrow, tangled paths veiled by forest and hill.

It was a day's ride from Valencia when trouble struck. The golden sun had just dipped below the horizon, casting an orange hue over the Sot de Chera Forest. Trees rose like ancient sentinels, their branches clawing at the sky as darkness fell. The pale glow of the full moon soon became their only source of light.

In the underbrush, a herd of wild Aurochs grazed in silence. These ancient beasts, with winding horns and heavy forelocks, were relics from another age—soon to vanish from the world forever. One such creature broke from the herd, drawn by the scent of fire and humans. It stumbled upon a group of ruthless Spanish huntsmen camped nearby.

The Auroch's curiosity was met with cruelty. Crossbow bolts flew. The wounded beast thrashed and charged the campfire in a dying frenzy, overturning it. In seconds, flames licked the surrounding trees. The forest ignited like parchment.

Sinan and his companions, not far from the blaze, struggled to navigate their frightened donkey through the choking smoke. Luís tugged at the reins while Blanquina tried to calm the beast. But it was Sinan who paused—his eyes catching movement amid the flames.

A lynx cub, it's fur charred, limped into view. It was badly burned and alone.

"No time!" Luís shouted, gesturing to move on.

But Sinan lunged forward, shielding the cub inside his tunic just before a flaming branch crashed onto the spot. Clutching the kitten to his chest, he helped Luís pull the donkey to the road, just ahead of the fire's reach.

That night, they moved carefully along the empty main road. Sinan sat beside Dr. Badoz, who lay wrapped in linens, his arm in a sling. The elder physician's breathing was labored.

Sinan gently unwrapped his tunic to show the lynx cub.

"Ah," Dr. Badoz rasped with a faint smile, "an Iberian Lynx cub... and all black. Ferocious things, you know."

"I don't want to keep it," Sinan said softly. "Only to help it live."

Dr. Badoz studied him with tired eyes. "You really do have the heart of a healer, don't you?"

"You are my uncle, aren't you?" Sinan offered with a smile.

But the smile didn't return. Dr. Badoz looked away, his expression shuttering.

Without another word, he guided Sinan's hands in how to clean the wounds and treat the lynx's injured eye. When finished, he turned his back to Sinan, facing the corner of the wagon.

Sinan laid the patched cub gently in a basket of cloth, then leaned against the wagon's wooden frame, confused and quiet.

Luís, watching from across the cart, limped over and sat beside him.

"My mother wants me to study at the University of Paris," Luís said after a long pause. "Philosophy. Come with me."

Sinan smiled, imagining it. But his smile faded when he saw Dr. Badoz's form shivering beneath his covers. Without a word, he rose and adjusted the linens, tucking them carefully around the older man.

"I understand," Luís said quietly.

Once Sinan returned, he looked at Luís, his eyes full of guilt. "Why don't you hate me? For how I treated you?"

"You didn't know," Luís replied simply.

"It doesn't matter. I had no right," Sinan whispered, tears welling. "No right to treat anyone that way."

"When the last Moorish stronghold fell in Granada," Luís said, "the Banu Rashid family—the final royal house of the Moors—escaped to Morocco. Their daughter married the governor of Tétouan. Her name was Hakimat Titwan."

Sinan furrowed his brow. "You're making that up."

Luís shook his head, smiling. "She's real. They say she treats Jews and Muslims as equals."

"That can't be."

"There's a bigger world out there than what we were taught, Sinan. The fall of Granada... it's no different than Masada. We've been fed lies our whole lives. But maybe—like Queen Hakimat—we'll find a new home out there, somewhere."

"I hope so," Sinan murmured.

Luís nodded. "We can regret what we've done. But we shouldn't regret who we are—or who we were born to become. Be proud, Sinan. Our ancestors laid down their lives for us to exist."

Something moved along the roadside, catching Sinan's eye.

A limping Auroch passed through the moonlight—injured but alive. It turned briefly toward them before disappearing back into the darkness.

And then the mirror dissolved. The older Sinan sat motionless aboard Captain Sayyida's ship. He gently closed the brass case of the astrolabe, the glow of the memory fading.

For the first time in many months, he slept. And his sleep was deep... and dreamless.

David Nobyl

10

The Pirate's Physician

Sinan crept from his hammock stealthily, and Samson's shadow followed, swift as a panther. The night was dark, and together they rose onto the deck of the Pirate Queen's ship.

The moonless sky mirrored the grim fate that was to befall the unsuspecting crew. With stealthy footing, Sinan and Samson entered the captain's quarters. After some time living on the ship, Sinan had a better understanding of the ship's layout.

The great Pirate Queen Sayyida Al-Hurra lay awake in anticipation. Silently, she handed Sinan a leather satchel with a loose strap. He inspected the contents, barely discernible in the dim light.

Satisfied with what was inside, he nodded to Samson, and they moved to the living quarters. Sinan whipped out a thick-leather handkerchief and tied it around his nose and mouth. The knot was tight, as he entered the eerie head, or restroom, of the ship.

Samson posted himself outside, his swollen arms crossed like a pair of meat hams. He was ready to take on anyone who dared to cross their path—even a giant kraken wouldn't stand a chance against him.

As Sinan waited in silence, the sound of the ocean seemed to grow louder and hotter. Suddenly, the first victim, Braman, stumbled into the bathroom. His breath reeked of alcohol, bladder full. But little did he know, he was about to face his worst nightmare.

As Braman made his way to the urinal, he was met with an odd sight. Instead of the usual hole in the floor, there stood a masked figure dressed in a horrible leather gown and mask. This was Sinan, the ship's doctor.

Braman froze in fear, his eyes bulging out of their sockets. But before he could react, Samson locked the door from the other side and held it steady. Braman was trapped, and there was no escaping this necessary intervention.

Ten minutes of continuous shrieking and pounding on the door followed, waking up the entire ship in the process. The crew members had no idea what was happening, but they knew it couldn't be good.

Once the pirate's shrieking had subsided, Sinan got down to business. He pulled out an ink bottle and quill in one hand and a moleskin notebook in the other.

"Braman, what brings you in here at this hour of the night?" Sinan demanded as he looked up from his notebook, his pen poised to write.

The pirate scratched his nether regions, a worried look on his face. "I—I have a problem, Doc," he stammered.

Sinan narrowed his eyes. "Is that so? Care to elaborate?"

Braman bristled at the tone, his anger bubbling to the surface. "I've been getting up all night, wandering around like a drunken sailor and waking up the whole crew! And during the day, I keep falling over like a drunkard and whining about not getting enough sleep. What do ya want me to do?!"

Sinan's lips thinned into a frown. "I want you to tell me what's going on, Braman. And I want you to do it without pulling your pants down."

The pirate scowled, his fists clenching. "I—I can't help it, Doc. It's driving me crazy!"

Sinan scribbled something in his notebook, his face a mask of concentration. "Can you tell me more about this problem of yours?"

Braman glared at him, his temper flaring. "More?! You want me to tell you more?!" With a grunt, he yanked down his pants, revealing a massive, swollen lump next to his privates. "Look at it, Doc! Look at what's been plaguing me!"

Sinan recoiled in horror, his face paling. "For the love of all that's holy, Braman, pull your pants back up! I don't need to see that!"

The pirate complied, his anger now replaced by concern. "Please help me. It itches and I hate it. And this rash on my hands and feet! What's wrong with me?"

Sinan took a deep breath, his mind racing. "Have you had any sexual relations in the past year or two?"

Braman's eyes widened in surprise. "Yeah, lots of them! In fact, more than the average pirate, if you catch my drift."

Sinan nodded, his face serious. "And do you prefer men, women, or both?"

The pirate recoiled, his face contorting in disgust. "What kind of question is that?!"

"I think I understand what's causing your problems," Sinan said quietly, his voice barely above a whisper.

Braman's eyes widened in horror. "No. No, it can't be!"

Sinan nodded grimly. "I'm afraid so, Braman. The Pox, or in medical lingo, Syphilis. But don't worry. I was taught how to make the cure by my uncle."

The pirate looked at him, his eyes pleading. Sinan pulled out two vials from his satchel and handed them to Braman.

"The first is for your urinary incontinence. The second is for The Pox."

Braman looked at the vials, his face a mix of disbelief and hope. "But that's impossible. How can you cure The Pox?"

Sinan smiled faintly. "Scrape the mold off of old bread and dissolve it in alcohol ether. That's all you need to do."

Braman looked at the vial of milky, viscous liquid and licked his lips. "Alcohol, huh?" Without further ado, he uncorked the tiny bottle and poured the entire contents down his throat.

"That vial," Sinan sighed, shaking his head in disbelief, "was meant to last a month."

Braman cocked his head to the side. "You know, I think I'm cured now," he grinned, eyeing Sinan's satchel, "Unless you've got some more medicine in there for me?"

Sinan rolled his eyes. "Let him out, Samson."

Braman grinned widely, his eyes sparkling with joy. "Thanks, Doc! You're a lifesaver!"

He swaggered out of the bathroom, feeling like a new man. As he passed by the other crew members, they stared at him in amazement.

"What's going on?" one of them asked.

"I just got cured of The Pox!" Braman exclaimed, his voice filled with triumph.

THE GREAT JEW PIRATE

The crew members looked at each other in disbelief, then formed a line outside the bathroom door, eager to receive the same miraculous cure.

"What have I gotten myself into," Sinan thought aloud as he watched the scene with a mixture of amusement and resignation.

A full day passed before Sinan finished tending to his last patient. With all the pirates seen, he entered the Pirate Queen's cabin, his hands thoroughly washed with trace amounts of ash and gunpowder.

"Ready for your checkup, Captain?" he half-joked.

"If you dare to even start," she warned, "I'll drive my scimitar straight up your..."

"75!" Sinan interrupted. "Your men, and one really poorly disguised woman, have a whopping grand total of 75 venereal diseases. What kind of ship are you running?"

David Nobyl

David Nobyl

11

Sayyida's Solemn Vow

The Pirate Queen chuckled, relaxing. "I'm the captain, not their mother. It's not my concern what they do in port. As long as they're on deck and ready to work when we depart, my concerns end there. What's with you and the gunpowder hand washing? No physician I've ever seen does that. And as reigning Queen of Morocco, I'm sure you can imagine the caliber of physicians I'm used to."

"My teacher wasn't very...orthodox, shall we say, in his ways. Let alone his opinion of the state of modern medicine," Sinan grunted.

"Who was your teacher?" she asked.

"His name was Dr. Badoz. He was my uncle and Chief Physician to the Queen...," he stopped himself.

"Which queen?" Sayyida inquired.

"Doesn't matter," Sinan quipped. "The past is gone now. All we have left is what lies ahead."

Just as Sayyida was about to press Sinan further, Samson entered the cabin. "Captain, we're set to reach Isle

Ischia tomorrow at dusk. That's where they're holding the child slaves."

"Excellent," Sayyida nodded. "Take our new doctor and help prepare the weapons and artillery. It's going to be a long, bloody night. Let's just hope our informant was right." She shot Samson a secretive look.

With that, Sinan and Samson bowed and left to prepare for the upcoming battle. The crew readied the cannons, gunpowder, and an array of weapons. Samson and Sinan worked tirelessly, the sunset casting a warm glow over them.

Samson and Sinan were nearly done when Samson decided to throw a curveball Sinan's way. The sun had dipped low in the sky, casting a breathtaking array of purples and pinks across the clouds as Sinan set down the last of the shields and swords.

"Catch!" Samson shouted, launching a scimitar in Sinan's direction. In a cat-like maneuver, Sinan dodged, the sword embedding itself into the wooden mast behind him.

"What was that for?" Sinan demanded, his neck hairs standing at attention.

"Battle awaits us. Are you ready?" Samson inquired, his tone authoritative.

"I don't know. I've never fought before," Sinan replied, only for Samson to fling another scimitar at his head. But this time Sinan leaned it and caught the spinning weapon mid-air.

Samson watched as Sinan caught the scimitar with ease, his own surprise mingling with that of the rest of the crew and the captain's. "For one who has never been in battle, you seem to know more than you let on," Samson spoke, picking up a third, even larger scimitar. But instead of throwing it, he held it tight in his hand, balancing it out so that his strokes gave off harmonic frequencies that reverberated through howling winds around them.

Sinan raised an eyebrow, his gaze locked onto Samson's movements. "Are you trying to impress me, or yourself?" he quipped.

Samson chuckled, his eyes glinting with amusement. "Who says I can't do both?" With that, he charged forward, his scimitar flashing through the air with deadly precision.

Sinan's eyes narrowed as he readied himself for the attack. He moved with a grace that belied his inexperience, his movements fluid and precise as he blocked Samson's strikes with ease.

The two of them danced across the deck of the ship, their scimitars ringing out in a deadly melody. The rest of the crew watched in awe, their eyes fixed on the two warriors as they battled it out.

For a moment, it seemed as though Samson had the upper hand. His strikes were swift and powerful, and Sinan was forced to take a step back to avoid being hit.

But then, something changed. Sinan's eyes seemed to flash with a newfound determination, and he moved with a speed and ferocity that Samson had never seen before.

In a blur of motion, Sinan disarmed Samson and had him at sword-point in a matter of seconds. "Perhaps I am not ready, but are any of us ever truly ready for that black void that lies before each and every one of us?" he said, his voice cold and steady.

Samson's eyes widened in surprise, his own sword arm lowering as he stared at his adversary in awe. "How? I do not understand. You know secrets of medicine others could scarily imagine. How can you also know the ways of the blade as if by instinct, all while being a pious man?"

Sinan smirked, his eyes gleaming with amusement. "I'm lucky in the teachers I've had in life."

"Who trained you to be such a master of the blade?" Samson requested.

Sinan's eyes flicked over to Queen Sayyida, who was watching them from the helm of the ship. "The one-armed man," he said, his voice low and dangerous.

"Who is the one-armed man?" Samson echoed, confusion etched on his face.

"Oruc Barbarossa," Queen Sayyida called out.

Sinan grinned, his eyes flashing with mischief. "So, you've heard of him? Or should I say his younger brother, Hizir Barbarossa?"

"You dare utter that swine's name!" Queen Sayyida yelled, her eyes flashing with anger.

Sinan let out a chuckle as he watched Sayyida storm off, her rage as hot as the desert sun. He turned to the crew, a smug grin spreading across his face like a spilled inkwell on parchment. "Looks like the captain has a bit of a temper," he said with a smirk.

The crew glared at him, their eyes full of anger and contempt. They may have been a motley crew, but they were loyal to their captain, and they didn't take kindly to anyone who insulted her.

"Watch your tongue, Sinan," growled one of the crew members. "We won't tolerate any disrespect towards the captain."

Sinan raised his hands in surrender, his grin still firmly in place. "Easy, easy," he said. "I didn't mean any offense. I just wanted to know if she knew who I was talking about."

"Well, now you know," said Samson. "And if you know what's good for you, you'll drop the subject and never bring it up again."

"Don't worry, I won't," he said. "I have no desire to feel the pointy end of the captain's knives."

The crew relaxed a bit at his words. He leaned against the mast, his fingers drumming a quick rhythm on the wood as he thought. He couldn't help but feel a twinge of guilt. He had accidentally reopened deep gashes of her past and he needed to make amends.

An hour or so later, Sinan made his way to the captain's cabin, rapping his knuckles against the door before inviting himself inside.

"I've come to apologize," Sinan began, but to his surprise, not only was Queen Sayyida sitting on the floor, but she had downed half a bottle of rum. Her eyes were swollen, red, and glassy with intoxication. She looked up at him, not with a piercing gaze, but with a dull and blunted one.

"I guess I should thank you," she slurred, turning back to her bottle.

"For what, bringing back bad memories?" Sinan retorted.

"Thank you...for, uh, reminding me of this mess that I—and you—that we are in," she stumbled through her thoughts. "You see, uh, you want the easy way out. You want me to kill you so you can go see your family. I get it, really, I do."

Sinan tried to interject, but Sayyida stopped him by raising her hand.

"I saw how you longed to eat that blade with your stomach. I saw how you say you're willing to help me, but you just can't wait for the next moment to throw yourself onto the nearest pike!" she scrutinized. "But you know why I haven't done that yet? Why haven't I helped you like someone who actually cares about your pain and suffering?"

Sinan waited for her to take another swig.

"You haven't earned it!" she spat. "Dying and being set free is a right to be earned! It's earned in battle, earned by saving lives, earned by protecting the people you love or people you haven't even met! But it's never selfish."

"I don't wish to die," Sinan protested. "Anymore."

"Yet, you don't fear death," she retorted, sarcastically. "What are you gonna do tomorrow? When we land on the beach, huh? Charge the sands like a buffoon and get yourself killed?" She looked up at him with the unsteady eyes of a drunkard, but with the resolution of someone who could fight through the haziness of alcohol.

Sinan froze in disbelief. He couldn't fathom how someone could see through him as thoroughly as she did, knowing his innermost desires and plans for the following day. He did in fact plan to do exactly that. Run headfirst into battle to be set free.

"How did you know?"

"You're not the first member of my crew," she let out a loud hiccup, "to come to me in desperation and peril. You won't be the last." She took another swig from her bottle and finished it with three large gulps. "I only hope you find what you need while you're here."

"And do you know what I need?" Sinan glanced around her cabin, taking in the assortment of maps, sketches of various men, and one particular image of a man, a woman, and a young child.

"I can't answer that for you. I have too many of my own unanswered questions," she sighed. "But it has something to do with this." She pointed at Sinan's pocket. He slid his hand inside and pulled out the magic astrolabe.

"So, besides viewing old memories, do you know how it works?" Sayyida tried to get up but failed. Sinan attempted to help her, but she held up her hand in protest.

"You're implying I know what 'it' is," Sinan replied. "I only know how to see old memories and sometimes the memories of people who've crossed my path. Do you know how it works?"

"Maybe," she said, forcing herself to get up on all fours at first and then slowly crawling up the side of her cabinet. "Maybe it's the same Kabbalah magic that took my son's life and destroyed my husband before my eyes," she spat, straightening herself beside the cabinet. "But what do I know?"

"Captain," Sinan pleaded. "Tell me what you know. It may be our only way to take down Andrea Doria."

She shivered at the name. "Kabbalah magic doesn't change, but the way it's used can," she shuffled her feet into her captain's chair and plopped into the cushioned seat. "Think of the person you love most in this world. Think of them and only them."

"Say I do, what then?"

"Then open your astrolabe," she continued, ignoring him, "and let it show you what you need to see."

With trembling hands, Sinan thought of the person he loved most in the world, his eyes misting, and he opened the brass case. The astrolabe glowed a fierce red now, and the wispy mirror formed quicker this time.

The memory began to play, and he was certain it was not his own. He had never even met this person when the memory had happened, years ago. But he knew whose it was.

"Rahel," Sinan gasped.

David Nobyl

David Nobyl

12

Catalonian Conversos

Dawn's shimmering light pierced the nautical twilight over Barcelona's coast, rousing the earliest risers from their slumber. It was late December of 1505, and the recent discovery of the New World had ignited a frenzy of ambition, exploration, and imperial greed. At the Port of Barcelona, a towering bronze statue of Columbus—hastily erected atop a lofty pillar—symbolized the city's hope for glory and prosperity. But that hope would soon dim. A political shift was coming that would siphon trade from Barcelona's harbor, plunging the city into economic decline and unrest.

News of Queen Isabella's death had spread rapidly through Christian Spain, and rumors soon followed: King Ferdinand planned to eliminate all conversos—converted Jews—still living among them. For the citizens of Barcelona, desperate and angry, this rumor provided the perfect scapegoat. Pogroms swept the city, and crypto-Jews were massacred with impunity.

David Nobyl

Barcelona, no stranger to such horrors, showed no sign of changing its ways. The looming shadow of the Spanish Inquisition had returned.

On a frigid December night, a twelve-year-old Catalan converso girl—the eldest daughter of the last crypto-Jewish family in Barcelona—climbed the treacherous path toward the Montjuïc watchtower. A small woven sack clutched to her chest, she crept through the darkness, careful to avoid patrolling guards. Montjuïc, meaning "hill of the Jews," had long been the site of a Jewish cemetery, though a Christian lighthouse had since been built atop its bones. That lighthouse, too, would one day be demolished, replaced by a fortress of empire.

At the cliff's edge, the girl gazed down at the crashing Mediterranean waves. Her fear of the sea was second only to the burning determination in her brilliant green eyes. Like an Iberian lynx cornered by fire, she refused to run. Not yet.

She knelt at the southeastern corner of the lighthouse and carefully laid a single red rose on a worn tombstone protrusion. Only two Hebrew letters remained visible on the stone—most had been erased by recent construction. But the girl knew the inscription by heart: "Funerary stele of Rivka, daughter of Rabbi Abraham Ha Levi. May her Rock and her Savior protect her."

Exactly two hundred years had passed since her great-great-grandmother was murdered in a pogrom. Her family had been forced to convert to Christianity. Those who refused were either burned alive or dragged through the streets until dead.

But the child's tribute did not go unnoticed. A guard found the rose. Moments later, the alarm bell rang, echoing

THE GREAT JEW PIRATE

through the city and signaling a high alert for "suspicious activity."

She fled quickly, back to the place she called home: a small underground textile shop that had once been the ancient synagogue of Barcelona. Her family—now the last known conversos in the city—was hunted. With the king's decree in force, the local populace had been granted the role of judge, jury, and executioner.

Back at the shop, Ester wiped her brow and knocked on the heavy door, hoping her daughter had already returned. Felipe, her husband, opened it with a look of strained worry etched on his face.

"She hasn't come back?" Ester whispered.

He shook his head and shut the door behind her. "I asked the neighbors. No one has seen her."

"You think those people would help us even if they had?" she snapped.

"Let's prepare Shabbat first," Felipe's elderly mother said softly from her bed in the corner. "It's not like she hasn't done this before."

"All right."

Ester locked the windows, ensuring no one could see inside. Then she lifted a kitchen floorboard and drew out a tall, golden teapot, its surface adorned with thick silver leaves. But this was no ordinary teapot.

Like a Russian nesting doll of Jewish memory, each piece of the teapot concealed another artifact: a dreidel tucked inside the lid, a spice holder bearing Hebrew script, an eternal flame holder hidden in the spout, and a tiny Megillah rolled into the handle. Within the belly of the teapot lay a full seder set.

Ester had just begun to place the sacred items on the table when a sudden knock froze them all.

In a flurry, the family reassembled and reburied the teapot. Felipe raced to the door—and flung it open.

There stood a Spanish commander in full armor, medals gleaming like trophies of conquest. In his grip was a frightened girl—Ester's daughter—her face pale and her small sack now gone.

Behind him, a pack of grinning soldiers loitered like hungry dogs.

Felipe didn't care. His daughter was home. That was all that mattered.

"Thank you, sir," Felipe said, bowing deeply and repeatedly. "My daughter has a habit of wandering off. We're grateful for your help."

The commander said nothing. His eyes slid over Ester, lingering too long—just as they had once before, years ago. Felipe, oblivious or choosing to ignore it, kept apologizing. When he finally stopped, the commander extended a gloved hand.

Felipe quickly produced several coins from his coat, placing them into the waiting palm.

The commander grinned. Satisfied, he released the girl, shoving her through the doorway.

As Felipe began to shut the door, the commander blocked it with one hand. "Careful," he warned, voice low and menacing. "If your family keeps disappearing, I might not bring them back next time."

Felipe laughed nervously.

The commander leaned close to Ester, his breath hot on her neck. "You would have a better life with me," he whispered.

Ester bowed her head, her eyes closed tight with rage and fear.

"Gracias, Diego de Cordoba," she said, voice thin as parchment. "But I must remain with my family."

Diego de Cordoba snarled and stroked his mustache with mock elegance. "For now," he muttered, stepping back into the darkness.

Felipe slammed the door and bolted it, his breath catching in his chest.

"Lo siento, Papá," his daughter wept, "I just wanted to leave roses for my great-great-grandma. And for my little sister. Today is her birthday. Please forgive me."

Felipe dropped to his knees and wrapped her in his arms.

"It's all right, Rahel," he whispered, voice thick with grief. "You did it for all of us. We miss her so much."

David Nobyl

David Nobyl

13

Valencia's Hidden Kingdom

Back aboard the Pirate Queen's ship, Sayyida and Sinan exchanged glances as the memory mirror rippled, blurring the last image before bleeding into the next. They turned their attention back to the swirling light, ready to witness whatever the magic had in store for them.

Valencia had long been the crown jewel of the Catalan-speaking territories, its port among the largest in Europe, famed for silks and clementines that perfumed the bustling air.

Together, Sinan, Dr. Badoz, Blanquina, and their friend Luís made the return journey to Valencia. Their mission was twofold: help a friend escape and bring Dr. Badoz to tend to Luís's ailing father. In the doctor's absence, a young Catalan girl named Rahel had taken on the role of caregiver.

She had lost her family in a brutal raid on Barcelona. Blanquina had taken her in, and she stayed behind while the others went to fetch the doctor. When they returned, Rahel's relief was palpable. None of them yet knew that both Sebastian de Olmedo and Diego de Cordoba were tracking them, closing in.

After the group settled in, Dr. Badoz examined Luís's father carefully. Once finished, he turned to Rahel.

"Excellent work," he said with genuine appreciation. "Your attention to detail is rare." He lifted a poorly bandaged arm and cast a sidelong glance at Sinan, who was busy entertaining his one-eyed pet caracal.

The feline playfully nipped at Sinan's fingers, holding his hand in its soft, spotted paws.

"May I ask," Dr. Badoz continued, addressing Rahel, "where are you from?"

"Barcelona," she replied tersely.

"Ah, then you must know the inscription on the grave atop Montjuïc," he mused. "You know the one, yes?"

"May her Rock and her Savior protect her," Rahel said instinctively—and immediately regretted it. Her eyes widened, realizing she'd fallen into a trap.

"There's no need to interrogate her," Blanquina interjected quickly. "She's the last surviving daughter of Ester and Felipe. They died in the raid. That's why she's with us."

Dr. Badoz bowed his head. "Then we must protect her. All of us. While we still can."

Rahel's shoulders eased slightly. But a new worry crossed her face. Dr. Badoz noticed.

He lowered his voice. "I've secured passage for Sinan and me to Venice. As soon as I finish treating Luís's father, we leave. You're welcome to come."

Rahel nodded deeply, emotion flickering in her eyes.

THE GREAT JEW PIRATE

Blanquina chimed in, half-skeptical, half-curious. "If I may ask—what exactly are you using to treat him?"

"Ricotta cheese," Dr. Badoz said plainly.

Blanquina burst into laughter, only to quiet when she realized he wasn't joking.

Modern medicine would later understand the symptoms as sideroblastic anemia—a condition mitigated by certain nutrients found in foods like ricotta.

"The cheese will strengthen his blood," Dr. Badoz explained. "Luís, could you go to La Lonja de la Seda and fetch more? Be extra cautious today."

"Why today?" Sinan asked. When everyone turned to him, he added, "What? You thought Tzitzi and I weren't listening?"

At the mention of her name, the baby lynx purred and butted her head affectionately against Sinan. He dangled a string over her head, and she tumbled after it, still adjusting to life with only one eye.

"Rumors say Sebastian de Olmedo is in town," Dr. Badoz said grimly. Sinan froze.

"That's why I'm sending Luís. And why I'm going to El Barrio Judío alone."

"The abandoned ghetto?" Blanquina gasped. "But if anyone sees you—"

"I know," he cut her off. "But there is something I must retrieve. I cannot leave Spain without it. And I must go alone."

His tone left no room for argument. Even Rahel sensed it: this was a man with unfinished business etched into his soul.

Sinan said nothing. He kept his head low, fingers toying with a linen napkin. Quiet suited him when scheming.

Dr. Badoz departed one way; Luís another. Sinan stayed behind, assisting Blanquina and Rahel in caring for Luís's father. He folded sheets and hung them to dry so Tzitzi could keep playing with the dangling strings.

"She's got quite a spirit, that one," Blanquina smiled.

"Who, the wild animal or my kitten?" Sinan quipped.

Blanquina arched a brow. "She's the last of the Barcelona conversos. There's no place for her here. But what if she joined Luís at the University of Paris? Dr. Badoz's letter got him in. I'm sure he'd write one for both of you."

Sinan paused. "I used to say I'd follow my uncle wherever he went. But maybe that wouldn't be such a bad detour."

Blanquina folded quietly. "We're all still healing. Especially Dr. Badoz."

Sinan caught her meaning. "He hasn't told me anything. Care to enlighten me?"

Blanquina froze. Then, realizing she'd said too much, turned away.

"I know something happened the night my mother died," Sinan pressed. "And I know it happened here. Please."

Her voice trembled. "The night your mother died... changed us all. The Inquisition demanded proof of our conversion. Terrible things were done. We did what we had to."

"What did he do? What happened to her?" Sinan whispered.

"No!" Blanquina cried. "He was our rabbi. He had no choice! And it is not my place to speak what you are not ready to hear."

THE GREAT JEW PIRATE

Sinan clenched a linen cloth so tightly water streamed from it onto the floor.

Blanquina lowered her voice. "There is a reason he hasn't spoken a single Hebrew prayer in thirteen years. One day, he may tell you. Or not. But that decision is his, not mine."

She gathered her basket and left quietly.

Sinan followed, his chest tight with frustration. Inside, he knelt beside his kitten and scratched her belly to calm his nerves.

"What did you say to Blanquina?" Rahel demanded.

"That's between us," Sinan replied, not looking up.

Rahel stepped closer. "Your uncle risks his life in the old Jewish Quarter, and you're playing with your kitten?"

"I've lived with him longer than you," Sinan said, still calm. "I know how stubborn he is. But that doesn't mean I'm idle."

He stood and revealed a torn piece of cloth—a piece of Dr. Badoz's tunic, ripped during their last escape.

"She can track him?" Rahel asked.

"She's smarter than she looks," Sinan said with a sly grin, wrapping a scarf around his neck.

Tzitzi leapt onto the windowsill, sniffing the breeze.

"I didn't know caracals could do that," Rahel whispered, impressed.

"Funny," Sinan said, glancing back at her. "I was actually talking about you."

Her face flushed crimson.

Sinan grinned. "You coming?"

The blush faded, replaced by a spark of anticipation. She nodded.

David Nobyl

David Nobyl

14

Fates Converge

In the bustling heart of Valencia's central market, Luís had been occupied with purchasing ricotta cheese from Italian merchants who traveled far to sell their wares. Unknown to him, outside the marketplace, in a coffee shop, the notorious Diego de Córdoba sat with his small but feared group of soldiers.
Diego sipped an invigorating cup of Spanish espresso, freshly imported with the earliest batches from the New World, while his men watched their four purebred Iberian greyhounds viciously fight over a large chunk of jamón. The dogs' brawl ceased when the ground rumbled—dozens of horses thundered through the cobbled streets.

The horses charged up to the Spanish soldiers at the café, their metal-shod hooves clanging on the stone steps, startling the greyhounds. The lead rider dismounted, revealing himself as Sebastián de Olmedo, who commanded a small army under King Ferdinand's orders.

Diego didn't even look up from his espresso until he'd finished his sip and placed the tiny porcelain cup back on its coaster. Finally, he glanced up at Sebastián, who stood over him, stiff with purpose.

"To what do I owe the pleasure?" Diego asked, stroking his well-trimmed goatee.

"I am on a mission to capture a certain group of conversos who've eluded me," Sebastián replied. "I need your help to find and eliminate them."

Diego smirked. "And what makes you think I'd help you? I have my own conversos I'm hunting down... twin brother."

A hush fell over the soldiers, and even the dogs quieted. It was true—the two men were twins, identical except for their facial hair. While Diego wore a goatee, Sebastián was clean-shaven.

"I am De Olmedo now," Sebastián snapped, aware of the eyes on him.

Diego scoffed. "You think getting a fancy title in the king's court, changing your family name to suit your Inquisition puppet masters, and convincing the crown to hand you an army makes you powerful?"

He stood, meeting Sebastián eye to eye. Though the same height, Diego's broader frame cast the more commanding shadow.

"You've never tasted real war—not like North Africa. My men and I bled for this empire. You, on the other hand, command torturers from behind velvet curtains."

Sebastián's temper flared. "Twin or not, if you refuse a direct order from the king, I'll see you and your dogs imprisoned."

Diego's men reached for their swords, but he raised a hand, signaling restraint. "True, you have the king's favor—but think carefully how you proceed. I know the crown's secrets."

Sebastián narrowed his eyes. "What secrets?"

"That the very wars against the Moors—wars I fought—were bankrolled by Jewish financiers. And when the fighting ended, those same royals passed the 1492 edict. Convert or die. Clever loophole: once Jews became Christians, they could no longer legally collect interest. And if they refused? No repayments at all."

Sebastián said nothing. The truth stung.

"Brilliant policy," Diego mused, finishing another sip. "But now? Burning conversos for sport? That's fanaticism."

"Then why play their game?" Sebastián demanded.

"That's personal," Diego replied coldly. "Press me again, and your shiny army will be scrap metal and horsehair. Understand, 'older' brother?"

Sebastián's men stiffened. He backed up—just one step. "Fine. Let's strike a deal. For your help, you'll earn the king's gratitude."

Diego raised an eyebrow.

Sebastián tried again. "By royal authority, I restore your title as Governor of Oran, effective immediately. Signed by sunset."

Diego's grin returned.

"With full absolution for past charges," Sebastián added.

Now Diego stood and clasped his brother's hand in a firm shake. "I knew you had it in you."

"So how do we find our conversos?"

"By listening to the ground beneath their feet," Diego said, turning toward the market. He glanced back at the confused faces. "Ask the bread and spice vendors. They see everything—and speak, if the price is right."

Sebastián nodded and gestured for his men to move.

Just as Sebastián stepped forward, Diego gripped his arm. His voice was low and firm. "If you find a young

Catalan girl—tell me first. Her mother is important to me. And if anything happens to the girl... your men won't live to regret it. Comprendes, hermano?"

"Sí," Sebastián wrenched his arm free. "But if you fail me, there will be no decree. Comprendes tú?"

Diego nodded slowly. He whistled, and the greyhounds snapped to attention. With his men in tow, he entered the marketplace—La Lonja de la Seda.

Inside, Luís had just finished purchasing three pounds of ricotta cheese at a bargain price from a one-toothed, cross-eyed Gypsy woman who knew far more than she let on. As he turned to leave, she watched him closely, already turning details over in her mind—details she would soon trade to Diego for her own protection.

David Nobyl

15

Into the Void

Dr. Badoz darted through the winding alleys of Valencia like a cat chasing not a mouse, but a clue. The buildings loomed around him, their stone faces worn and weary from centuries of neglect. He had once found the "kissing" style of architecture—where buildings leaned toward one another—quaint, even romantic. Now it felt suffocating.

The farther he went, the more the neighborhood decayed. Cracked windows gaped like broken teeth, walls slumped, and peeling paint flaked off like shedding skin. Turning onto Calle de la Paz, he squeezed through a narrowing corridor, exhaling heavily as he emerged on the other side.

He stopped to catch his breath. Memories surged—his beloved, the birth of his son, the grandeur of the Major Synagogue of Valencia's Jewish Ghetto. Then came the darkness. The secrets, the betrayals, the lies buried deep beneath his role as a physician. All of it pressed down on him like the buildings around him.

He forced the past back into its cage and focused. His eyes scanned the crumbling architecture until he spotted it—a ruined house wedged between two taller ones, like a forgotten book crammed into an overstuffed shelf.

Heart pounding, Dr. Badoz ascended the crooked steps. The door, barely hanging on its hinges, creaked with the building's silent plea for rescue.

This was it—the Major Synagogue. His former home. This time, he didn't push away the memories. He let them come. Then, candle in hand, he stepped inside.

Glass crunched beneath his boots. A metallic clang echoed from behind. He whirled around, fists clenched—but there was only darkness.

He pressed on, deeper into the ruin. The stairs groaned beneath his weight, but held. On the second floor, where once his family's Megillah had been kept, he found nothing but charred ash.

He moved aside a shattered cabinet, revealing a rug layered in dust. Beneath it, a trapdoor. He yanked it open and uncovered a stone box, its surface engraved with the Seal of Solomon. His hands trembled.

Sliding in the key Sinan had reclaimed from Sebastian, he opened the box with a quiet click.

The air seemed to crackle—though it may have only been his nerves. The box had been protected for generations, seen only by the most venerated rabbis. Now, it fell to the last rabbi left in Spain. A man escaping with a boy he claimed was his nephew—but who was in truth his only son.

Tears welled in Dr. Badoz's eyes as he remembered the brutal edict of 1492. Jews expelled, slaughtered, or forced to convert. He had lied to protect his son. And now he lied to live with himself.

THE GREAT JEW PIRATE

Inside the box lay silver coins and a relic: an ancient Hebrew astrolabe, the last of its kind. Its three bronze plates revealed maps, but only to the worthy. He tucked it into his leather physician's satchel, then shut the box, leaving it hollow—like himself.

There was no more time for mourning. He bolted downstairs and exited into the courtyard.

Soldiers awaited him.

Spanish troops, armed and mounted, encircled the ruins. Their leader, garbed in red and black, sat atop a pristine white steed. Sebastián de Olmedo.

"Well, well, Dr. Badoz," Sebastián sneered. "You've led quite the chase. But all games must end."

Dr. Badoz froze, scanning for an escape. There was none.

Sebastián dismounted, triumphant. "I knew you'd return eventually. I just didn't expect it so soon. Thank you for your... predictability."

A guard handed him a pair of iron shackles—the same ones used during Dr. Badoz's time in Diego de Deza's dungeon. Their rusted hinges were still stained with his blood.

Sebastián held the cuffs in place, savoring the moment.

"I waited years for this," he hissed. "Every time I tried to rise in court, to get close to the Queen, you were there. She trusted you. Listened to you. Praised your medicine—'so far beyond any Christian physician,' she'd say." He spat at the ground.

Then—a rock.

It struck Sebastián squarely in the head. He collapsed.

Chaos erupted. Stones rained down from the rooftops. Soldiers panicked.

Dr. Badoz sprinted into the chaos, ducking behind a statue of the mayor. Above, Sinan and Rahel launched their ambush, a barrage of well-aimed stones.

A soldier galloped by, carrying the limp body of Sebastián slung across his lap like discarded cloth.

"What are you doing here?" Dr. Badoz gasped, breathless.

"Oh, nothing," Sinan said, smirking as Tzitzi purred beside him. "Rahel's never thrown stones at Spanish soldiers before. Thought I'd show her a good time."

"Not true!" Rahel interjected. "It was his idea."

Sinan winked. "What can I say, uncle? I like saving you. It's becoming a habit."

That word— "uncle"—stabbed at Dr. Badoz like a knife. It was the barrier he'd built between himself and the boy. A lie for survival, but a cruel one.

"Enough," Dr. Badoz said, pulling himself together. "We're leaving. To Puerto Natzaret. Now."

"We can't abandon Luís and Blanquina!" Sinan protested. "His father's still sick!"

"He's recovering. He'll survive. But if we go back, they'll be killed."

Sinan's face fell, his fists clenched tight. But he nodded.

With Rahel and Tzitzi, they ran through the city. The midday sun glared off the cathedral's scaffolding as they reached the port.

"That one!" Dr. Badoz pointed to a modest vessel. They boarded quickly.

Inside the cramped captain's office, a plump, bearded merchant sat among a map of the Mediterranean, an hourglass, and a broken astrolabe. When he saw Dr. Badoz, his face lit up.

"Right on time," the merchant said, his grin wide. "Do you have what I asked for?"

Dr. Badoz placed silver coins on the desk. "As agreed."

"And the astrolabe?" the merchant prodded. "Mine's broken. No other ship will get you where you need to go."

Dr. Badoz frowned, suspicious. Before he could respond, heavy boots echoed on the deck. Barking dogs followed.

Tzitzi bristled.

The merchant's grin faded. "They're here. I tried."

Footsteps thundered. Luís's voice rang out in panic.

The cabin door flew open. Diego de Córdoba's soldiers stormed in. A blade pressed to Luís's throat. He clutched a ball of ricotta cheese, his arms trembling.

"He cornered me! I had no choice!" Luís cried.

"You sold us out!" Sinan shouted.

"No! I didn't!"

"How could you? I trusted you!"

Tears streamed down Luís's face. "I swear!"

"TRAITOR!"

Diego shoved Luís aside. The boy fled, sobbing, dropping the cheese. Diego didn't bother to pursue. He saw the act for what it was—and respected the cunning.

Now his attention turned to Rahel.

"As we agreed?" the merchant asked timidly, extending his fingers.

Diego smiled. Then sliced off the merchant's hand with one smooth stroke.

The man shrieked. Diego kicked him overboard.

"I hate greedy merchants," he muttered.

He turned to Fernando. "Cuff them."

Rahel dashed for the ship's edge.

Fernando chased. Sinan rolled beneath him, sweeping his legs. Years of mischief had taught him armored guards' weak points.

Fernando stumbled, recovered, grabbed Sinan, and flung him hard against the deck. Tzitzi lunged, biting his leg.

Fernando cried out in pain. Dr. Badoz rushed forward, seizing Fernando by the nerve points in his neck.

Fernando gasped, flailed. Sinan kicked his face, stunning him. But a heavy object crashed into Dr. Badoz's skull. He collapsed.

Diego stood behind him, dagger hilt stained with blood.

In his other hand, he held Rahel by the hair—unconscious.

Sinan struggled to rise, only to feel a brutal blow to the back of his head. Lights burst behind his eyes. He hit the deck.

The last thing he heard was Diego's voice: "Load them onto the Cavalleria. We sail for Naples."

And then—

Darkness.

The memory mirror through which Sayyida and Sinan watched flickered... then fizzled out completely.

David Nobyl

16

Slaves and Survivors

Sinan left Sayyida's quarters with the astrolabe safely tucked away in his pocket. As he descended the stairs to the lower quarters, he heard Samson and Braman whispering from their hammocks.

"Braman," Samson said, still awake, "Sayyida never told me—how did you get that information? About the slave children. It gave her hope again, after all these years."

"Ah," Braman chuckled, swirling his ale, "a man like me always finds things out—especially with a few coins and the right pretty face."

Samson rolled his eyes. "This battle... it's something she's been waiting for her entire life."

"If we survive," Braman muttered, taking another swig.

"For the chance to save Sayyida's child, I'd gladly lay down my life," Samson said. "I've already lived through worse."

"Oh yeah?" Braman raised an eyebrow. "Like what?"

Samson shifted in his hammock. "You know I'm from Djidjelli, east of Algiers. My family lived in the palace."

"Sure," Braman nodded. "But that's old news."

"What I never told you—or any crew member—is that we were the royal family," Samson revealed. "Only Sayyida knows. I told her back when I was part of her Queen's Guard in Morocco."

Sinan's foot creaked on the floorboard. He froze.

"We already knew you were there, Sinan," Samson called calmly.

"We did?" Braman blinked.

Sinan stepped forward with folded arms. "At least I know why Sayyida keeps you around. Couldn't sneak up on you even if I tried."

"Exactly," Braman said.

"Don't let me interrupt."

Samson nodded. "We ruled peacefully. On the night of my older brother's coronation, my uncle poisoned the entire royal family. Everyone died—except me, the smallest and weakest."

"Poisoned?" Sinan asked. "How do you know?"

"The Red Death."

"What?"

"You might know it as the Lockjaw Toxin."

Sinan gasped. "That's a deadly muscle paralytic. First the jaw locks, then violent seizures. No cure. A death sentence."

Samson nodded. "We used it for hunting—never on people. My uncle used it to stage his coup and made me a warning. Let me live, then scarred me as an example." He gestured to the thick keloid scars lacing his body.

"I'm sorry," Sinan said, glancing at his own charred hand.

Samson noticed. "What happened?"

"Burned. Andrea Doria made me hold it in fire. Burned something out of me. I feel nothing now. Not pain. Not touch. Not even softness."

"But that's not what haunts you, is it?" Samson asked gently.

Sinan winced.

"We've heard your screams at night," Samson continued.

"I see them every time I close my eyes—Rahel, my father, Chava. She was calling to me, begging me to help, and I was..."

"Helpless," Samson finished.

Sinan nodded.

"How did you come to work for Sayyida?" Sinan asked.

"My uncle sold me to the Sultan of Tunisia. Sayyida was a guest in his court and bought my freedom. Offered me a position by her side. I never left."

Sinan narrowed his eyes. "The Sultan... you didn't happen to see a lynx with one eye, did you?"

"Don't think so. Why?"

"Tzitzi. I rescued her as a cub. She saved my life more than once."

"A one-eyed lynx?" Braman laughed. "You two have lived interesting lives."

"Believe me," Sinan sighed, "we could both use a little less interesting."

Braman belched. "Well, since we're all confessing... I once had a wife and a daughter. Lost them both because of my drinking and gambling. I came home one night, and they were gone. Taken by those I owed. Instead of fighting, I turned to the bottle. That bottle led me to piracy."

Sinan and Samson exchanged solemn glances. Each of them carried ghosts.

Before anyone could respond, an explosion rocked the ship.

"What was that?" Sinan barked.

A bell clanged.

"They've spotted us!" Samson shouted, springing up.

The three men dashed up the stairs. Above, Sayyida stood poised, eyes fixed on the enemy ship.

"To your stations!" she commanded.

Cannon fire shook the deck. One projectile tore through the red sails and snapped the mast, flames licking up into the darkening sky.

Crew members doused the fire with a thick orange compound, creating a smokescreen that enveloped the ship and scattered in all directions.

But relief was short-lived. The retreat signal was called. Panic spread. The ship turned sharply and fled.

White surrender sails rose.

Suddenly, Sinan was yanked from behind and thrown into a lifeboat. Sayyida and Samson leapt in after him. Braman was already at the oars.

"Catch!" Braman tossed one to Sinan.

As they rowed furiously, Sinan couldn't resist, "Weakest in the family, huh?"

Sayyida smacked the back of his head. "Shut up and row."

They glided into a hidden grotto, concealed by cliffs from the Spanish watchtowers. From the shadows, they watched enemy warships board Sayyida's vessel.

The Spanish flag rose.

Sayyida didn't flinch. She handed Sinan her second scimitar. "You know how to use it. Time to fight."

Sinan accepted the blade with a grim nod.

THE GREAT JEW PIRATE

They dragged the lifeboat deeper into the grotto, but armed Spanish soldiers surrounded them. The soldiers aimed sleek, new hand-rifles at their chests.

Sinan raised his blade, ready to strike. But before he could swing, a shot rang out.

He froze.

He looked down, expecting blood—but he was unharmed. The soldier who fired stared in confusion.

"Halt!" a booming voice commanded.

A tall man with a salt-and-pepper goatee emerged.

Sinan's heart skipped.

Sebastián de Olmedo.

He was supposed to be dead.

But Olmedo didn't recognize him.

"A stunning sight," Olmedo chuckled, gold-threaded armor glittering. "The Pirate Queen herself."

"Like how?" Sayyida snapped.

Olmedo locked eyes with Braman.

Braman hesitated. Then he lifted his rifle and aimed it at Sayyida.

Samson's scimitar dropped. "Braman... how could you?"

"They got to me months ago," Braman mumbled, ashamed. "Cornered me in a tavern. Said they'd... cut something off. Told me what to say. I had no choice."

Sayyida sank to her knees. Her scimitar fell with a dull thud.

Sinan had never seen her look so crushed.

"You see?" Olmedo declared to his troops. "Even the fiercest can break when pressure is applied just right."

He waved his hand.

"Take them to the dungeon. Tomorrow, we burn the Pirate Queen and her loyal dogs."

Sinan, Sayyida, and Samson were dragged up to the fortress and thrown into a stone chamber. No crew. Just them.

Silence.

Then Samson broke it. "You look like you've seen a ghost."

"That commander..." Sinan's voice trembled. "I saw him die."

"People survive more than we know," Samson said, tapping the bandage on his own side.

But Sinan's gaze was locked on the dungeon door. "His name is Sebastián de Olmedo. I watched Hizir Barbarossa drive a scimitar through his chest... over a decade ago."

David Nobyl

17

Shards of Truth

"That's impossible," Samson whispered in the dark cell after the guards had gone.

"Let me show you," Sinan replied quietly. He withdrew the astrolabe and opened it. Samson watched, astonished, as a mystic mirror shimmered into view between them.

In its reflection, a Spanish ship cut through the waves. Below deck, young Sinan, Dr. Badoz, and Rahel sat among other prisoners in the barracks of Sebastián's warship, La Cavalleria.

"It's been ages, and I've missed you so much," Dr. Badoz murmured in his sleep. "Don't worry, I won't be much longer."

"Who are you talking to?" young Sinan asked.

Dr. Badoz stirred, eyes fluttering open. Shackled at the wrists and ankles, he glanced around the dim hold. "No one," he muttered.

A few stray beams of light filtered through the cracked wood above, while the ship creaked and groaned around them. The salty sea air stung their throats. On the third day without food or water, conversation had vanished, leaving only the clink of chains and the occasional moan of despair.

Even in the gloom, Sinan could make out Rahel. She sat chained across from him, silent and solemn. Her black hair shimmered faintly in the shadows, framing her sun-darkened skin. Her green eyes, sharp with awareness, refused to meet his.

On Rahel's right sat a bearded man and his pregnant wife. On her left, two skeletal Moorish brothers who had already been aboard when the others arrived. Dr. Badoz, shackled beside Sinan, muttered to people who weren't there, lost in fevered dreams.

The doctor gave Sinan hope. Without him, Sinan would've felt completely alone.

Suddenly, heavy boots thudded overhead. Light spilled into the hold as the hatch opened, and soldiers descended the wooden stairs. Sebastián followed close behind.

He stepped over the Moorish brothers and knelt beside Dr. Badoz, who was still mumbling incoherently.

Grabbing the doctor's chin, Sebastián forced his face upward. Dr. Badoz's eyes were clouded, distant.

"What a fall from grace, Lorenzo," Sebastián hissed. "You were once the man who killed the great Tomás de Torquemada."

Gasps rippled through the prisoners. Rahel stirred, her chains clinking.

"I couldn't touch you," Sebastián seethed. "Queen Isabella adored you. Called you a miracle worker for saving her child. But she's dead now. Things have changed."

He leaned in, voice low and venomous. "Her death... so well-timed, don't you think?"

Dr. Badoz blinked slowly. "You?"

Sebastián smiled, teeth gleaming in the flickering light. "Tomás would be proud of me. His most loyal student."

With a vicious shove, he slammed the doctor's head against the wooden planks. The crack echoed through the hold.

Straightening his coat, Sebastián turned to the rest of the captives. "Under King Ferdinand's orders, we sail to Naples. A new Holy Office has been established there, and they need examples."

He smirked. "And you will serve quite nicely."

Rahel's voice cut through the silence. "Where is Diego de Córdoba?"

"Oh, your gallant suitor?" Sebastián chuckled. "He follows behind in his shiny new ship. Reappointed Governor of Oran. He wanted to give you some space—before escorting you to Venice."

Rahel's jaw clenched. Her fists tightened around the iron chains, but she said nothing more.

Sebastián turned with a theatrical swish of his cloak and climbed the stairs. The soldiers followed, slamming the hatch shut behind them. The darkness returned.

The silence was broken by soft scratching.

"Tzitzi?" Sinan called softly. From under a floorboard, a small, one-eyed lynx cub squeezed out, her tiny claws clicking against the planks.

Sinan grinned. Tzitzi nuzzled against his chest, then clawed weakly at the chains around his wrists. Defeated, she curled into his lap and closed her one good eye. The other had never healed properly, but she'd survived—thanks to Sinan. Her loyalty was fierce and unwavering.

From the shadows, a voice spoke. "Is it true? Did you really kill Tomás de Torquemada? That viper?"

A long pause.

Dr. Badoz finally answered, his voice thin, almost disembodied. "He sought a cure. I gave him one."

"We wouldn't be here if not for him," grumbled the unseen man, his tone bitter.

"If not him, another would've taken his place," Badoz replied calmly.

"Tell me how," the voice asked, cracking slightly. "Let me savor that story."

Dr. Badoz took a deep breath. "After what he forced me to do to my own family... it was the least I could give him. A tincture here. A touch of poison there. His fear of death did the rest."

A silence followed.

"He welcomed it, in the end."

"If only we could be so lucky," muttered one of the Moorish brothers. "The fate that awaits us is far worse."

David Nobyl

18

Barbarossa Brothers Attack

Dr. Badoz drifted into a surreal slumber aboard Sebastián's ship as a storm churned elsewhere along the Mediterranean coast of Tunisia. Dark skies cracked with thunder while lightning revealed a small xebec sailing into Houmt-Souk Port on Djerba, the fabled island of the Lotus-Eaters. Though the island now boasted a growing population and the sacred El Ghriba Synagogue, its mythic Lotus remained elusive.

As the Spanish Inquisition spread its grip across Christendom, Djerba's Jewish community sought liberation for their persecuted brethren. In desperation, they reached out to an unlikely ally: the Ottoman Empire. On this tempestuous night, the Barbarossa Brothers prepared for a bold strike against the heart of Spanish naval power.

A young man in a tattered cloak leapt from the xebec onto the rain-soaked sand, clutching fragile documents. This was Hizir, the youngest Barbarossa brother, his patchy ginger beard unable to hide the fire in his dark eyes. Several men followed him to a small stone fort that overlooked the beach.

Inside a cavern, three men huddled around a map. A rustic scimitar with elaborate inscriptions pierced the table's center. Hizir threw the documents down, interrupting their strategy.

"Welcome back, brother," said Oruc Reis, the eldest. His crimson beard and thunderous rage had earned him the infamous name Barbarossa. Though feared by many, his gaze on Hizir was soft.

"The Sultan approved it," Hizir said, not smiling.

"Then celebrate! He gave us La Goulette to expand our base. This is good news."

"There's a catch," Hizir muttered. "He demands a third of our spoils. Add the taxes we pay to the Jews of Djerba, and we're nearly broke. We lost two ships last month. We can't afford this."

Oruc studied his brother, then turned to the other men. One wore a mookleh—a scholarly Jewish turban—and a prayer shawl. "This is Maimonides, Chief Rabbi of El Ghriba. He comes on behalf of his people. In exchange for helping liberate their kin from Spain, they'll remove their tax."

Hizir didn't even glance at the Rabbi. "Sounds suicidal. You want another Ilyas? Count me out. We're Ottomans, not their saviors."

Oruc's smile vanished. He seized the scimitar and swung it, stopping the blade a hair from Hizir's neck. "Don't speak of Ilyas like that. Our roots are mixed—Christian, Greek, Muslim. Our father, Yakup Aha, was Albanian Christian. Our mother was Orthodox. These people are no different from us."

THE GREAT JEW PIRATE

"Fine," Hizir relented. "But do we have a plan?"

Oruc turned to the second man beside the Rabbi. "Kurtoglu brings news: a Spanish warship, the Cavalleria, carries 380 soldiers—and likely, prisoners. We intercept it, keep the loot, and satisfy the Sultan."

"Any risks?" Hizir asked.

"Avoid Ischia. It's Spanish territory, guarded by Admiral Andrea Doria. Never engage him."

"Understood," Hizir nodded.

"The ship's name?" he asked as Oruc turned to leave.

Oruc grinned. "The Cavalleria."

***

Weeks passed, but back aboard the Cavalleria, Dr. Badoz's mind gave him no rest. It replayed a haunting memory.

Rain fell on Valencia as a woman, limping and cradling a child, ran through the narrow streets. She reached a door, pounded, and collapsed into a young man's arms. From the shadows, a Dominican friar handed the young man a ruby-hilted dagger.

She pleaded. The man sobbed. Then he plunged the dagger into her stomach. She slumped, lifeless. But the child in her arms lived.

Dr. Badoz screamed awake, then drifted again into unconsciousness.

Sinan, wide awake, stared at the wooden ceiling. He couldn't bring himself to ask about the dream. Something inside the doctor had broken.

Rahel slept nearby. Tzitzi hid in the shadows. Sinan feared her discovery.

David Nobyl

He looked through the cracks in the hull. Something stirred in the mist, but vanished before he could focus. He sighed and turned to the Moorish brothers, huddled for warmth.

He thought of Luís. The betrayal. Would he ever forgive him? Would they meet again?

Then he heard a whisper.

"Young man," said the old man near Rahel, cradling his pregnant wife. "Your name?"

"Sinan."

"Ah. Like Sinai. Are you a Jew like me?"

"What's Sinai?" Sinan asked.

"Where G_d gave Moses the commandments."

"Then why does He let His chosen people suffer so?"

The old man sighed. "Have you heard of the Golem?"

"No," Sinan muttered. "More ghost stories? What's your name, anyway?"

"Ramón. But my friends call me Rabbi Samuel Joseph Pallache."

"You just liked the name Ramón?"

"Indeed," he smiled. "But back to the Golem..."

He leaned in. "My son," he whispered, gesturing to his wife's belly, "is the 91st descendant of King David. And that's the name we have picked out for him."

Sinan blinked. "Wasn't he Greek?"

"No," Pallache chuckled. "You know David and Goliath? One stone, blessed by G_d."

"Sounds like a big kiss on a pebble."

"G_d chose David to save the Jewish people...and unite them. Haven't you heard the story?"

Sinan nodded, but before he could answer, an explosion rocked the ship.

THE GREAT JEW PIRATE

"They're here! The Barbary Pirates!" one Moorish brother shouted.

Above, chaos erupted. Steel clanged, guns misfired, and screams filled the air. The Spanish defenses crumbled.

Sebastián burst into the hold, wild-eyed. He grabbed Dr. Badoz, shoved a pistol in his mouth, and pulled the trigger.

Click.

Nothing.

He looked down. A scimitar burst through his chest. Sebastián collapsed.

Behind him stood Hizir Barbarossa.

"Spanish and their guns," he muttered.

***

Later, as Diego de Córdoba's ship approached the smoldering wreck, Fernández reported the damage.

"The Barbarossa brothers, based on the attack pattern. We found your brother's body. Scimitar through the heart. Surviving crew say it was Hizir Barbarossa."

Diego didn't flinch. "Good riddance."

He patted a document tucked in his coat—Sebastián's signature, now his ticket to power.

"And the girl?"

"Gone. Not among the wreckage."

Diego let out a howl that echoed across the sea.

Fernández rested a hand on his shoulder. "We have greater plans. Don't let one woman undo all this."

"I did this all for her!" Diego snapped.

"Then don't lose it all because of her."

Diego turned back to the horizon.

"Barbarossa Brothers," he murmured. "You owe me a debt now. And one day... I will collect."

David Nobyl

19

Slave Children of Isle Ischia

Back in the dungeon depths of Aragon Castle on the Isle of Ischia, Sinan snapped the astrolabe shut, and the vision fizzled out. He leaned against the cold stone wall and closed his eyes, the weight of everything pressing down on him. It felt like they had been imprisoned forever. But Samson's quiet voice pulled him back.

"It's not over yet," Samson whispered, his tone laced with defiance. "The captain has a plan."

Sinan snorted. "Oh, wonderful. Is she going to summon a demon to distract the guards?"

"She's already faced worse," Samson replied, his voice steady. "Don't underestimate her."

Before Sinan could respond, Sayyida spoke from the shadows. "Four times now, Sinan. That's four times I've refused to kill you."

"Worse than demons," Sinan grinned. "Really?"

Sayyida didn't respond immediately, and when she did, her voice carried a heaviness that silenced them.

"I made a deal with a dybbuk to save my son," she said, her voice raw. "But the demon tricked me. Killed my husband. Took my son."

Sinan's sarcasm faded. He knew that kind of loss.

"I tried to outsmart it... made a second deal," Sayyida continued, her voice faltering. "It didn't end any better."

Sinan exhaled. "So, we're just as doomed. Braman tricked us too."

But Sayyida's lips curled into a sly smile. "Did he?"

Before Sinan could ask what she meant, Braman appeared like a shadow from the corridor, holding a ring of keys—and their confiscated weapons.

Sinan blinked. "Did I miss something?"

"Don't you love it when a plan comes together?" Sayyida said, pulling a scroll from her vest and unfurling a detailed map. She pointed. "There. That's the cave. That's where the children are. We'll use the old tunnels."

Sinan groaned. "More tunnels. Fantastic."

Braman quickly unlocked the cell. "We need to move. Now. The guards will sound the alarm any minute." He gave Sinan an apologetic glance. "Sorry for the act."

Weapons in hand, they followed Sayyida down—not up—the staircase.

"The exit's that way," Sinan pointed, confused.

"We're not escaping," Sayyida said. "We're rescuing children."

The corridor led to a dead end.

"They blocked the tunnels?" Samson asked.

Sayyida's eyes narrowed. "No. This isn't the tunnel's beginning."

THE GREAT JEW PIRATE

She drove her sword into the stone beneath her feet. The ground gave way, and they were sucked into darkness.

Braman screamed all the way down, but Sayyida stayed focused, guiding their fall with her blade. They landed hard in a subterranean grotto, lit by the shimmer of a glowing lake. Sinan slid in last, tumbling onto the stone floor.

But wonder turned to horror.

Children—dozens—stood frozen like statues, their faces twisted in agony, bodies locked in rows between long steel tables.

Sayyida ran forward, scanning them for life. Samson crouched beside one, his eyes narrowing.

"I've seen this before," he said.

"Where?" Braman asked.

"The Lockjaw Toxin," Samson replied. "But this is stronger. Their entire bodies are petrified."

Sinan wandered deeper into the chamber. His steps slowed as he saw her. A girl. Ten, maybe eleven. Her face was carved with sorrow.

Samson came up beside him. "Who is she?"

"Chava," Sinan whispered. "She's my sister."

David Nobyl

David Nobyl

20

Wrath of Asmodeus

Above ground, Diego de Córdoba seethed. "They escaped? And Braman is missing?!"

"The prisoners are headed to the caves!" cried a soldier.

Diego slammed his fist against the stone wall. "Sound the alarms! Get to the grotto. Sayyida will not leave this island alive!"

Spanish troops surged into the tunnels.

Inside the grotto, Sayyida shouted, "Barricade the children! They're going to open fire!"

Gunshots erupted. A bullet struck Sayyida in the shoulder. She screamed, and Samson shielded her with his body. Sinan and Braman flipped steel tables for cover.

"I'm out!" Braman yelled, dropping his empty gun.

Sinan turned to Sayyida for a plan—only to see her curled in Samson's arms, whispering like she was praying.

Was this it?

Then, Sayyida rose, bloody but resolute. She raised her arms. "Come forth, Asmodeus!"

A burst of blinding light exploded above her. From the glare emerged a monstrous creature—lion's head, horse's body, serpent's tail.

Sayyida's summoned demon charged the Spanish soldiers. Screams filled the cavern.

Sinan peeked through a crack in the barrier—just in time to see a cannon blast hurl him across the room. He slammed against the ground. Everything spun.

Through the haze, a masked figure appeared—cloaked in black, wearing a wide-brimmed hat and a white plague doctor's mask. He knelt beside Sinan and quietly bandaged a bleeding wound.

Sinan's body buzzed with pain as consciousness returned.

The figure placed a large vial in Sinan's hand.

"For the children," the plague doctor whispered. "Two drops. Each eye."

Then—another explosion.

When the smoke cleared, the demon vanished in a puff of sulfur, and the plague doctor was gone. The battle was over.

Sayyida and Samson stirred beside him.

"What happened?" Sayyida asked, groggy.

Sinan sat up, heart racing. "What happened?! You didn't see the demon? Or the plague doctor?"

Sayyida blinked. "You saw Asmodeus?"

"Giant lion-horse-snake thing? Kind of hard to miss!"

Sayyida said nothing, her expression unreadable.

Sinan steadied his breath. "Forget it. We need to unfreeze the kids."

He inspected the vial, then approached Chava. Her mouth was sealed tight. He hesitated—then carefully dropped two glistening drops into each of her eyes.

THE GREAT JEW PIRATE

Her eyelids fluttered. A cough. She fell into his arms.

Sayyida stared. "That... shouldn't be possible."

"Eyes absorb fastest into the bloodstream," Sinan said, handing her the vial. "Go. Help the others."

Working fast, they administered the antidote to every child. One by one, the frozen bodies returned to life, their groggy eyes adjusting to the dim light.

Using Sayyida's map, they led the dazed children through the narrow passageway to the grotto's mouth. Outside, in the pouring rain, lifeboats waited—manned by loyal pirate crew.

And beyond, under black storm clouds, Sayyida's grand ship rocked gently on the sea—free once again.

Sinan stared in disbelief. "How... how did you pull this off?"

Sayyida gave a tired grin. "A few demons and a lot of planning."

Sinan laughed, helping a child into the boat. They had done it.

They had saved the children.

And escaped with their lives.

David Nobyl

David Nobyl

21

Sayyida's Suffering

Queen Sayyida's ship surged through the churning sea, its sails taut with wind despite the dark storm roiling overhead. Rain hammered the deck as Samson secured a makeshift sling around Sayyida's wounded arm using a torn strip of cloth.

She gave him a quiet nod and slipped into her quarters, the weight of their battle still heavy on her shoulders.

"So," Samson said, turning to Sinan, "where did you get the antidote?"

Sinan, cradling his groggy sister Chava in his arms, shook his head. "I don't know. A figure in a plague doctor mask handed it to me—black robes, beaked mask. I couldn't see who it was."

Samson's brow furrowed. "These children... Were they isolated cases? Or part of a larger, darker scheme? That toxin—it wasn't ordinary Lockjaw. It was something more."

Sinan nodded grimly. "The real question is: who is it for?"

After settling Chava into a hammock below deck, Sinan approached Sayyida's cabin. He knocked, found the door ajar, and stepped inside—only to freeze.

Sayyida sat slumped at the edge of her bunk, her head bowed, a pistol pressed against her temple. Tears streaked her cheeks, her strong features hollow with despair. The lantern beside her flickered dimly, casting long shadows that mirrored the turmoil in her eyes.

Sinan closed the door behind him, his voice barely above a whisper. "Sayyida."

She didn't look up.

"I failed," she said, her voice ragged and hoarse. "He wasn't among them. Not one of those children was my son."

He took a step closer, careful not to startle her. "I'm sorry."

She laughed, brittle and sharp. "Sorry? What does that matter now? I abandoned a kingdom, left my people to burn while I chased a ghost. I lost my husband. My son. My title. Everything. And for what? A whisper of hope?"

She shook her head, eyes wet and wild. "They think I killed him, you know. My husband. My own people think I murdered the only man who ever truly saw me. Maybe I should have. Maybe then there'd be a reason for all this madness."

"You're not mad," Sinan said gently, stepping closer. "You're in pain. And you've been carrying it alone for too long."

Her hand trembled around the pistol. "I should have died with him. At least then... there'd be peace."

Sinan knelt in front of her. "You gave up everything for love. That's not weakness. That's courage. And even now, you're still fighting. You brought those children back from a nightmare. You gave them life again. You saved my sister. You saved me."

She met his eyes, her voice breaking. "But I couldn't save him. I couldn't even find him."

"Then keep looking," he said. "Not because you've failed, but because you still can. Because you're the only one who can."

Her gaze dropped to the pistol in her hand. After a long, shaking breath, she lowered it to her lap.

"You think I still have a purpose?"

"I know you do," Sinan said. He gently reached out and took the pistol from her hand, placing it aside. "This world needs you. Now more than ever."

She closed her eyes, exhaling slowly. Then, with great effort, she whispered, "You're a stubborn fool."

"Takes one to know one," he smiled.

A faint laugh escaped her lips, the first real one in what felt like an eternity.

"What's next, then? Where do we go from here?"

Sinan stood. "Samson is right. If the Spanish Empire is running these experiments, they must be preparing for something big... invasion. I remember how King Ferdinand wanted to wipe out the Barbary Pirates so that he could not just invade parts of North Africa, but conquer all of it."

"How can we fight against something like that?" Sayyida asked.

"I'm not sure. But we would need to enlist the help of the Barbarossa Brothers," Sinan mused.

Sayyida scoffed at the suggestion, but ultimately relented. "Hizir is an arrogant swine, but he cannot be matched in battle."

She picked up her gun and set it on the table, symbolizing her acceptance of Sinan's plan.

Their moment of calm was shattered by cannon fire from a Spanish Galleon, commanded by a furious Diego de Córdoba.

"I thought we'd gotten clear?" Sayyida shouted as she raced on deck with Sinan close behind.

"His ship tore through the sea towards us!" Samson roared between their own cannons' firing.

The ship rocked violently. Diego had attacked with such swiftness that soon, he and his men were able to force-board the pirate ship, plunging into hand-to-hand combat over artillery fire.

Sinan and Sayyida snatched their scimitars and pistols, hurling themselves into the fray to fight for their lives and those of the crew and children below.

"They're trying to break into the lower deck to recapture the children," Samson shouted.

"Astute observation! I thought they just wanted a rematch!" Sayyida quipped, battling fiercely and shooting Spanish soldiers with her pistol. Several Spanish soldiers breached the pirates' defense and rushed below deck.

Sayyida signaled to Sinan beside her, "Go below deck and protect the children!"

Sinan nodded and, under cover of her pistol fire, descended below deck where he fought off two armed Spanish guards. Behind them, however, loomed a third, taller Spaniard, holding a terrified Chava in a chokehold with one hand while brandishing his long, Toledo broadsword with the other.

"You died," Sinan growled. "I saw Hizir Barbarossa run you through—Sebastián de Olmedo!"

The man laughed. "Sebastián? No. I'm Don Diego de Córdoba—his twin."

THE GREAT JEW PIRATE

Sinan paled. He had mistook Diego for his twin, Sebastián!

"I'm now General of the Royal Spanish Armada," Diego said, then flung Chava against the wall. She crumpled unconscious. "And now, the Barbarossa Brothers are crushed! Doria took care of them in Djerba." He grinned. "I'm sure you're intimately aware, Sinan.'

He lunged. Sinan blocked, but the force shook his scimitar. Blow after blow, Diego pressed the attack. Sinan fought with desperate precision, but the seasoned general was too skilled.

Diego's dagger slashed Sinan's side, sending him crashing into the wall beside his sister. He raised his blade for the killing stroke—

—and the ship rocked violently.

An explosion threw Diego off-balance. Seizing the moment, Sinan snatched Chava and fled to the deck, dodging cannon fire and bodies locked in combat.

He reached the nearest lifeboat, laying Chava inside. But as he turned to climb in, a shard of timber struck the back of his head.

He collapsed into the boat.

Ropes snapped. The lifeboat plunged into the sea below, unnoticed in the storm's fury.

Above, Sayyida's crew roared with renewed force, overtaking the Spanish boarders. With their main guns disabled, Diego barked a retreat. His battered ship turned and limped toward Ischia.

Sayyida's vessel was swept into open waters by the storm. When the skies cleared, her crew cheered, raising mugs in celebration.

"We've losses," Samson said, frowning. He pointed to the missing lifeboat.

"Not bad for your first naval battle, Sinan," Sayyida said—then paused. "Sinan?"

She and Samson searched the ship. No sign.

"Captured?" Samson asked.

"No," Sayyida said. "Sinan would die before being taken. But that missing boat..."

They examined a frayed rope and a bloodstained splinter of wood.

Samson stared out to sea. "He's out there."

"We go to Morocco," Sayyida said. "The children must be safe. Then Tunisia. If Sinan wants the Barbarossa brothers, that's where we'll find him."

"You think he'll survive the storm?" Samson asked.

"He already survived one," Sayyida replied, her gaze unwavering. "The one inside."

***

Back on Ischia, Diego's crippled ship returned to port. But another vessel loomed offshore—a larger, more fearsome one, flying Genoese colors.

Down the gangplank came Admiral Andrea Doria, leaning on a carved cane. His long silver beard blew in the wind as he approached Diego.

He planted his cane between his feet.

"So," Doria said with a cruel smile, "your efforts against the Pirate Queen have gone... poorly."

Diego bristled. "I am General Don Diego de Córdoba."

"To me," Doria murmured, stepping close until their noses touched, "you're a bug. Careful I don't squash you."

.

22

Storm at Sea

The tempestuous sea battered Sinan and Chava's tiny wooden lifeboat, shaking them from the depths of unconsciousness. Upon regaining their senses, they shared a fleeting, stunned moment of reunion—before the storm, like a jealous god, roared louder, assailing them with renewed fury.

Driven by raw instinct and the will to survive, they bailed water and paddled with aching muscles. Every wave was a mountain. Every hour a battle. The wind whipped against their salt-burned skin, and the rain stung like needles. The storm stretched on for days, blurring into an endless haze of effort, pain, and survival.

By the seventh day, the sea calmed. The sun returned, pale and indifferent, casting light on bodies gaunt with hunger and eyes dulled with exhaustion. Their supplies were gone. Hunger gnawed at their stomachs, and the silence between them grew heavy.

Sinan noticed Chava hadn't spoken since waking. She avoided his eyes. Whether from fear, trauma, or something else, he couldn't tell. He chose not to press her.

That night, as the stars returned to the Mediterranean sky, Sinan pulled out his astrolabe. The device shimmered as he activated the memory mirror. The glowing surface stirred, catching Chava's attention. Wordless, she leaned against his sunburned arm, eyes fixed on the swirling images.

The projection unfolded like a dream: a much younger Sinan aboard the ship of Hizir Barbarossa, rescued from captivity only moments ago. There, too, were Rabbi Pallache and his pregnant wife, Rivka. Chava's eyes widened at the sight of the woman. Her lip trembled. A single tear slipped down her cheek.

"I've been digging into our past," Sinan said softly. "I think it holds the key to understanding what's ahead."

She nodded, wiping her face, still silent but listening.

The memory shifted. Dr. Badoz sat upright beside a young Sinan, clear-eyed and lucid for the first time in weeks. The Barbary pirates had seized the Spanish ship Cavalleria, and the freed captives adjusted to their strange new freedom.

"Learn the language of your enemy if you wish to vanquish them," Hizir said as he sliced through Sinan's chains.

Rabbi Pallache was shouting for help—his wife was in labor. The barracks filled with the sounds of panic. Even the seasoned pirates looked lost.

Oruc entered, taking stock. "No midwives aboard? Just soldiers, slaves, and sea-thieves?"

Dr. Badoz and Sinan exchanged a glance. "I'm a physician," the doctor said. "But we need supplies. I need my satchel."

Soon, Dr. Badoz, Sinan, and Rahel were crouched beside Rivka, preparing for the birth.

"She won't make it past the brim without help," Dr. Badoz murmured. "Remember what I showed you in Medina del Campo?"

Sinan nodded. With practiced focus, he helped guide the baby into the world. At last, a cry pierced the room. Newborn lungs filled the air with life. Even the pirates stared in mute astonishment.

Hizir blinked slowly, unreadable. Oruc just shook his head in disbelief.

"It's a girl," Dr. Badoz said, smiling.

Rabbi Pallache blinked. "Girl?"

Rivka shot him a warning look.

"A girl is perfect," he amended quickly, dodging Sinan's grin.

"And her name?" Sinan asked. "Now that 'David' is taken."

"Chava," Júlia offered quietly. "My grandmother's name."

"Chava," the parents echoed.

But Badoz's smile faded. Rivka's hand had gone cold. Sweat beaded her brow. He checked her pulse—weak and racing.

"She's crashing!" he barked.

Sinan's stomach dropped. Her blood was draining too fast.

Then a spark of memory. He leapt to his feet and ran topside.

He returned moments later with a sealed leather pouch, carefully sterilized needle, and a bladder of warm, salted water.

He tied a cloth around Rivka's arm, searching for a vein. The ship rocked, but his hand remained steady. He slipped the hollow needle into the vessel at her elbow. Blood welled at the edge. He attached a reed to the bladder.

The fluid began to flow.

Color returned to Rivka's cheeks. Her breathing steadied. Her eyes flickered open.

"Where did you learn that?" Badoz asked.

"Torralva used a similar method to save you. I improved it. Saltwater draws moisture into the blood. Restores pressure."

Rahel watched in quiet awe, memories of her own mother's healing hands flashing behind her eyes.

Hizir narrowed his gaze, studying Sinan like a newly discovered treasure. This boy wasn't just clever—he was dangerous in the best of ways.

But before he could open his mouth, Oruc leaned in, voice full of amusement. "Worth his weight in gold, wouldn't you say?"

"I was about to say that," Hizir muttered.

"Sure you were," Oruc grinned.

Hizir rolled his eyes. "You just want credit for recruiting him."

"No," Oruc said, patting Sinan on the back. "I want him on our ship when the world begins to burn."

Sinan smiled slightly, unsure if they were praising or drafting him—or both.

***

Back in the lifeboat, the aged Sinan stared at the glowing mirror as it shifted again.

A new image began to form. One he hadn't seen before.

Chava sat up straighter, her expression sharpening.

THE GREAT JEW PIRATE

Was this the missing piece Sayyida had alluded to? The key to understanding what came next?

The light of the mirror pulsed, waiting to reveal the truth.

David Nobyl

David Nobyl

23

Tempest on the Horizon

As the sun rose over the azure Mediterranean waters, a cry echoed from a high tower perched on a rugged cliff: "We are the Italian-Sicilian Resistance!" Below, circling in the surf like a great predator, was the fearsome, armored flagship of Admiral Andrea Doria, the Genoese mercenary and enforcer for the Spanish Monarchy. His sleek warship gleamed in the morning light, a terrible beauty carved for conquest.

The resistance had grown bold, swelling in number and resolve against Spanish oppression. Their leader, Rinuccio della Rocca, stood defiantly atop the watchtower, his voice clear above the crashing waves.

"My name is Rinuccio della Rocca," he shouted to the vessel below, "and we will never surrender!"

No reply came. Frustrated, he sneered down at the deck. "Show yourself, coward!"

The door to the Admiral's quarters creaked open. Out stepped Doria, tall and thin, his black beard flowing like dark silk. He limped forward, dragging a boy by the hair in one hand, a massive, double-barreled pistol in the other.

Gasps erupted from the tower.

Doria stopped at the ship's bow, leveled the pistol at the boy's temple, and locked eyes with Rinuccio.

Rinuccio's blood drained from his face. "My son..."

The pistol roared.

The boy's lifeless body plunged into the churning sea.

Without a word, Doria turned and hobbled back into his dark quarters. As he disappeared, he muttered coldly, "I'm Genoese."

Inside the cabin, a window stood open to the crisp morning air. Across from him sat Domenico, his aging uncle, tuning a beautiful violin etched with the Doria family crest.

"The storm, Uncle Domenico... isn't it beautiful?" Doria murmured.

Domenico glanced up. "What storm? The sky is clear."

Doria pointed toward the horizon. "You're not looking far enough. Out there."

Domenico squinted but saw nothing. "You've grown poetic in your madness."

Doria smirked. "A tempest can capsize a fleet before it's ever seen."

His uncle sighed. "You've done much for Genoa, Doria. Perhaps it's time to retire. Find a village. A peaceful life."

"Genoa's sovereignty, or nothing," Doria whispered. "We are on the brink."

"Of what? Genoa is no more. Ferdinand will never give it back. He'll swallow it as the French did—then send inquisitors to devour what remains."

"Perhaps. But it is not Ferdinand I serve. It is his grandson, Charles. The boy sees beyond blood and empire. He's sharp. Merciful."

Domenico scoffed.

THE GREAT JEW PIRATE

"He will become Emperor," Doria continued. "With a force unlike any the world has seen."

"And you think he'll turn it toward Genoa?"

"He will," Doria said, rising. "Because we share a common enemy."

He pointed to a faint speck on the horizon.

"Commander!" he barked.

A soldier entered.

"Set a course for that storm. We've got company. Time to teach the Barbary Pirates who rules these waters."

***

The memory mirror through which Chava and Sinan watched shifted once more and showed the crew aboard the Cavalleria. Only now, several weeks had passed since Chava's birth, and they were in the midst of a raging tempest.

It was all hands on deck as they battled the wind and rain, trying to save their lives from the merciless sea.

Sinan and Rahel were busy hoisting the remaining sails when Dr. Badoz and Rabbi Samuel came to help with the rigging. Together, they worked like a well-oiled machine, each person playing their part in the effort to keep the ship afloat.

Oruc kept the ship steady while Hizir and several men helped to dry up and catch their breath. Once the ship was stabilized, Oruc and Hizir headed below deck, followed by Dr. Badoz.

"Sorry, Doc," Oruc said, wringing his drenched tunic. "Venice is controlled by King Ferdinand. Taking you there would be like juggling knives blindfolded. The Sultan, on the other hand, welcomes all Jews to his land. You'll be treated well there."

Dr. Badoz bowed his head in acknowledgment, and Oruc and Hizir locked themselves in a storage room. Hizir grumbled, "I don't understand these Jews. We rescue them from the devils, and they jump right back into the flames."

Oruc gave him a knowing look. "Home is a powerful thing to lose. Don't underestimate the aftermath of loss."

Meanwhile, Sinan sat outside the locked room with Rahel and a disgruntled Tzitzi. "What did he say?" Sinan asked Dr. Badoz.

"He said they won't take us to Venice," Dr. Badoz replied coldly, holding his leather satchel slung over his shoulder. "We're headed to Tunisia."

Rahel's face fell, and Sinan tried to console her. "Maybe this could be a fresh start, a new beginning."

Dr. Badoz hesitated before continuing, and his words came heavier than before. "This is just the beginning for you. You'll come to love the things that lie ahead for you. But for me... all that I ever loved is gone. I was once regarded among the greatest physicians in Castile, taught by the finest minds of Córdoba and Salamanca. But in the Ottoman world, Sinan... their medical knowledge is generations ahead. There are procedures there I've only ever imagined. The instruments they use—tools I could barely dream of. What I know is already obsolete."

Sinan looked at him, puzzled. "But you can still practice. Learn, adapt. You always do."

Dr. Badoz shook his head slowly. "Even the best stone cracks under enough weight. My hands shake now, Sinan. My mind falters. And there is more than just science haunting me."

THE GREAT JEW PIRATE

He paused, then added with a quivering voice, "I promised your mother I would keep you safe, and I have tried. But not as an uncle, Sinan. As a father."

Sinan blinked. "What?"

Dr. Badoz stared into the sea. "The Inquisition gave me a choice. Kill my wife or lose you both. She—she insisted I take her life. She begged me. Her last words were a plea to make sure you survived. I told the world you were my nephew to keep you hidden... and to shield myself from the shame."

Sinan was frozen.

"I couldn't bear to raise you as my son while carrying the memory of what I'd done. And every time I looked at you, I saw her. Her eyes. Her fire. Her sacrifice."

Tears spilled down Sinan's cheeks.

"I'm so sorry for how coldly I treated you," Dr. Badoz whispered. "It was never because I didn't love you. It was because I loved you too much."

Sinan buried his face in Dr. Badoz's chest. "You never stopped being my family. You never stopped protecting me."

Dr. Badoz laid his head against Sinan's, releasing a sigh he held inside for decades. "My son."

David Nobyl

David Nobyl

24

Dead or Alive

Dr. Badoz released Sinan and reached for the astrolabe in his satchel when a thunderous explosion rocked the ship. Sinan found himself catapulted backwards.

The air left his lungs in a violent gasp as his back slammed against the deck. Before he could rise, another blast shattered a support beam, sending a cascade of timber and debris crashing down. One heavy plank pinned Rahel beside him, and splinters rained like shrapnel.

Sinan groaned, half-blinded by smoke and salt, his ears ringing with a high-pitched whine. Through the dust and ruin, he forced himself up, every limb screaming in protest. A burning ache in his ribs warned of cracked bones, but he pushed forward, driven by something far deeper than pain.

"Father!" he shouted hoarsely, stumbling across the shredded planks.

The word tore from him before he even realized it—father, not uncle. The truth had broken free in his heart just as violently as the ship around him.

He flung aside shattered crates and smoking beams, hands bloodied and trembling. Panic clawed at his chest. He was too late. Again. The ship's stern was obliterated, a jagged maw of broken timber yawning into the sea. Nothing remained of the room where Dr. Badoz had stood moments ago—just splinters and silence.

Sinan dropped to his knees, gasping in desperation. In his shaking hands was the astrolabe, but it was no longer whole. The main body remained, but its seven plates—each representing knowledge passed down through generations—were gone, likely swallowed by the sea.

He clutched it to his chest like a relic of a man he had just begun to know. A father he had barely spoken to. A father who had died the moment their souls had touched. It was too cruel. Too brief. The ache inside him wasn't just grief—it was a scream of years stolen, of questions unanswered.

He wanted to cry out, but rage stifled his sobs. He turned toward the source of it all, rising to his feet, spine stiff with fury.

There, sailing just beyond the wreckage, loomed a monstrous warship. Its crimson-stitched sails flared like wings of a vulture, its black hull glinting with menace. On the upper deck, the sharp silhouette of Admiral Andrea Doria stood—slender, cold, unmoving. His profile, with its eagle nose and stone-cold posture, was etched into Sinan's mind like a curse.

Etched into the ship's flank, in bold Gothic lettering: ANDREA DORIA.

"That ship," Sinan seethed, his voice trembling with hatred. "I'll never forget that ship."

***

THE GREAT JEW PIRATE

The memory mirror flared once more, showing a new scene. Sinan and Chava leaned closer, eyes wide.

Doria's vessel circled the detritus not with haste, but like a predator savoring its kill. The wreckage from the Barbary Pirates' ship he had just attacked mere moments ago floated like scattered bones upon the surface of the sea. Then, movement—barely noticeable. A lone figure clung to a piece of driftwood, coughing, bleeding, but alive.

Doria raised his cane and pointed. "Bring him aboard!"

His crew moved with precision, hauling the survivor aboard. The man collapsed to the deck, coughing up seawater, his hands shaking.

Doria stepped forward slowly, the tip of his cane rapping against the wood in perfect rhythm. He gazed down at the soaked, battered man, his expression unreadable.

"Are you a pirate?" he asked coolly, drawing a sword hidden within the cane, letting the blade catch the light.

The man looked up with bloodshot eyes. "No. My name is Dr. Lorenzo Badoz."

Recognition bloomed across Doria's pale face, and a smile twisted his lips.

"Ah, yes. The physician to the Queen," he drawled. "Let me make my offer again, Doctor. Slower, this time."

The mirror's glow dimmed, then vanished entirely. Sinan clutched the astrolabe to his brow, trembling.

His breath caught in his throat.

"He's alive."

David Nobyl

David Nobyl

25

The Demon King

Sayyida and Samson sailed back to Morocco, their ship heavy not with treasure, but with children rescued from enslavement—orphans needing homes, safety, and a second chance. As their vessel pulled into the harbor, the city's skyline shimmered in the Mediterranean sun, but the welcome was anything but warm.

Rumors of Sayyida's absence had festered into open resentment. Whispers of abandonment, betrayal, and scandal echoed through the marketplace. Many viewed her journey not as a righteous crusade but a dereliction of duty—an insult to her station and a shameful departure from the economic and political responsibilities she had been entrusted with.

Beneath the grumbling, though, was the deeper truth: her power, as a woman, had never sat easily with many of Morocco's citizens. Her strength, her command, her refusal to be meek—it had earned her the crown, yes, but also enemies. Some called her pirate. Others, tyrant. Few still called her queen.

But when protests erupted and fists raised against her return, Sayyida acted not as a diplomat but as the Pirate Queen. She crushed the dissent swiftly, and without apology. Her armada, stationed just offshore, reminded the people of the steel beneath her silks. History would one day paint her in nobler colors, but in that moment, she restored order, not through sweet words, but by sheer force.

Only then were the children delivered to sanctuaries across the kingdom—homes, and orphanages that would tend to their healing. It was not trust that returned to Sayyida's reign that day. It was fear.

Once the streets had quieted, Sayyida retreated into her castle—into the silence of her chambers, accompanied only by the ghost of her grief. There, behind thick doors no one dared knock on, she shed the armor of leadership and became only what remained: a mother, a widow, a woman who had given everything and still lost what mattered most.

She barred Samson from entering. He understood, and left her to the shadows.

The grandeur of her bedchamber did nothing to lift her spirit. Golden tapestries, carved cedar pillars, and the scent of myrrh could not hide the truth stained into the room's fabric. The sheets on her bed, though darkened by age, still bore the faint, rust-colored evidence of a murder committed long ago—a wound that time refused to let scab over.

Her husband's death had been sudden, brutal. A blade in the night. Her son had been found nearby, trembling and bloody. But Sayyida refused to believe the child she had loved could be capable of such horror. No—she had chosen to believe a dybbuk, a vengeful spirit, had taken hold of him. It was the only explanation her heart could endure.

And now, as she stared at those old stains, the weight of it pressed down again. Her husband lost. Her son missing. Her country hostile. Her people ungrateful. The anguish she had held at bay for so long came crashing down like a tidal wave. Her grief festered into rage, until at last, she screamed into the emptiness.

"Where are you? Show yourself, you vile demon!"

A rasp, dry and mocking, slipped from the shadows. "You needn't shout, Pirate Queen. I may be tired and withered, but I'm not deaf."

Sayyida spun, snatching her scimitar and swinging it in a deadly arc that stopped just shy of the creature's neck. A grotesque figure loomed in the shadows, its leathery wings folded and eyes glowing like burning coals.

"Are you not Asmodeus, King of Demons?"

"Asmodeus I am," the creature replied with a grin that stretched too wide. "But I haven't held that title in centuries."

"Who holds it now, then?"

"The Demon of Semites," it said, voice thick with ancient malice. "Older even than I, we know it by no other name. A dybbuk of annihilation—of Jews, Muslims, all Semitic bloodlines. It whispers through the empires, orchestrating ruin. A phantom behind history's curtain."

Sayyida's jaw tightened. "And let me guess—Sinan is meant to oppose it? A Great Jew Pirate prophesied to save us all?"

The demon chuckled. "Just as Goliath had David and Ramses had Moses, the Demon of Semites once more has its mortal foe. Sinan is fated to find the lost Sword of Solomon. Only it can destroy the demon's hold. If he fails, both your people will suffer endless torment for millennia."

"What does any of that have to do with me?"

"You are the spark," the demon rasped. "You found Sinan. You forged his will to fight. Not by force, but by igniting his purpose."

"I never agreed to that," she hissed.

"But you did. In exchange for a chance to see your son again. And that promise remains—if you complete one final task."

A single tear slid down her cheek. She let it fall.

"You told me you'd return my son. WHERE IS HE?!"

The demon shifted, wings rustling. "Patience, Pirate Queen. You are close. Bring the master of Sinan to the battlefield, and your bargain will be fulfilled."

Sayyida's expression darkened. "You mean Hizir Barbarossa?"

"Close... but no scimitar."

She stiffened. "Oruc Reis. The One-Armed Barbary Pirate."

"He goes by a new name now," the demon whispered. "The Man with the Silver Arm."

Sayyida scoffed. "And where do I find this overgrown brute?"

"In Djerba," the demon said, voice fading. "Hiding in plain sight."

"And if I fail?"

"Then your son will remain a whisper. Forever lost."

Then it was gone, vanishing into the darkness like a breath on the wind.

Left alone, Sayyida stood in the dim light, her hands trembling. But her voice—when it came—was steel. "Then to Djerba I go."

David Nobyl

26

The Holy Roman Emperor

Far across the sea, within the looming fortress of Aragon Castle on Ischia, Admiral Andrea Doria stood high upon the battlements with Don Diego de Córdoba. They watched the ocean as a ship bearing the golden crest of the Spanish Royal Family approached.

Doria's hawk shifted restlessly on his gloved arm.

"You think he lives up to the legends?" Diego asked with a smirk.

"Hoping for an autograph on your helmet, Governor?" Doria replied, chuckling darkly.

"I'll laugh last."

"You didn't see him, did you?" Doria said, turning serious.

"Who?"

"Sinan."

"That pathetic street-rat? Please. He's no threat."

"He's eluded you more than once. That makes him dangerous."

Diego folded his arms. "You had your chance years ago. Why not kill him then?"

"Because he's key to the storm we're conjuring," Doria murmured. "A storm that will swallow North Africa—."

Prince Charles stepped into the sunlit courtyard, flanked by his royal guards. Young, poised, and already ruthless, he carried the gravity of an empire in his stride.

"Your Highness," Doria bowed, voice rich with reverence.

Charles waved off the pleasantries. "Enough. Are we ready to destroy the pirates or not?"

"We suffered a minor interference on Ischia," Diego began, eager to redirect blame. "But the larger operations remain unharmed."

"Wasn't that our main research hub?" Charles asked.

"One of several," Doria replied, eyes narrowing. "The toxin development continues elsewhere."

"Is it ready for mass use in the North Africa campaign?"

"Our top alchemists are close. The vapor toxin is nearly weaponized."

Charles's voice dropped to a growl. "Then why the delay? We received the tetanus toxin shipments from King Sālim months ago."

Diego puffed out his chest. "I secured Sālim's allegiance—"

"Spare me the ceremony," Charles cut him off. "I want decisive destruction."

"Then allow me to demonstrate," Doria said, signaling to a guard. He produced a crimson vial, uncorked it, and held it under the guard's nose.

THE GREAT JEW PIRATE

Moments later, the soldier's body seized. Panic filled his eyes. His mouth opened to scream, but no sound escaped. Slowly, his limbs froze—ankles, knees, shoulders—until he stood immobilized like a grotesque statue.

"He'll die within minutes," Doria explained to the prince. "Unable to breathe. A perfect weapon."

Prince Charles turned pale. "Deploy it as soon as it's ready."

As the prince left, Diego glared at Doria. "Multiple facilities? You kept that from me."

Doria only smiled. "All in due time."

Diego gestured at the still-frozen soldier. "Can we reverse it?"

"That's the best part," Doria said, snapping his fingers.

A hooded figure emerged—a man in a plague doctor mask and flowing black cloak. The masked figure handed Doria a green vial. The procedure was repeated. The soldier unfroze, gasped for breath—then stiffened again, locked back into place.

The plague doctor shook his head.

"Still unstable," Doria sighed. "But we're close."

He turned to the masked man. "You have a new mission. Go to Venice. Protect our interests there. And send word when the formula is complete."

The figure nodded once, then vanished into the shadows.

David Nobyl

David Nobyl

27

Forgotten Kabbalah Library

The North African coast of Tunis was littered with the wreckage of many ships and boats, their splintered remains nudged gently by the lapping sea foam. One boat, in particular, had been dashed violently against the rocks, leaving no sign of its passengers. Only a pair of dragging trails in the sand led inland—silent testaments to two unconscious bodies hauled toward the ancient ruins of Carthage.

Once the mighty capital of Hannibal's Carthaginian empire, Carthage now lay in ruins—a graveyard of broken columns and scorched earth. Scipio Africanus had long ago razed it to ash, and in its place had risen a haunt for outlaws, scavengers, and spirits best left unnamed. It was here, among the debris of a fallen civilization, that Sinan and his sister Chava had disappeared.

Under the cover of a moonless night, a sturdy, inhumanly strong creature dragged two unconscious bodies through the crumbling remnants of the once-great city. Sinan, one of the castaways, drifted in and out of consciousness, each flicker of awareness offering only a glimpse of shattered columns and stone walls swallowed by vines.

The North African coast of Tunis was littered with the wreckage of a small lifeboat, its shattered remnants pushed lazily to and fro by the lapping sea foam. One particular boat had met a violent end upon the shoreline, but its two shipwrecked occupants were conspicuously absent. Only a winding trail in the sand hinted at their fate — the tell-tale drag marks of bodies pulled painstakingly toward the ruins of ancient Carthage.

Once the proud home of Hannibal, Carthage had long since fallen from glory, its ashes swept into history by Scipio Africanus and the might of Rome. Now, the fallen city was home to something altogether different: bandits, exiles, and things best left in shadow. A fine place for a mystery — or a resurrection.

Under the cover of a moonless night, a sturdy, inhumanly strong creature dragged two unconscious bodies through the crumbling remnants of the once-great city. Sinan, one of the castaways, drifted in and out of consciousness, each flicker of awareness offering only a glimpse of shattered columns and stone walls swallowed by vines.

"Chava!" he gasped into the darkness, voice cracked and feeble.

"She's safe," answered a raspy voice from nearby — one that sounded like it had smoked its way through centuries. A candle flickered to life, illuminating the deeply wrinkled face of an old woman who looked like she could bake baklava and curse a sultan in the same afternoon.

THE GREAT JEW PIRATE

Behind her, two glowing orange eyes blinked in the dark.

Sinan tried to sit up but winced as his ribs screamed in protest. He looked down and noticed his wounds had been bandaged with surprising care. "Should I be concerned that I'm alive and patched up by a cackling stranger and her... pet demon?"

The old woman raised a brow. "Fresh meat and wit. How rare."

Sinan squinted at the glowing eyes in the shadows. "...Please tell me that thing's not going to eat me."

"Eat you? Don't flatter yourself, boy," she said with a chuckle. "He's on a dirt-free diet."

With a low, grumbly purr, the creature emerged — a squat rock-being with stubby limbs, owl-like eyes, and an expression that somehow radiated sarcasm.

"This charming heap of gravel is Ach Ha-Katan. Achi, for short. A Golem — soul within stone. And you, I presume, are Sinan the Clueless."

Sinan blinked. "Okay, now I'm more concerned. How do you know who I am? Where is my sister?"

"I'm still trying to figure out how G-d keep sending me idiots," the old woman muttered, mostly to Achi, who gave a theatrical shrug.

She rose slowly, leaning on a cane that looked older than most countries. Achi scampered at her side as she shuffled toward a hidden staircase.

"Wait — where are you going? Who are you?"

"Oh hush. Follow me if you can keep up without tripping over your own questions."

"Lovely," Sinan muttered, dragging himself upright. "Saved by a crypt keeper with a pet boulder."

As they descended the spiraling stone staircase, the walls lit up with candles, each bursting to life as Achi exhaled little puffs of flame.

"Welcome," the old woman announced grandly as they reached the base, "to the Forgotten Library of Kabbalah."

Sinan's eyes widened. The chamber stretched for what seemed like miles. Rows upon rows of ancient tomes, scrolls, and odd contraptions filled the space. It was both overwhelming and oddly peaceful.

"Okay," Sinan said, breathless. "That's impressive. And you are...?"

"Madame Miriam. Keeper of this glorious mess. And part-time babysitter, apparently."

From the corner, Sinan spotted Chava seated on a pile of cushions, lost in a book the size of a tombstone.

"Chava!" he called, rushing forward — but a sharp whack of Madame Miriam's cane blocked him.

"Careful. She's reading. And not everyone bounces back from trauma like it's a stubbed toe."

Sinan bristled. "I don't care what she's reading. I just need to know she's okay."

"Then ask her," Miriam said, stepping aside with a gesture that somehow managed to be both gracious and condescending.

Sinan knelt beside his sister. "Chava? It's me. You okay?"

She turned to look at him — but her eyes were distant, as if seeing through him. She gave a vague shrug and returned to her book.

Sinan stood, his heart sinking. "What happened to her? Why won't she talk?"

Miriam leaned on her cane, unamused. "Because she can't, genius. She's been through horrors most grown men wouldn't survive. You think she's going to snap out of it because you gave her a hug and a guilt trip?"

Sinan clenched his fists. "I'll do whatever it takes to help her."

"Good," Miriam snapped. "Because right now, you're about as helpful as wet parchment."

Achi mimed an explosion with his stubby fingers. Jazz hands included.

Chava let out the faintest snort.

Sinan blinked. "Is your rock making jokes?"

"Yes. He's funnier than you too."

"Fantastic," Sinan muttered. "Insulted by a sand sculpture and a grandmother-shaped thunderstorm."

Madame Miriam laughed, full-bellied and wicked. "Oh, I like you. You've got bite. Like getting slapped with a sarcasm fish."

She reached into her robes and pulled something gleaming from within.

Sinan groaned. "Don't tell me I lost that again."

She held up the astrolabe. "Let's talk about this little trinket, shall we?"

"You've been using it as a memory mirror," she said, spinning it in her hands. "Cute. But it can do far more than dredge up your past."

Sinan crossed his arms. "Let me guess. But only if I'm 'worthy'?"

"Pfft. Worthy? Please. I've seen foot fungus more worthy. But with the right teacher... maybe you won't completely botch it."

"And I suppose you're that teacher?"

She peered at him. "If I ask how stupid you can be, just know — that's not a challenge."

"Charmed."

"Oh, you will be. Once I'm done slapping the ego out of you."

"Why help us at all?"

She sobered slightly. "Because some threads in the tapestry of fate are too thick to ignore. Yours, Sinan, is practically strangling destiny."

Sinan looked down at the astrolabe, then back to Chava.

"She has a magnificent mind," Miriam said softly. "But yours... yours is overcrowded. War, grief, vengeance. If you don't clear it, you'll never see what you need to."

"You want me to just forget everything?"

"No. I want you to face it. Forgetting is for cowards."

She tossed him the astrolabe. "Open it. Finish what you started. And remember — there is no turning back."

Sinan sat slowly, fingers hovering over the ancient device.

"This is going to hurt, isn't it?"

"Oh yes," Miriam nodded, satisfied. "But on the bright side, it'll be character building."

Achi gave him a thumbs-up. Sort of.

With a sigh, Sinan activated the astrolabe. The memory mirror shimmered into being.

"Here we go," he murmured.

"Life is hard," Miriam said behind him. "It's harder when you're stupid."

Despite himself, Sinan smirked. Then he looked into the mirror — and the pain returned.

David Nobyl

28

Master of the Scimitar

"The boy's pathetic, useless," Hizir scoffed in Oruc's cabin.

"Then train him," Oruc laughed. "He's young. He's been through much—more than most men twice his age—and he has spirit. He'll be a great ally to us one day."

"I'd rather train a goat to shave itself," Hizir grunted.

"That... wasn't a suggestion, Hizir. You'll train the boy, or you'll be swimming back to Tunisia," Oruc replied with a pleasant smile. "And you know I'll make you do it."

Hizir gritted his teeth. "Fine. But I do it my way."

He stormed out, grumbling curses under his breath, and spotted Sinan on the forecastle deck, studying Hebrew with Rabbi Samuel and Rahel. Without warning, Hizir grabbed him by the arm and dragged him away.

Tzitzi the cat raised her head in confusion, indignant at the theft of her favorite pillow.

Hizir tossed a wooden practice sword at Sinan, who barely caught it with an awkward thunk against his chest.

"Was I supposed to catch that or something?" Sinan asked, blinking.

"Do you have any skills in fighting for yourself? Any at all?" Hizir barked.

Sinan shrugged. "I mean, I've dodged a lot of things in my life—arrows, slurs, expectations. Does that count?"

"Pick. Up. The sword," Hizir growled, voice taut with restraint. Sinan obeyed, though he wobbled slightly under its weight.

Hizir assumed a battle stance, holding his own wooden scimitar with trained precision. Sinan mimicked him, sort of.

"Ready?"

"For what exactly?" Sinan squinted, the blade nearly blocking his entire view of Hizir.

Hizir charged. Sinan instinctively threw his sword up and rolled beneath the pirate, managing to clumsily whack Hizir in the face on his way through.

Hizir tumbled backward.

From outside his cabin, Oruc cackled. "You're doing great, Hizir. Another lesson or two and he'll be training you!"

Hizir's face flushed red as laughter erupted across the deck. Even Rahel cracked a smile from the upper level, though her concern lingered in her furrowed brow.

"You'll pay for that!" Hizir snarled. He retrieved both swords, tossing one back at Sinan.

The two circled each other, steps echoing in rhythm. Hizir studied Sinan carefully, probing for a weak point.

"You have no home. No family. No one," Hizir said coldly.

Sinan's jaw tightened. He gripped the sword, fingers whitening.

THE GREAT JEW PIRATE

"You can't protect yourself. You couldn't protect them. What is your worth in this world?"

Sinan trembled.

"Tell me," Hizir hissed, eyes burning. "Do you truly believe you could've saved your mother and father from the Inquisition?"

With a howl torn from his soul, Sinan charged, rage surging like a tidal wave.

"Finally," Hizir muttered, pleased.

They clashed—wood against wood, fury against finesse. Hizir struck four times. Sinan barely blocked three. The fourth hit his knee, and Sinan dropped with a scream.

The deck fell silent.

"Had enough?" Hizir asked.

Sinan howled again and sprang at him. Hizir met the attack with a blow to the chest that sent Sinan gasping.

Rabbi Samuel moved forward, but Oruc raised a hand, halting him.

"Enough! You've lost!" Hizir barked.

"Never!" Sinan roared, grabbing his sword, only to be hit again—this time in the stomach.

Rahel turned away, unable to watch. Even the crew winced.

"Stay down!" Hizir ordered. "Idiot—stay down!"

But Sinan didn't. He crawled forward and bit Hizir's leg.

"OW! You bit me?!"

Sinan took advantage, reclaimed his sword, and turned—only to find Oruc standing in front of him.

Sweating, trembling, and maybe bleeding, Sinan halted.

"Sinan," Oruc said softly, "we are not the Inquisition. I take responsibility for this. It was wrong."

Sinan's chest rose and fell in shallow gasps.

"From now on, I will train you—if that is what you still want."

"I want to fight," Sinan rasped. "To protect those I love. So what happened to them... never happens again."

Oruc nodded. "Then so it shall be. But please, try to calm down."

Without a word, he descended below deck, eyes hollow. He didn't glance at Rahel or the rabbi. He disappeared into the dark.

The following days passed in fog and fever. Sinan was consumed by exhaustion. His body burned, trembled. A sickness deeper than mere illness clawed at him.

The grief of losing his father—of realizing the man he barely got to know was gone forever—weighed like chains around his chest. Self-loathing bloomed in his soul: for failing to protect his parents, for biting Hizir like a mad dog, for not being stronger.

Even Oruc was shaken. "When we reach La Goulette tomorrow," he said to Rabbi Samuel and Rahel, "we'll find a doctor. But until then... all we can do is pray."

He pulled Hizir aside, eyeing the Cavalleria off the port side. "I don't trust the Tunisian court. Prepare yourself."

Hizir nodded, subdued. Later, watching Sinan writhe in his bunk, he whispered, "I didn't understand. I didn't see the weight he was carrying. I'm sorry."

That night, Rabbi Samuel prayed.

Rivka tended to Sinan, dampening his forehead.

"Sinan," she whispered. "We can be your family. Chava, Rabbi Samuel... me. Just come back to us."

When the others went to sleep, Rahel knelt beside Sinan.

THE GREAT JEW PIRATE

Her heart pounded not only with fear but with something softer, more tender—something she had never felt before.

She dipped the cloth into the basin again and wrung it out gently, then pressed it to Sinan's flushed forehead. His skin was burning, his breaths shallow and uneven.

"Sinan," she whispered, brushing a damp strand of hair away from his face. "You're the most infuriating boy I've ever met. You're reckless, and honestly? You smell like someone stuffed sardines into a goat's sock."

She gave a weak chuckle at her own joke, her fingers curling around his trembling hand.

"But..." Her voice cracked, and she blinked away tears. "You're also the bravest person I've ever known. You jump headfirst into danger just to protect others. Even when you're hurting. Even when you're bleeding. Even when you can barely stand. And I think... I think you might be the only person who's ever made me feel like I'm not alone."

He stirred, murmuring unintelligibly, and squeezed her fingers ever so faintly. It was enough to unravel her composure. A tear slid down her cheek.

"I don't want to lose anyone else, Sinan. Not after everything. Not after everyone. So please, don't go where I can't follow. I'm not asking you to be strong right now. I just want you to come back."

She leaned closer, her forehead resting gently against his. "I need you here. We all do. But I think... I need you most of all."

She stayed that way for a long time, her fingers tangled in his, listening to his ragged breathing. And though he didn't answer, she swore something shifted in him—like a tide pulling back from the edge.

Unseen, Rabbi Samuel—only pretending to sleep—heard every word.

***

Dawn.

Sinan stirred.

He rose slowly, moved to the back of the ship, and washed his face. He looked down at his reflection.

Gone was the boy.

In the water, he saw cheekbones sharper, eyes deeper, jawline stronger.

A new version of himself. A more realized version of the man he intended to become.

He turned and headed for Oruc's quarters.

Hizir opened the door and stepped aside with a silent nod.

Oruc looked up, a broad smile breaking across his face.

"I'm ready," Sinan said. "To learn from both of you."

Oruc raised an eyebrow. "Swordplay, I assume. And Hizir can handle..."

"Romance?" Hizir deadpanned.

Oruc snorted. "Ah yes, the famous affair with Sayyida Al-Hurra. A tragic tale of unreciprocated insults."

"Please," Hizir sighed.

Sinan stood tall. "Each of you fights differently. I want to learn both styles. And forge one that's mine."

Oruc nodded.

Hizir hesitated. Then said, "Only under one condition."

Sinan braced. "I'll endure any insult."

"No more insults," Hizir replied. "You've earned that. My condition is simpler."

Sinan blinked. "What is it?"

THE GREAT JEW PIRATE

"Promise me one thing."
"Anything."
"Never. Bite. Me. Again."

David Nobyl

David Nobyl

29

The Boy & The Lynx

For the many weeks that followed, Sinan trained relentlessly under the watchful gazes of Oruc and Hizir. His days were split between grueling sword drills and quiet hours learning Arabic with Rahel, her voice patient but firm as she prepared him for life in what might soon become their new home.

Their ships sliced through the narrow strait leading into the port of Tunis. Excitement simmered in the air, mingled with unease. As the coastline unfurled before them, Sinan found himself captivated by the crumbling ruins scattered across the rocky terrain.

"That," Rahel said, her tone reverent, "was once the mighty empire of Carthage. Led by Hannibal himself, the only general who truly threatened the might of Rome."

Sinan turned, eyebrows raised. "How do you know all this?"

"My uncle studied at the University of al-Qarawiyyin in Fez," she replied, a small smile playing at her lips. "I always dreamed of joining him on his diplomatic missions. We used to write letters about visiting Carthage one day."

Sinan gazed out at the ruins with newfound interest. "How did Hannibal manage to challenge Rome?"

"He was a master strategist. And Carthage—at its height—was the final stronghold against Roman domination. By the time of the Punic Wars, Rome had already conquered most of the Mediterranean."

"Did Hannibal win?" Sinan asked, hopeful.

Rahel winced. "He came close. He even led an army of war elephants over the Pyrenees."

Sinan's eyes widened. "War elephants? Now that I would've liked to see. But if he lost, why do people still admire him?"

Rahel's eyes sparkled. "Because he had foresight. The Rabbis of Carthage were said to possess Kabbalistic insight, and some say they gifted Hannibal with visions of the future."

"But he still lost?" Sinan pressed.

"Only because Scipio Africanus outwitted him at Zama. Hannibal was forced to abandon his gifts." Her voice turned wistful. "Some believe that beneath these ruins lies a hidden library of those ancient texts."

Sinan smirked. "A secret Kabbalistic library under a dead empire? That's oddly specific."

"So is every legend worth believing," Rahel shot back.

As the ruins faded into the horizon, the ships finally arrived at La Goulette, the bustling port of Tunis.

"Lower the anchor!" Hizir barked, setting off a flurry of crew activity. From the deck, he waved frantically at a tall man waiting on the docks.

"If you don't move, Ishak, you'll be flattened!"

"What's going on?" Oruc emerged from his cabin.

THE GREAT JEW PIRATE

"Him," Hizir pointed with a grin. "You can crush."

"After six months, this is how you greet your eldest brother?" Ishak called back, arms outstretched.

Hizir leapt onto the docks, embracing his towering brother with a twist and flourish. Oruc followed, the wood groaning beneath his weight as he picked them both up in a bear hug.

"How long since we stood together like this?" Oruc beamed.

"Too long," Ishak murmured. "If only Ilyas could see us now."

The mood sobered. Oruc nodded and set them down gently.

"How's our mother?"

"She's well... though worried about your dealings with the Bey."

"Then let's not keep him waiting," Oruc said with a sigh. "Where does he want to meet?"

"Inside the Grand Market," Ishak replied, sarcasm not lost in his graceful bow.

From the deck, Sinan observed the interaction with curiosity. Rabbi Pallache appeared beside him.

"They saved us, yes," the Rabbi said quietly. "But nothing is ever free."

Sinan nodded and jumped down to the dock.

"I want to go with you," he said. "To speak on your behalf."

"This is not your fight," Hizir said sharply.

"But the Sultan accepts Jews—"

"The Ottoman Sultan does," Oruc corrected. "Not necessarily the Bey of Tunis."

"He barely tolerates us," Hizir added.

"That's... not encouraging," Sinan muttered.

"Stay here," Ishak said. "Please."

With disappointment on his face, Sinan stepped back as the brothers carried a chest full of spoils toward the city.

Once the Barbarossa brothers departed for the market, Rahel was nowhere to be found on deck. Sinan scanned the ship but quickly spotted her leaping from the deck onto the rooftops of the surrounding marketplace, swift as a falcon in flight. Without a word, she was off.

Sinan gawked at the agility with which she moved and scrambled after her, clutching the railing before following her with far less grace. Tzitzi, as ever, needed no prompting. She sprang to the edge, tail flicking once before she launched herself after Rahel.

Sinan landed awkwardly on the rooftop, slipping on a pile of dusty tiles. He stumbled, nearly tumbling off the edge, only saved by Tzitzi, who dug her claws into his tunic to anchor him.

"Careful," Rahel hissed from above. She didn't stop. She was already halfway across the tiled expanse, bounding from one rooftop to the next with the precision of someone who knew this terrain far better than she let on.

Sinan muttered a quiet curse and followed.

They weaved through the market's chaos above, the rooftops giving them a perfect view of the winding stalls below. The Grand Market of the Port of Tunis was a maze of vibrant colors and pungent aromas—trinkets, rugs, herbs, incense, live chickens, brassware, and a thousand haggling voices.

Rahel crouched low and signaled them to stop. She pointed toward the towering limestone building at the far edge of the market. "There," she whispered. "That's where they're going."

THE GREAT JEW PIRATE

Sinan nodded, panting heavily. Soon Rahel perched high among the branches of a broad-leafed fig tree overlooking the limestone courtyard. She balanced with uncanny poise, her keen eyes fixed on the unfolding scene below. She had slipped away from the ship before Sinan or anyone else had noticed, following her instincts and the uneasy feeling in her chest. She needed to see for herself what kind of man ruled Tunis—and who the Barbarossa brothers were really dealing with.

Behind her, with far less grace, Sinan clambered up the same tree, huffing as he pulled himself onto a branch. Tzitzi leapt after him, landing on his shoulder and promptly climbing atop his head.

"You're going to get us caught," Rahel whispered harshly without turning. "Try not to knock the tree down."

Sinan narrowed his eyes at her back. "You're welcome for the reinforcements."

From their vantage point, the trio surveyed the central courtyard nestled in the heart of the limestone fortress. Below, the Barbarossa brothers approached with measured confidence, carrying a chest filled with their hard-won spoils. Oruc, Hizir, and Ishak stopped before the dais, where the Bey of Tunis reclined atop a plush zebra rug, lazily puffing on a gold and glass hookah. Four guards surrounded him, stoic and silent, their blades glinting ominously.

On one side of the Bey, a woman sat cross-legged, her son beside her. A red sash adorned her waist, and a gold-encrusted scimitar lay casually at her side—a clear badge of Moroccan royalty. A younger Sayidda Al-Hurra, still only a Princess of Morocco. Behind her, silent and immovable, stood a towering young man—barely more than a boy—with long dark curls and deep-set eyes. It was a young Samson. His quiet demeanor masked a power that rippled just beneath the surface.

Opposite them stood King Sālim al-Tūm of Djidjelli, Ruler of Algiers, armored and imposing. Two burly archers flanked him, their arrowheads slick with the dreaded Djidjelli "Lockjaw" toxin—capable of paralyzing a man before he could draw breath.

Upon settling the treasure before the Bey, Ishak bowed first. "We thank you for honoring us with this visitation. We had no idea that when you requested we meet, it would be in secret inside the Grand Market itself."

Bey Abu waved him off with an air of indifference. "Desperate times call for special measures," he hissed. "If my people knew I was meeting with you—" he glanced at Oruc, a smug grin forming. "What is it they call you? Baba Oruc? Papa Oruc?"

Oruc's grip on the chest tightened, his eyes ablaze. "Is there something wrong with it?"

"Not the title, but who bestowed it," Bey Abu countered, blowing fragrant smoke toward him. "Those Marranos and Moriscos—those Jews and Muslims who left their faith behind, correct?"

"You suggest those banished don't deserve a second chance to live?" Oruc growled.

"I, for one, think Oruc's actions have noble merit," Sayyida Al-Hurra interjected smoothly.

Bey Abu laughed, the sound hollow. "And what are they calling you these days, Hakimat Titwan? You're no better than him in my eyes."

"Are you not equals in sovereignty?" Hizir asked, drawing a flicker of interest from Sayyida.

Sālim scowled at Samson. "And yet she travels with a dog of war," he sneered. "A slave gifted as a favor to be permitted an audience with the Bey is disgraceful." He spat at Samson's feet.

Sayyida's gaze snapped to Sālim. "Say another word and I will have your tongue removed," Sayyida said coldly, her hand twitching toward her blade. "Don't think I don't know how you murdered your entire family for the right to your throne."

The courtyard thickened with tension. Bey Abu puffed again, bored. Ishak tried to intervene. "What my brothers are trying to say—"

Bey Abu silenced him with a wave.

"There are already too many Jews in our lands," he drawled. "My coffers can't support more mouths."

"I couldn't agree more," Sālim bellowed, laughing. "If even one Jew sets foot in my lands, I'll feed them to the beasts in the arena!"

"Isn't that what you did to your family?" Oruc snapped, eyeing Samson. "Or did one escape your stubby little fingers?"

Sālim's laughter died and his eyes narrowed. He leapt to his feet, sword drawn. His guards raised their toxin-laced arrows. Oruc and Hizir followed suit, blades out, the cold whisper of steel hanging in the air.

Samson tensed but stayed back. Sayyida stepped forward, shielding her son.

Then, without warning, a shimmering bolt of green energy—barely visible—shot from one of Sālim's guards. Hizir deflected the blow intended for Sayyida with his shield. It ricocheted through the air, grazing Rahel and causing her to lose balance.

The brittle wood cracked with a loud SNAP.

Rahel gasped—then fell.

"Rahel!" Sinan lunged after her instinctively as the branch gave way beneath them both. Tzitzi leapt free just in time.

Rahel hit the carpet first, limp. Sinan tumbled after her, landing with a hard thud beside her unmoving form.

The courtyard erupted in chaos. Swords were drawn again. Tzitzi growled, and the Bey noticed the unusual lynx. She intrigued him.

"Poison!" Sayyida shouted, kneeling beside Rahel. "They used the Djidjelli poison!"

"What have you done?!" Oruc bellowed, storming toward Sālim, his blade raised.

"She was spying," Sālim smirked. "And so was he."

The Bey of Tunis rose slowly from his couch, a rare gesture. "ENOUGH," he commanded, and silence dropped like a blade.

He eyed the fallen girl and the boy. "You bring spies to my courtyard, Oruc. I should confiscate your payment entirely."

"You'll get your payment," Oruc growled, looking at Rahel's unconscious body, then at Sinan, who was cradling her.

"And I want double," the Bey added coolly. "For the insult of this intrusion—and for the beast." He gestured to Tzitzi.

"No!" Sinan shouted as a guard yanked Tzitzi from his arms. "Don't take her—she's mine!"

"She's collateral," the Bey replied, exhaling smoke. "She stays. My new pet."

Sayyida stood. "Let the girl receive medical attention," she demanded. "What's done is done."

The Bey waved a lazy hand. "Take them and go. I tire of this spectacle."

THE GREAT JEW PIRATE

Sinan looked back one last time as Tzitzi was dragged behind a curtain, her eye wide with fear. Rahel was carried out gently by Ishak, her limbs slack, her face pale and still. And then the limestone doors slammed shut behind them with a hollow, final thud.

"This isn't finished," Hizir growled to Oruc as they made their way through the city streets, Rahel still unconscious in their arms.

"No," Oruc said grimly. "We'll see Sālim on the battlefield soon enough."

With that, the memory mirror dissolved into a shimmer of light, the echoes of the past vanishing into the amber glow of the astrolabe. Sinan closed its lid with trembling fingers, the metallic click sounding louder than it should have in the stillness of the underground Kabbalah Library.

The scent of ancient parchment and sandalwood hung heavy in the air. He glanced around to confirm he was alone—only the shadows of unread tomes and forgotten truths kept him company.

He slumped forward, resting his head on a stack of worn books, their spines inscribed with languages lost to most of the living. And there, beneath the weight of memory and the silence of stone, Sinan let the tears come—quietly, fiercely, without shame.

David Nobyl

David Nobyl

30

Djidjelli Desert Raiders

"Can't sleep, huh?" rasped Madame Miriam, her voice cutting through the night air as she gazed out over the cliffside from the entrance of her Carthaginian cave.

Sinan stepped into the moonlight beside a hollowed-out oak tree, its brittle leaves whispering in the breeze. Below, waves crashed violently against jagged stone, echoing the storm inside him.

"I find solace in the sea's embrace," he murmured, watching the water clash endlessly against the shore.

Madame Miriam let out a dry chuckle. "It seems the sea was made for you."

Sinan smirked. "Can't argue with that."

"Ah, I knew there was a brain rattling around in that head somewhere," she teased. Her tone shifted. "But on a more serious note... there's something I've been meaning to show you."

From within the folds of her robe, she drew two brass discs, no larger than teacup saucers. Each was carved with concentric circles, cryptic geometries, and script unfamiliar to Sinan—but eerily similar to the language in Chava's books from the Carthaginian library.

"Stolen straight from your astrolabe," she said, handing them to him. "Engraved with ancient Hebrew. They were your father's, weren't they?"

Sinan turned them over, eyes narrowing. "That's right. But what are they?"

"Maps," she said plainly. "Crafted by Hebrew Talmudists to guide our people home—even after centuries of exile and persecution by the Demon of Semites."

Sinan raised a brow. "Demon of Semites? I've heard of Asmodeus, the demon king who fought King Solomon for his throne, but that sounds more like a bedtime story for children."

Miriam gave him a withering look. "You really think centuries of massacres, exile, blood libels, inquisitions, pogroms... were coincidence? I've called you an idiot before. Don't make me right."

Sinan blinked, caught off guard.

"They say," she continued, voice low, "that when Hashem unleashed the final plague in Egypt—"

"The locusts?" Sinan guessed.

She glared. "No, the death of the Egyptian firstborns sons. Legend goes that when Pharaoh Ramses lost his son, his soul twisted into hatred for all of Hashem's children. It was quite literally torn from the cycle of life and death—and it became a dybbuk. Over the centuries it fed off the pain and suffering of Jews and Muslims. It didn't take long before it gained enough strength to ascend into demonhood."

"The Demon of Semites," Sinan repeated, frowning. "Never heard of it in any of my readings."

"You will," she said, flatly. "Because you have something it wants."

Sinan hesitated. "What?"

"Show me the astrolabe."

He pulled it from beneath his tunic and handed it to her. She clicked one disc into the center. The mechanisms aligned with a soft snap. Raising the astrolabe to the stars, she turned the gears until the etched letters pulsed with a glowing light.

"What does it say?" Sinan asked. "I recognize the Hebrew, but not the rest."

"To read Kabbalah magic, one needs more than knowledge," she said. "Chava was born with this gift. You—weren't."

She continued, reading from the disc: "Travel east, find what you seek." She adjusted the position. "But beware: travel west, and doom you'll meet."

Sinan scoffed. "I don't even know what I'm seeking."

"The Demon does," Miriam replied. "That astrolabe is the last of its kind—a key to the Sword of Solomon."

He let out a breathless laugh. "What, the mythical blade of the wise king?"

"Do you think Solomon used a stick and a prayer to banish Asmodeus and build the Second Temple?" she snapped.

His grin faded.

"This map—and the sword may reveal—are our people's last hope. A final defense against a rising evil. Perhaps even a path to a future homeland."

She placed the second disc atop the first. The plates began to spin in opposite directions. New glyphs ignited in radiant light.

Miriam read: "When man turns to dybbuk and dybbuk to demon, only the Sword of Solomon can restore order. Find the sword in—"

She stopped.

"Well?" Sinan prompted.

Her voice softened. "The third plate is missing. It holds the sword's location. But I warn you, Sinan—the path ahead will bring despair. You don't have to walk it."

"I'm already living a fate worse than death," he replied coldly. "I'll find the third plate. I don't have a choice."

"You always have a choice," she said, firmly. "It's just that our worst regrets often come from the ones we make freely."

His voice rose. "Was it my choice when the Inquisition tore my family apart? When I was burned? When they took—everything? Was that my choice?!"

Her gaze dropped. "It is your choice to protect your sister."

"She can't come with me," Sinan said, voice steadying. "It's too dangerous. I want her to stay with you. She'll be safe here."

Miriam sighed. "I wish she could. But I've seen what's to come. I can't stop it."

"You've seen?" he said, incredulous. "You're a seer now?"

"I never wanted to be," she murmured. "I've lived in these ruins for fifty years, away from everyone I loved—not for fun, Sinan. I had a family. Grandchildren."

Her voice cracked.

"My little Hania," she whispered. "I wanted to see her grow. But after what I saw… the pain coming to our people—I lost myself. I left them. I couldn't explain. I just vanished."

Sinan remained quiet.

"I came here, alone," she continued. "But one day... a stone golem with a human soul bound it found me. He's kept me company ever since."

Sinan's voice dropped. "It's someone you knew, isn't it?"

"No," she said, surprising him. "But the soul needed purpose. And so did I."

"What did you see when you looked into our people's future, exactly?" he asked softly.

She shook her head. "Enough to break me for decades. And when I returned to myself, my family was gone. Forgotten me. But I waited—because I saw you. You, and especially Chava."

Her eyes flicked toward the horizon. "Never again will I look ahead."

She turned to Sinan. "The memory mirror offers answers from the past and future. But if you ever try to see ahead—know that you risk true madness. Promise me you won't."

"Ignorance can be educated, craziness can be medicated, but there's no cure for stupidity," Sinan said, cracking a weak smile.

She let out a breath. "I guess I've been the fool here all along."

She handed him back the astrolabe. Then, brushing dust from her sleeves, she turned toward the cave.

"Now go. Chava's practicing in the amphitheater with Achi. Tell them to come—I'll make breakfast."

Sinan watched her vanish into the shadows. The cliff no longer whispered danger. Sunlight warmed his back. He turned toward the path.

But unbeknownst to him, hooves pounded. Their riders hunting for the elusive rock golem of legend. Whispers from the nearby townsfolk had grown loud enough to attract the King of Djidjelli and his Desert Raiders to come hunt for sport.

Clad in black, their cowls pulled low and curved shamshirs swinging at their sides, the Djidjelli Desert Raiders rode swiftly over the hills. Silent and focused, they fanned out, eyes scanning the amphitheater ruins like wolves circling prey.

At their helm rode King Sālim of Djidjelli and Algiers, his face partially obscured but his presence unmistakable—grave, calculating, and merciless. At his side, Commander Ibn al-Wazzan followed, one hand on the hilt of his curved blade, the other gripping the reins.

Sālim raised a gloved hand, pointing toward the amphitheater where Chava practiced alongside the Golem and little Achi. The girl's back was turned, oblivious to the eyes fixed upon her.

"Bring me the Golem," Sālim commanded coldly.

The commander relayed the order. The raiders moved into formation, tightening their approach. Their voices rang out in unison: "Yes, my king!"

With a subtle gesture, the signal was given. The men erupted forward, hooves pounding as they let out a guttural war cry that broke the silence of the dawn.

Behind them, a covered cage quivered. The thing inside snarled and thrashed with unnatural force, rocking its iron frame.

Sālim turned, voice sharp. "Quiet, beast. If you behave, you shall have your fill."

Below, Chava froze mid-motion. The sudden shout, the charging horses—it was happening too fast. Achi clung to her leg, trembling. She tried to call for help, but her voice

THE GREAT JEW PIRATE

caught in her throat. She clutched her book tight to her chest, backing against the Golem instinctively.

Then came the hiss of rope cutting through the air.

A lasso twirled overhead—faster than her eyes could follow. Its whistle pierced the air as it arced toward them, aiming to bind the Golem... or her.

But just before it struck, an arm shot out and caught it mid-flight.

The rope coiled tightly around Sinan's forearm.

In that split second, his eyes flicked up to the riders—and locked on the embroidered sigil on their cloaks: a golden flame atop a black crescent.

He froze.

King Sālim.

He knew what that meant. Djidjelli. Executioners. Burners of villages. They hadn't come to negotiate.

There was no time to think, no room for talk.

He acted.

With a surge of strength, Sinan yanked the rope hard, pulling the raider clean off his horse. The man hit the stone with a sickening thud.

Sinan was on him in an instant. A sharp blow to the temple dropped him. Sinan wrenched the shamshir from the raider's belt and turned, blade gleaming.

One clean slash—and the ropes fell away from Chava and Achi.

"Go!" he barked, eyes never leaving the rest of the advancing riders. "Run—now!"

But their hesitation cost him time.

The remaining raiders, snapping out of their shock at what they'd just witnessed, charged as one.

Sinan spun on his heel and darted through the ruins, using the crumbled arches and fallen columns for cover.

Another rider lunged—Sinan ducked beneath the swing of a saber and drove his shoulder into the horse's flank, sending the beast rearing. Its rider tumbled backward, and Sinan struck, sharp and fast.

Up above, King Sālim watched, his fury simmering beneath a cold exterior.

"This worm... he dares?" the king seethed. "Bring me that scoundrel!"

"But Your Highness," the commander replied, "what of the Golem—?"

"To the abyss with the Golem!" Sālim snapped. "We've found something far more valuable."

Without waiting, he turned and tore the heavy cloth from the iron cage behind him.

A low growl echoed across the hilltop.

Inside, a beast shifted—a monstrous hybrid of tiger and cheetah, with lean muscle, curved claws, and a single burning-yellow eye glowing like a coal in its skull.

Sālim said nothing, only pointed.

The creature understood.

The cage door slammed open.

It leapt.

The beast bolted down the slope, a blur of muscle and fury. Its paws tore up stone and dirt alike. Even on horseback, Commander Ibn struggled to keep up. But the beast never slowed.

In the ruins, Sinan barely had time to turn.

It hit him like a battering ram—fangs sinking into his shoulder, claws raking across his chest. Blood burst from the wound as he crashed to the ground, shamshir skidding from his grip.

Sinan cried out in pain, the sound raw and sharp.

THE GREAT JEW PIRATE

The beast stood over him, snarling, pressing its weight down. Behind it, the commander approached, whip in hand.

"Off him!" Ibn shouted, cracking the whip toward the creature.

It growled in protest, baring its fangs but refusing to let go.

Sinan, dazed and bleeding, looked up into the beast's face—into that lone, luminous eye.

Recognition flickered.

Through the haze, through the agony, he whispered—broken, sincere:

"Forgive me."

The beast froze.

Its snarls fell silent.

Then, slowly, it unlatched its jaw and stepped back, leaving Sinan's shoulder drenched and torn.

His body slumped against the limestone, his vision dimming.

And as darkness closed in, he exhaled one final, faltering breath:

"Forgive me, Tzitzi."

David Nobyl

David Nobyl

31

King Sālim's Gladiator Arena

"King Sālim Al-Tum of Djidjelli, I presume?"

Diego de Cordoba's smile curved like a rapier, pleasant but meant to cut. "Admiral Doria has spoken of you often. Colorful stories. Apparently, you've captured the so-called Great Jew Pirate."

Sālim chuckled, lounging on his throne as though Diego had delivered a compliment. "Admiral Doria?" he echoed with a theatrical yawn. "That overpaid mercenary knows little of real power. But go on. Enlighten me—what have his lips been flapping about now?"

Diego hesitated, just for a beat. The light in Sālim's eyes was sharper than he expected.

"He's... been vocal," Diego offered carefully.

"Is that so?" Sālim's voice curled around the words like smoke. "Vocal about what, exactly?"

Diego straightened. "I think we have more pressing matters to discuss."

"Indeed we do," Sālim agreed, the words steeped in condescension. "But what are matters of diplomacy without a little polite preamble? I'm sure Doria has told you of my grandeur. How I toppled my own brother, rid myself of his Ethiopian wife and mixed-blood children... and sent the weakest of them wandering the earth as a living legend of my wrath."

The Spaniards stiffened. Diego's smile grew tight.

"Point taken," he said coolly. "Spain seeks an alliance. Not war."

"I'd hope so," Sālim said, rising from his throne. "For I rule Algiers now. Every neighboring kingdom kneels before me."

"For now," Diego muttered.

Sālim's eyes narrowed. "What was that?"

"I asked what comes next," Diego said innocently. "What does the future hold for a man like you, Your Highness?"

Sālim gave a toothy grin. "Next, I take Morocco from that insolent Queen Sayyida Al-Hurra. She thinks the sea protects her. Fools make fine ornaments for the ocean floor."

"We've met," Diego replied. "Her... and an accomplice of hers. A man you claim to have in custody."

Sālim chuckled, deep and dark. "Ah yes. The Jew Pirate. Or as your Emperor nearly called him—problematic inspiration."

Diego's expression sharpened. "We're not here to aid your conquest of Morocco. We're here for one reason. To retrieve Sinan."

Sālim's grin widened. "And what if it's not that simple?"

Diego didn't blink. "Then we'll make it simple."

Sālim raised a brow, amused. "Sinan offered himself, you know. Gladiator's honor. Said he'd rather die fighting than see his sister harmed." He leaned forward. "A noble fool, wouldn't you agree?"

Diego's hand shot to his sword. "He was to be returned alive."

The room exploded with tension as Spanish steel rang out, swords half-drawn.

Sālim didn't flinch. "Forgot your cannons, did you? Or left them outside as a peace offering?"

Diego's voice dropped to a deadly whisper. "Break this deal and Spain will erase you."

Sālim threw back his head and laughed. "Where's the fun in threats, Diego? Stay. Enjoy the show."

Diego scowled. "Why should I?"

Sālim gestured toward the arena beyond the court. "Because Sinan's opponent is a crowd favorite. The most dangerous gladiator in my domain. They call him... the Spirit of Vengeance."

A flicker passed over Diego's face.

"Oh?" Sālim asked with mock curiosity. "That name means something to you?"

"I'm beginning to think you know far more than you let on," Diego said quietly.

Sālim's laugh was dry and cold. "At least I know who I'm dealing with. Come. Let's be entertained."

They were guided through a narrow corridor, eventually spilling into the colosseum—a sprawling timber arena crowned with roaring crowds and an arrogant Sultan's perch.

Below, in the dungeon-barracks, Sinan sat against the cold stone wall of his cell. Chava lay beside him for comfort. Nearby, an old woman, skin like parchment, poured water into a young man's mouth—his front teeth chipped deliberately, creating a funnel.

"What's the matter with him?" Sinan asked.

"Lockjaw toxin," the woman rasped. "He's been paralyzed for years."

"Was it Sālim's doing?"

She nodded. "My family was thrown in here long ago. My children poisoned slowly. Only one was sold as a slave to the highest bidder."

"Why?"

"To be the Sultan's terror-tale. The frail one, supposedly harmless."

"The boy... what was his name?"

"Samson."

Sinan's breath caught.

He leaned in closer to whisper, but footsteps interrupted him.

Djidjelli guards appeared, scowling.

"You! Time for your divine thrashing," one sneered.

"That's the Great Jew Pirate?" a prisoner muttered.

The cell door creaked. Sinan was dragged to his knees. A thick steel mask was forced onto his face. His screams echoed through the dungeon. One guard's mallet swing missed and hit Sinan in his side, breaking the astrolabe hidden in his robes.

Chava stirred awake just in time to see him dragged away.

On the floor, half-buried in gravel, glinted a broken half of Sinan's astrolabe. Chava clutched it to her chest as though her prayer could tether him to life.

Above the dungeon, the crowd roared, hungry for spectacle.

THE GREAT JEW PIRATE

Sinan was thrown into the arena. There, the Spirit of Vengeance awaited.

David Nobyl

David Nobyl

32

Spirit of Vengeance

Overlooking the battlements of King Sālim's colosseum, the white sands of the wooden arena shimmered under a harsh desert sun. In the center, a sword stood buried to the hilt, a lone shield leaning beside it like a relic from an abandoned war.

King Sālim raised his hand. A single clap, sharp and deliberate, echoed across the arena.

"Tonight!" bellowed the announcer, appearing at the podium like a conjurer unveiling his latest trick, "we gather from every corner of the realm for an event as rare as a blood-red sun! A spectacle of legends!"

A dramatic pause. Then, with a smirk: "And none of them are here."

The crowd erupted into booing.

"Ah, forgive me! I jest!" the announcer said with a wink. "Our first warrior tonight: a brute of blood and vengeance! The man who eats nightmares for breakfast! I give you— THE SPIRIT OF VENGEANCE!"

The gates creaked open. From the shadows emerged a towering figure clad in glinting iron and crowned by the golden Mask of Agamemnon. He held twin broadswords slick with dried blood, each swing of his arm a threat unto itself.

The crowd chanted: "VENGEANCE! VENGEANCE!"

"And his opponent," the announcer continued, his voice reaching a theatrical pitch, "a thief of winds, a conjurer of Kabbalistic magic, a pirate of Hebrew legend—the Great Jew Pirate!"

From the opposite gate, a slender figure stepped into the light. Sinan's face was masked in steel, his eyes barely visible through the slits. A dagger hung from one hand. In the other, a rope.

A hush fell. Then laughter.

"Now," the announcer said with relish, "for those afraid of blood or shy of death, I suggest you avert your eyes."

The crowd cheered wildly.

The Spirit of Vengeance lunged first—a blur of muscle and rage. Sinan ducked low, rolled into the sand, and snatched up the shield just in time to absorb the blow. Metal clanged against metal. The crowd roared.

Sinan darted around the Spirit like a shadow, rope trailing. With one swift flick, he looped it around his opponent's ankle and pulled hard. The titan stumbled and fell.

Sinan seized the moment, sprinting toward the sword embedded in the sand. He dropped into a slide, grabbed the hilt, and pulled with everything he had. Nothing. It wouldn't budge.

Too slow.

The Spirit was on him again. A broadsword crashed against the shield, shattering it like glass. The impact drove Sinan to his knees. Another slash grazed his leg. Pain flared.

He collapsed, dropping everything.

"Had enough?" the Spirit growled.

THE GREAT JEW PIRATE

Sinan spat blood and screamed, yanking the sword from the earth with a burst of raw adrenaline.

He swung.

Missed.

The Spirit countered. The strike hit Sinan square in the chest, sending him flying.

"Stay down!" the Spirit hissed. "I'm trying to save your life!"

But Sinan rose again, eyes wild. He lunged. The Spirit kicked the sword away and pinned him.

"It's over!" he barked.

Then—a scream. Sinan sank his teeth into the man's thigh.

"You devil!" the Spirit howled. "I told you never to bite me again!"

Sinan froze.

"Hizir?"

"Of course it's me, you lunatic!"

Above, Sālim stood. His fury was volcanic.

"UNLEASH THE BEASTS!"

The announcer repeated it, voice booming. Gates creaked. The crowd gasped.

Two predators emerged: a massive lion and a sleek black lynx, one eye gleaming with madness.

Diego grabbed Sālim. "You break the deal, the Spanish Empire retaliates."

Sālim sneered. "Spain needs our Lockjaw Toxin. And your experiments on Ischia? Testing on slaves? I know. You have no leverage."

Sālim vanished into the shadows, his announcer following.

The lynx sprinted toward Hizir.

Tzitzi?

It tackled him.

Sinan, desperate, hurled half a shield at the beast, knocking it away.

It lunged at him next. He raised his arms, but it bit the steel mask instead. Sinan stared into its eye.

"I'm sorry," he whispered. "I failed you."

The lynx bit down harder—and the mask popped free.

Sinan's face was revealed.

Tzitzi stared, her one eye softening.

"You... want to explain?" Hizir muttered.

"Later," Sinan panted.

The lion approached.

Tzitzi leapt at it, claws flashing. But the lion grabbed her and flung her aside like a rag doll.

The lion turned to Sinan and Hizir, eyes cold. It leapt.

Sinan was struck hard, pain flooding his leg. Blood gushed.

He found the steel mask nearby, slick with the lion's own blood—it had hit the beast in the face.

The lion prowled closer. Sinan touched something in his pocket: the broken half of his astrolabe. He touched it and squeezed it hard, focusing on Madame Miriam's instructions in times of great peril.

Time... slowed.

Everything moved like syrup. The crowd was frozen. Hizir. The lion. Even the dust in the air hung still.

Blue light bled from Sinan's hand, healing his wounds as it travelled. Hebrew runes lit up his arm, spiraling upward.

A bolt of blue lightning tore through the sky and slammed into the lion. It spasmed. Went limp. Fell.

The soft blue light wrapped around Tzitzi. Her wounds closed. Her breath returned.

THE GREAT JEW PIRATE

And then—time snapped back.
The lion's corpse landed on Sinan.
Silence.
Then cheers.
Sinan rose, bloodied, glowing faintly.
Hizir gaped. "What are you?"
Sinan gave a crooked smile. "Let them decide."
The chant began low. A murmur.
"The Great Jew Pirate."
It grew. Louder. Stronger. The entire colosseum shook.
"THE GREAT JEW PIRATE!"
The name rang like prophecy.

David Nobyl

David Nobyl

33

Jews of Djerba

As the thunderous symphony of the gladiatorial ring echoed from the arena above, Chava held the fractured astrolabe half in her hand.

She held out as long as patience allowed, but eventually, the suspense overwhelmed her. Cross-legged on the cold ground, Chava cradled the astrolabe half like a delicate bird. Her lips moved in a hushed rhythm, each word a sacred prayer, a plea to the obstinate device.

The astrolabe, like a startled beast, responded with fits of sparks and reluctant crackles. It seemed to resist, to test her resolve—then finally, it gave in. It opened, and blue light flooded out of it. Outside, Sinan's astrolabe half would begin to glow as well, both halves activated at the same time with two incredible wills.

Chava heard a lightning strike, followed by a loud thud and silence. She dared not to breath. The crowd erupted into cheers, chanting, "The Great Jew Pirate"!

Chava let out a sigh of relief. In her lap, the glowing astrolabe began to pulse with its own volition. The memory mirror swirled into view, as if communicating with her.

It guided her, an unseen hand leading her through the labyrinth of Sinan's past. She became a ghost in his memories.

***

On the sunlit shores of Djerba Island, in the small Jewish city of Hara Sghira, the island bustled with life. The El Ghriba Synagogue at the center of the city was one of the oldest in the region, dating back to 586 BCE.

It had been a month since the events in the Tunis Grand Market. Since then, Oruc and Hizir's ship arrived in Djerba where they unloaded their cargo and passengers. Rahel was still in a coma, and was brought to the island infirmary by Sinan and Rabbi Pallache as soon as they arrived.

It was on this island that Hizir sought to find a brief respite. Oruc had other plans.

"Oruc, give it a rest! We both heard Madam Miriam's prophecy—and even if it's true, it isn't about Sinan! He's cocky and impulsive," Hizir grumbled.

"Maybe," Oruc replied calmly, "But I won't risk being wrong."

With a grin, Oruc produced a letter, the seal of the Ottoman Sultanate gleaming in the sun.

Hizir blinked. "You didn't."

"Oh, I did," Oruc said, clearly enjoying himself. "I figured the Bey of Tunisia would pull something under us just as he did. So, I wrote to the Ottoman Sultan months ago in case we were in need of a new benefactor."

Breaking the seal, Hizir scanned the ornate script. His eyes lit up. "The Sultan agreed!"

"Sultan Bayezid II himself," Oruc confirmed.

"This changes everything!"

"Yes," Oruc said with solemn gravity. "It does. Now, we have an entire Ottoman fleet at our disposal."

While Oruc and Hizir celebrated, Sinan took up a job as an assistant in the makeshift hospital in Djerba. It wasn't much more than a vast tent with countless beds. But this way he could be near Rahel every day. Her condition had remained unchanged and the physicians on the island had no idea how to cure her condition. Instead, Sinan poured himself into work. He tended to the wounded to make some money to buy medical books from the local libraries, reading anything he could to amass knowledge. Maybe there was something he could learn that could save Rahel and bring her back to him.

"Starving yourself won't bring her back faster," Rabbi Pallache said one morning, eyeing the dark circles under Sinan's eyes. "You need to rest. You may not be my blood, but you're my son. I'd give my life for you."

Sinan looked away, ashamed. "Don't say that."

"Do you think she'll survive?" Sinan said.

"I don't know. But I have hope."

"How can you?"

"Because I see you. You care for her with no expectation. That is faith. Even if you don't call it that."

Sinan choked back tears. "Teach me. Teach me how to have hope again."

Rabbi Pallache pulled him into a fatherly embrace. "I will. You have more strength than you know."

A familiar voice rang from the tent entrance. "Truer words have never been spoken."

Oruc entered and Rabbi Pallache bowed.

"May I speak with Sinan alone?" Oruc asked.

"If he wishes," Pallache said.

"It's alright," Sinan nodded.

Oruc sat beside him. "You've suffered much, and for that I am sorry. But there is something very obvious to me. You have a gift. A fighting spirit. And I want you to join me in my dream–building a kingdom of tolerance for Jews, Muslims, Christians. Together."

Sinan shook his head. "I don't want to fight anymore. I just want a peaceful existence. Just peace and quiet."

"So long as tyrants rule, peace is an illusion."

"Then let me live in illusion. It's all I have left."

Oruc studied him. "For now, do as you wish. I will not force this life upon you. But just remember, it may be thrust upon you regardless. If that happens, do not fight your fate."

Sinan nodded as the pirate left.

***

Over following months, Sinan became a fixture in the infirmary. He read to Rahel daily—texts on Hebrew, mysticism, monsters, and messiahs. Through his reading he created a nutrient extract for patients who could not tolerate solid food. One physician noted Sinan's invention and the news spread. With it, Sinan's reputation within the island's medical community grew.

That did not prevent Sinan from pounding his fists into the clay walls of his hut each night, the agony of waiting for Rahel's condition to improve eating him alive. Only the Torah and ancient texts soothed him.

He devoured them all. Their stories—of exile, despair, hope—became his own.

In time, he learned the Temple Mount sat under Mamluk control. The idea of a Jewish homeland teased him, a whisper of possibility he couldn't afford to believe.

THE GREAT JEW PIRATE

One day, Rabbi Pallache took him to the cemetery. Before a marble grave marked "Dr. Lorenzo Badoz," they recited the Yizkor together.

Sinan sank to the grass. He looked at the grave. "How do we know he's at peace?"

"We don't. We choose to believe. For our own peace."

Sinan kissed two fingers and pressed them to the cold stone and stood back up.

They descended the hill in silence, the wind brushing past them like a whisper of old prayers. As the city of Djerba stretched beneath them, its sunlit domes and palm shadows unaware of the heartbreaks it sheltered, Sinan's steps quickened. He clutched the Torah close to his chest, his other hand brushing the spine of the book he'd been reading to her.

He slipped into the infirmary tent, the scent of herbs and sea air clinging to the canvas. Threading his way past the cots, he reached her corner—his quiet sanctuary for months.

But the bed was not as he left it.

The sheets were smoothed. Her blanket, folded. Her body—gone.

Sinan froze.

The book in his hand slipped through his fingers and hit the floor with a muffled thud.

She wasn't there.

Rahel was gone.

David Nobyl

David Nobyl

34

Seven Years

Rahel stood ankle-deep in the warm, foamy waters just outside the medical tent—the very place where she had miraculously awoken from her coma and taken her first uncertain steps.

"Do you remember me?" Sinan asked softly, his steps measured with cautious hope.

Rahel kept her gaze on the glittering Mediterranean. "I'm not sure... it's all still so fuzzy."

"What's the last thing you do remember?" Sinan asked, a thread of curiosity winding through his voice.

A sly smile tugged at the corners of Rahel's lips. "I remember this remarkably idiotic boy who came and read to me every night for months. It was dreadful. I couldn't even tell him to stop reading with that atrocious lisp."

"I don't have a lisp!" Sinan scoffed, instinctively defensive.

Rahel laughed, the sound light and airy like sea foam. Her smile faded into something softer as she turned to face him.

"For the longest time, I thought I'd lost you," Sinan admitted, his voice barely above a whisper.

"I thought you'd lost me too... but you didn't walk away." Her voice held both wonder and warmth. "You stayed."

Sinan looked down, shame creeping into his expression. "Not always. I lost faith. I... I stopped believing you'd wake up. I'm sorry."

Rahel stepped closer, her eyes bright with unspoken truths. "I couldn't move. Couldn't speak. Couldn't even open my eyes. But I heard you. Every word. Every story. Every prayer. I held onto them. They gave me something to come back to."

Sinan's face flushed. "Maybe you dreamt it."

"I didn't. And I'll never forget it." She reached up and brushed his cheek, her thumb gently tracing the hollows of his tired face. "Thank you for talking to me. For keeping me safe. For seeing me, even when I couldn't see myself."

She leaned in, the scent of seawater and sun on her skin. Their lips met in a kiss, tentative at first, then filled with the gravity of time lost and time regained. Sinan wrapped his arms around her, holding her like something fragile and precious.

They broke apart, breathless.

"I don't know what happens next," Rahel said, her voice steady despite the thundering surf. "But I want to find out. With you."

Sinan gave her a lopsided grin. "That sounds... more terrifying than any sea battle I've ever fought."

She laughed. "Then we'll face it terrified. Together. We'll grow old and grumpy and argue about nothing. But we'll do it side by side."

"Deal," Sinan said, sealing it with a pinky entwined around hers. "And for the record, I still don't have a lisp."

***

THE GREAT JEW PIRATE

The memory mirror trembled, its light rippling like water under a restless wind, then lurched forward in time. Moments blurred and fractured, scattering like shards of pottery on stone.

Chava saw Sinan and Rahel spend the next seven years growing up on Djerba. Many of those memories she shared with them as this was her own childhood, too.

But beyond the island's shores, the world hardened. Oruc and Hizir swept across North Africa with their raids, harrying Spanish strongholds. In Spain, the boy prince Charles—once timid, almost gentle—was being forged under King Ferdinand's stern hand into something colder. By seven, Charles spoke the tongues of empires: Spanish, French, Italian, German. By ten, he commanded territories across Europe and far into the New World. His was the first Christian realm where the sun never set, yet his eyes remained fixed on the restless North African coast.

The Barbary pirates were his persistent thorn, and he meant to pluck it out. With Admiral Andrea Doria and Don Diego de Córdoba at his side, Charles tightened Spain's grip on its key Mediterranean holdings. One such jewel was Bougie. When its exiled king offered Oruc land and riches to retake his home, Oruc—fresh from a string of victories and swollen with reputation—accepted without hesitation. His mind was on more than plunder; he dreamed of freeing prisoners, of planting the seeds of a lasting dominion.

Hizir, for his part, cared less for vision than for wealth. But the promise of land, of something permanent, was enough to tempt him too—despite Ishak's grim warnings that the venture was folly.

David Nobyl

In 1512, the Barbarossa brothers set sail for Bougie. What awaited them was no crumbling fortress, but an ambush—Spain's Armada poised like a predator in wait, a trap woven by Doria and Córdoba on behalf of the newly crowned Emperor Charles V.

What should have been a swift victory unraveled into chaos. In the retreat, Oruc's left arm was torn from him, and his blood soaked the deck. Gripping Hizir's vest with his remaining hand, he rasped, "Find Sinan. I need him."

Hizir, incredulous, shouted over the din, "That boy? What could he possibly—"

"Meet me in Tunis," Oruc cut him off, his voice thin but unyielding. Then the brothers split—Hizir bound for Djerba, nearly seven years after leaving Sinan to survive, to build a life, to become a man.

The memory mirror flared red, as if warning Chava this next vision was its last.

***

The sun climbed over Djerba in a slow burn, spilling gold across the beach as if to bless the day itself. On most mornings, Sinan would have welcomed its warmth without a thought. Today, though, it arrived with an unwelcome companion: apprehension.

From somewhere in the courtyard below, a violin sang a lilting melody—light and sweet, entirely at odds with the tangle of thoughts in his head. He stood before the mirror, a pair of shears in hand, deciding the best cure for frayed nerves might be the simple ritual of taming his beard.

Despite twenty-five years of life—and seven of them lived in the safety and stability of Djerba—there were still patches that refused to grow properly. He trimmed and shaped the rest into a perfect five-o'clock shadow, tilting his head to admire the effect. The man in the mirror looked nothing like the boy who had first staggered onto this island. The wildness had softened into something more assured; his face was fuller now, the result of good living and generous hospitality. A slight double chin teased him, but with the trim high enough and his chin lifted, he could pass for the lean, dashing groom he wanted to be—at least until he exhaled.

He chuckled at his own vanity, sucking in his stomach for good measure before giving up the effort entirely.

Seven years ago, he'd been a fearful, hunted boy. Now he was a man respected by the Elders, woven into the fabric of Djerba's traditions. That transformation was not lost on him.

Stepping to the window, he let his gaze fall to the chuppah standing on the sands below. It looked almost like a miniature palace—wood and cloth made regal by care and intention—its shadow touching the emerald lip of the Mediterranean. This would be their new beginning, Rahel's and his, built as much from their stubborn endurance as from joy.

The weeklong separation, as Jewish custom demanded, had been harder than he'd expected. Yet it had given him time to deepen his prayers, to turn the pages of the Torah slowly, and to imagine not just the day's vows, but the decades that might follow them.

A knock on the door gave way to a burst of energy.

"It can't be—the steel-nerved groom actually fretting?"

Leo's grin entered first, followed by the rest of him—tall, lanky, a friend whose presence made rooms warmer.

"Very funny," Sinan said, though his smile was thin. "You could at least pretend to admire my composure."

Leo clasped his shoulder. "Your composure? I think you left it in the kitchen. Luckily for you, I brought a gift."

From behind his back, Leo produced a violin—its three strings gleaming beneath a Star of David made from tiny, precious gemstones. The wood shimmered in the morning light.

Sinan's breath caught. "Leo..."

"A masterpiece from the Mediterranean's finest hands," Leo said with mock grandeur. "For the groom who apparently needs reminding that he's the chief medical officer of Djerba, inventor of magnificent prosthetics, and—most importantly—about to marry the most patient woman on this island."

Sinan hugged him, the moment loosening something in his chest. "You always know how to calm my nerves."

"That's my role today, not just your medical assistant," Leo said, though his smile softened into sincerity. "You've earned this, my friend. Don't let old ghosts crowd the doorway."

"Easier said than done," Sinan admitted. "Some days they still find a way in."

Whatever reply Leo might have offered was cut short by a flicker of movement at the window. He leaned in, squinting.

"Not to ruin your special moment," he said slowly, "but did you know there's a ragged pirate crew heading for your front door?"

Sinan didn't even flinch. "The work never stops. See who it is, will you?"

Leo was halfway to the door when a voice thundered from outside.

"Sinan! You in there? It's Hizir Barbarossa!"

THE GREAT JEW PIRATE

Sinan's eyes widened. He crossed to the window and pressed himself against the frame for a better view. There stood Hizir—broad-shouldered, his beard thick and glossy enough to rival Oruc's—and beside him, Ishak, along with several men Sinan didn't recognize. Even from this distance, there was a hardness in Hizir's stare.

"Who is that?" Leo asked.

"He saved me from slavery once," Sinan said flatly. "But we've never been... harmonious. And that look? He's not here for the wine."

He stepped outside. "What brings you here on my wedding day, Hizir?"

Hizir's jaw worked before answering, like a man deciding whether to bite or speak. Ishak, ever the diplomat, jumped in before his brother could unleash whatever was brewing. "We heard the wondrous news. Our congratulations to you both."

"That's kind of you," Sinan replied. "But where's Oruc?"

"He's—" Hizir began, his tone sharp enough to cut, but Ishak overrode him. "After the wedding. Today, let us be part of your joy."

Sinan inclined his head. "The ceremony begins in an hour. Make yourselves comfortable near the chuppah."

Hizir's snort was quiet, but heavy with something unspoken.

Back inside, Leo muttered, "That one's holding a storm behind his teeth."

Sinan nodded. "And I think it's headed this way."

On the sand, Hizir crossed his arms and claimed a seat like a man seizing a fortress. His gaze tracked Sinan like a hawk watching prey, flicking only occasionally to the sea, where the horizon seemed to mock his absence from it.

"Sir, I believe that seat is taken," came a high, squeaky voice.

Hizir turned to find Chava standing there, chin up.

"Little girl, you don't know to whom you speak," he growled.

"True," she said sweetly, "but I do know that seat is for the late Dr. Badoz and the family members of the bride and groom. Which you're not."

Hizir stared at her for a beat, then—without a word—shouldered a guest from another front-row seat instead. He sat with the same contained restlessness as before, one hand unconsciously flexing as though it missed the grip of a sword.

When Sinan and Leo emerged beneath the chuppah, the crowd rose to see Rahel approach. She moved with a grace that seemed to hush even the sea breeze. Her eyes found his, and Sinan felt his grin stretching helplessly wide.

Rabbi Pallache, shawl draped across his shoulders, escorted her forward. Behind them, Chava tossed fistfuls of rose petals, flung with exuberance.

"Dear guests," the rabbi began, "not only do I have the honor of delivering the bride, but I shall also lead us in prayer for this wonderful wedding—"

He stopped abruptly. "What do you mean you lost them? The rings, Chava!"

With a magician's flourish, Chava produced both from her sleeve. The rabbi grumbled, glancing skyward. "If your mother could see you now..."

Sinan took the gold band, Rahel the black one, etched with the Seal of Solomon—Dr. Badoz's final gift. They exchanged vows, broke the glass, and the crowd erupted in cheers.

Rabbi Pallache's voice boomed. "You may now kiss the bride!"

Rahel leaned in, and the kiss was not hurried, nor shy—it was the quiet sealing of something meant to endure. In his ear, she whispered, "Promise me we'll never stop seeking the road ahead. That we'll grow old chasing it."

He whispered back his solemn promise, and her laughter—light and certain—carried into their second kiss.

Champagne corks popped. Music swelled.

At the edge of the celebration, Hizir's fingers drummed against the arm of his chair, the rhythm growing sharper as the minutes passed. His eyes followed the dance floor without truly seeing it, his expression caught between resentment and restraint.

And then—glass shattered.

At first, the guests laughed, assuming a drunken toast had gone awry. But Hizir stood there, scimitar drawn, his voice cutting through the merriment.

"You disgust me, Sinan! While you feast and dance, my brother Oruc lies in a pool of his own blood!"

Ishak moved to steady him, but Hizir swung the blade overhead.

Sinan stepped forward, voice unflinching. "You come here, on this holy day, and speak as if I've forgotten what you and your brothers have done for us. We remember, Hizir. But today is for life. For prayer. If you can't share in it, leave."

Hizir's scimitar came down, cleaving the main table in two. "Pray all you want," he snarled. "The table is already broken."

David Nobyl

David Nobyl

35

Crimson Sails

Sinan slammed the door behind him, the sound swallowed by the gentle hiss of the tide outside. He stood in the dim light of their beachside house, chest rising and falling, voice trembling with rage.

"I refuse! I won't let him storm in here and twist this day into something else."

Rahel, already seated at their small cedar table, didn't flinch. "And why not take the chance to help the man who has given us so much?" Her voice was calm, deliberate.

He stepped forward and laid both hands over hers, his frustration carrying through the pressure of his palms. "Because today was meant for us."

"And so will the rest of our lives," she said, her gaze steady. "But this—this is a chance to repay Oruc in a way we never could before."

"We?" His brows drew together. "This isn't some invitation for a romantic honeymoon."

Her tone shifted, quieter now. "Do you remember when our ship was attacked, and you lost Dr. Badoz?" She didn't let the silence stretch. "After that, Oruc wrote to every Jewish community in North Africa. I saw the drafts he threw away—so many of them. He found us a home, Sinan. This home."

He exhaled slowly, the resistance in him fading.

"Very well," he said. "We leave tomorrow. But tonight—"

She cut him off with a faint smile. "Tonight is ours."

By the week's end, they were in Tunis. Sinan made straight for the Sultan's castle. The others wandered toward the Grand Market—a lattice of wooden walkways above the tide, a place where spice smoke clung to the air and candlelight glowed on steel and silk.

The Sultan's guest chamber smelled faintly of cedar and seawater. Oruc lay propped on pillows, the sheet pulled high, his breath shallow. Hizir and Ishak kept vigil.

"Well, aren't you a sight," Oruc said as Sinan entered with Leo. He tried to sit, but Hizir's palm pressed him back.

"How bad?" Sinan asked.

"Ah, a scratch," Oruc grinned. The linen wrappings told otherwise—amputation above the elbow, flesh ragged rather than cleanly severed.

"Cannonball?"

"Damn right."

Sinan shook his head and reached for his satchel. Leo laid out parchment, ink, quill. Sinan began sketching—lines and curves spilling out in precise order. Hizir's eyes, usually anchored to his brother, strayed to watch.

When he finished, Sinan handed the papers to Leo. "Blacksmith. Solid iron. Assemble exactly as drawn."

Leo was halfway to the door when Oruc called after him. "Wait. Make it silver."

Sinan turned, incredulous. "All of it?"

Oruc smirked. "Iron's for tools. Silver... is remembered."

Meanwhile, the market had its own battles. Rahel spotted Chava at a shawl stand, tossing scarves into the air while Rabbi Pallache tried to catch them mid-flight.

"No more bambalouni for you!" the rabbi huffed.

"It's still kosher!" Chava crowed, darting toward the docks with Rahel in pursuit.

The chase ended when Chava froze at the edge of La Goulette. On the horizon—crimson sails. Andrea Doria's fleet. Then the first strike: a flash, a boom, and the market canopy shattered.

Her bambalouni dropped into the sea. Rahel reached her, grabbed her arm, and pulled her into the water as another volley tore through the stalls. Tunis was burning.

Sinan tore through the chaos until he found Rabbi Pallache. "Where are they?"

The rabbi pointed toward the harbor. "They took them. Out of the water."

On Doria's flagship, Rahel and Chava were hauled dripping onto the deck.

The admiral stood some paces away, leaning on his cane, head slightly tilted—not sizing her up like a commander assessing a prisoner, but like someone considering how best to hang a portrait. His clouded eyes seemed unfocused, yet the weight of them pressed against her skin as though they could see too much.

He didn't speak. Not at first. The quiet stretched, letting her hear the rigging strain, the lap of water against the hull, the slow inhale-exhale of his breathing.

Then—softly— "I wonder."

She felt her spine stiffen before she realized why: with each small movement she made—shifting her stance, straightening her back—he copied it, almost imperceptibly. His breathing began to match hers. A trick, she thought. Or maybe instinct. But the effect was... wrong. As if her own body had been claimed and was no longer entirely her own.

By the time he stopped in front of her, her pulse was trying to break its own rhythm.

He didn't snatch—he extended a hand, palm up, fingers slightly curled. She felt herself loosen her own without intending to, and he slid the black wedding band free as though she had offered it.

The metal disappeared onto his finger. The haze left his eyes. He grew taller—no, she realized, he simply straightened—and let his cane drop with a hollow clatter.

"You keep it polished," he murmured, turning the ring in the light. "That means you value what it stands for." His gaze stayed steady, as if willing her to speak. "Though I doubt you know where it came from."

Her throat was dry.

"King Solomon," he said, almost conversational, as though remarking on the weather. "Found it in a grotto at Rosh Hanikra, long before you were born. It was patient, waiting for me. And now"—he glanced at her hand— "it found its way back."

She moved for the rail, hauling Chava with her, but hands caught them both before they'd taken a step.

"My husband will come for us," she said.

He tilted his head in the exact way she had when she'd spoken, mirroring it so precisely it felt like mockery. "Of course he will. That's why you're still breathing."

The masked plague doctor arrived with Sinan and Leo in ropes.

"Sinan," Doria said, his voice low, not rising to meet the chaos of battle outside. "I've been looking for something you carry."

THE GREAT JEW PIRATE

When Sinan denied him, Doria didn't snarl. He breathed in through his nose, slow, measured, and looked past him—as though deciding whether this conversation was still worth his time. crossbows angled at Rahel's and Chava's throats.

"Where is the astrolabe?"

"I have no idea what you're talking about," Sinan said.

After another brief silence, Doria lifted his hand bearing the ring. The cloudless sky swelled with heavy thunderclouds, cracking and booming overhead. Lightning followed, striking Sinan and searing his arm. Sinan screamed as his wedding band melted off his skin. The Plague Doctor averted their gaze.

Sinan held the charge until it sank into him, curling into glowing Hebrew script along his arm. Doria's eyes tracked the marks with the same interest a jeweler gives a flawed gemstone—curious, not impressed. He lifted his ringed hand once more.

Across the bay, Hizir's fleet was falling apart. Then another blue lightning cracked over Doria's deck, hurling Sinan into the sea. Hizir dove, searching for Sinan, but the water gave nothing back.

One by one, the Barbary ships slipped beneath the black water, their masts vanishing like burned matchsticks.

David Nobyl

David Nobyl

36

Man with the Silver Arm

The memory mirror fizzled out for good this time, the last spark collapsing into darkness.

Chava sighed. Achi lost his balance, landing on his stony backside with a resonant thump. He'd been hiding behind her since they were first thrown in the barracks.

Above them, the Djidjelli dungeon trembled with the roar of the crowd. Somewhere overhead, Sinan and Hizir were fighting for their lives in the gladiator arena.

Achi scrambled up with a wriggle and a defiant puff of his chest. Chava tilted her head, unsure what had sparked the sudden bravado. The little golem strutted toward the cell bars, slid one arm through the gap—and to both their surprise, it passed straight through.

He glanced back at her, bouncing on his heels. Chava grinned and gave an enthusiastic silent clap. Encouraged, Achi inhaled dramatically—though his rocky belly didn't exactly budge—and tried to shove himself through sideways.

A screech of stone on metal rang out. His middle was firmly wedged between the bars. Achi looked down at his protruding tummy, then up at Chava, then back down again, as if hoping one of them had changed shape. He squirmed, grunted, wobbled—but no. He was stuck fast.

Chava tried to tug him back, but the effort sent her tumbling onto her rear. When she looked down, horror dawned—she was holding Achi's arm.

The golem stared at the empty socket where it had been, eyebrows raised in stone-faced shock. His gaze darted between his body, the arm in her hands, and back again. Finally, he lifted his remaining arm and shook a little fist at the injustice of it all.

"I'm sorry!" Chava mouthed. She tried to reattach the limb, jamming it between his head and shoulder, but it plopped back to the floor. Achi buried his face in his single arm, shoulders shivering in silent lament.

"It's okay. I can fix this," Chava whispered. She dug under a mound of hay and pulled free her hidden Kabbalah tome, flipping frantically to the right page.

As she chanted, the hay and sand at their feet began to swirl. The cell walls trembled. Achi rose into the air, eyes wide at the whirling force around him. Chava read faster, knowing the guards could return at any moment. She finished the last line—and the magic subsided.

Achi patted himself down. Still one-armed. He looked at her, shrugged, and then—thud—his other arm dropped off entirely.

Chava gasped. He wagged his feet in annoyance, still trapped in the bars.

"I'm sorry, I'm so sorry..." She curled up, head in her hands, tears threatening.

A poke at her side made her glance down. Achi's detached hand was tapping her. She looked from it to his face—he was smiling. The hand folded into a thumbs-up, then pointed at her book before returning to the thumbs-up.

"You're right," she said, sniffing. "One more time."

She began again. This time the sand moved in a smooth spiral, the air humming with precision. Achi rose higher—then sneezed. His body burst into a spray of pebbles.

Chava yelped and stopped reading. She scrambled to gather the pieces, but they crumbled between her fingers.

"You have talent, child."

The voice was rasped thin by age, but it froze her where she sat. Chava turned. In the shadows of the opposite cell, an old woman leaned forward, pale eyes milky with blindness.

"I may not see," the woman said, "but I am not blind to all things."

Chava stayed silent.

"You've lived through much," the woman went on. "Fear rests in your throat. But one day, you will have to speak. And I hope you do it before it's too late."

The words pressed against Chava's chest, but she only looked down at the lifeless stones.

"As for your friend," the woman said gently, "he isn't gone. Try again."

Chava inhaled, steadied her voice, and recited. The sand gathered itself into a mound. Slowly, a head emerged, then arms, then the rest of Achi—now formed entirely of fine golden-brown grains.

He twirled, wiggled, and strutted forward like a miniature conqueror. Chava cupped her hands, and he climbed in before scaling up her hair to stand triumphant on her head. She laughed, cutting it short at the sound of approaching footsteps.

The blind woman retreated into shadow. Chava shoved her tome under the hay and dropped Achi into her pocket.

Diego appeared at a sprint, flanked by guards.

"Open it!" he barked.

"Only King Sālim can—" The guard's protest ended when Diego grabbed him and shook until keys, trinkets, and even a small doll hit the floor.

"It's for emotional support," the guard muttered.

Diego rolled his eyes, snatched the keys, and fumbled at the lock—dropping them twice before snarling and forcing the door open himself.

Chava darted to the far corner. Diego lunged—slipped on her hidden book—and crashed flat. She seized the chance, snatched the tome, and bolted.

A shadow blocked the hall ahead—a towering man with a silver arm and scimitar.

She screamed.

"You see, Oruc!" came Sayyida's voice from behind him. "I told you it's ridiculous!"

"What's ridiculous?" Oruc growled.

"Strapping a metal arm to your stump—worse than the sheep incident."

"That was brilliant!" Samson called from somewhere behind her.

"It's not natural!"

Oruc ignored them, raised his silver arm in triumph—only for the scimitar to slide from its grip and clatter to the floor.

"See?" Sayyida said. "Useless. And you're frightening the girl."

"She's fine," Oruc said cheerfully—then bent to retrieve his weapon and watched the whole arm drop off.

"...a tad disarming," he admitted.

THE GREAT JEW PIRATE

In seconds, the arm was back on—and being swung like a mace to send Diego's men flying.

"See?" Oruc beamed.

"Yes. You used it as a whip," Sayyida deadpanned.

The fighting roared to life, Oruc laughing as he clashed blades. Sayyida and Samson hustled Chava clear.

Down another corridor, Diego tried to escape—only to meet Hizir face-to-face.

"You killed my brother!" Diego spat.

"He earned it," Hizir said flatly. "Just like you will."

But Diego smiled. "You're watching my hands. You should watch my feet."

A kick of sand blinded Hizir. When his vision cleared, Diego was gone—leaving only blue-green dye smeared in the dirt, smelling faintly of copper and rot.

"Lockjaw toxin isn't red," Hizir muttered.

Elsewhere, freed prisoners poured from their cells. An elderly blind woman clutched her son to her chest. "Samson! My boy!"

He embraced her fiercely, then took the frail man beside her into his arms. "We have the antidote now, Mother. Brought enough from Morocco for everyone."

She wept.

As they moved to leave, a massive feline blocked the exit. Samson readied his weapon—

"Wait!" Sinan called. "She's a friend."

Recognition rippled through Oruc, Sayyida, and Samson. "This must be Tzitzi," Samson said.

Sinan barely finished introducing himself before Tzitzi's nose led her straight to Chava. One sniff of her pocket—and Achi was inhaled. Chava froze. A mighty sneeze restored him to her hands.

Sinan blinked at the tiny sand creature. "Is that Achi?"

Chava pulled out her book, flipping to the page.

"Soul transference," Sinan read aloud. "You can... move a soul between objects?"

Even Oruc looked impressed. Sayyida just said, "All the more reason to leave before someone else tries to steal her."

They started toward the exit. Oruc leaned to Sinan. "By the way—Sayyida's got a demon inside her."

Sinan chuckled. "Yeah, I know."

David Nobyl

37

Revelry & Revelations

The moon spilled silver over the dunes outside Sālim's gladiator arena, bleaching the sand where, only hours ago, the earth had shaken with the clash of steel and the roar of the crowd. The siege of Djidjelli was over.

Inside Oruc's encampment, the air was thick with smoke, laughter, and the tang of strong wine. The "dining hall" was nothing more than a cluster of stitched-together tents, but it thrummed with victory—men dancing to the wheeze of a fiddle, tankards clinking, voices raised in half-sung toasts. Many of these faces had survived Doria's massacre at the Grand Market. Tonight, they celebrated that they were still here at all.

In a quieter corner, away from the raucous circle of dancers, Sinan and Chava hunched over the ancient astrolabe. Achi patrolled her shoulder like a sentry; Tzitzi paced behind them, tail flicking, curious but kept at bay by the press of Sinan's body over the table. Chava clutched her Kabbalah tome tight to her chest, but her gaze wasn't entirely on the device—it drifted now and then toward the floor, toward the shadows between the tent seams. She'd seen too much in the memory mirror to trust that joy lasted long.

Sinan noticed her distraction and nudged the astrolabe closer, drawing her focus back. "Stay with me," he murmured. She nodded, forcing a small smile, but her fingers tightened over the book until her knuckles paled.

Across the tent, Oruc stood with his silver arm catching every pulse of torchlight. He looked like a man who owned the room, even if the "room" was made of patched sailcloth.

"Raise your glasses!" he called, his voice booming over the music. "Tonight, we feast like champions!"

Samson, seated nearby, arched an eyebrow. His tone was polite, but edged. "You have a talent, Oruc. Only you could turn a supper in a sandpit into a royal banquet. Tell me—how do you stay so merry when the entire Holy Roman Empire plots our demise?"

Oruc clapped a broad hand on Samson's shoulder. "Because, my friend, we have the incomparable Sayyida al-Hurra at our table! She only joined me in the attack on Djidjelli because she recognized your rightful claim to the throne."

Sayyida, lounging with her drink, cut him a look sharp enough to slice fruit. "Let's not gild the cannonball, Oruc. We allied because it suited us both."

Hizir scoffed. She turned to him slowly, like a cat catching movement in the corner of its eye.

"Well, well. The hairy little red man has something to say?" she asked, swirling her drink. "Or are you tongue-tied? Wouldn't be the first time."

"Watch your mouth," Hizir said tightly. "You fork-tongued seductress—"

"Oh? Am I?" She leaned forward.

THE GREAT JEW PIRATE

"Yes! You kissed me. And then left the next morning as if I were—"

"So what?"

"I fell in love with you!" he blurted.

She laughed without warmth. "That was your mistake. My husband was dead. My son was gone. I'd left my country in exile. I was drunk, Hizir—and you were warm. That's all."

"My apologies for feeling something for the black-hearted Pirate Queen."

"Humble apologies?" she snorted. "Learn the word before you use it. And before you paint yourself the victim, remember that little rumor you spread."

"What rumor?"

"Oh, you know—the one where I murdered my husband and tried to kill my son. That I've been hunting him across the seas to finish the job."

"I never said that!" Hizir's voice cracked with fury.

"Admit it!" Her shout cut the music dead. Dancers stopped mid-step.

"I would never say something like that!"

"Don't flatter yourself. You're not even man enough to own your own lies."

Ishak stepped in quickly, hands raised. "Ah, the wine's strong tonight! Too strong. Let's not choke on old bones."

Sayyida drained her cup and smacked her lips. "Some bones don't rot away, Ishak."

At the back, Chava flinched slightly, as if Sayyida's words brushed against something she'd rather forget. She lowered her head over the astrolabe, shoulders drawing in, and Sinan placed a steadying hand on her arm.

The tension shattered—obliterated—by a burst of light from the corner.

The astrolabe hung in mid-air, whole again, bathed in a slow-turning blue glow. Chava stood with her arms tight around her tome; Sinan's grip on her shoulders was white-knuckled. His eyes were raw, bloodshot, his breath uneven.

"What is it?" Oruc asked. Sayyida's gaze narrowed.

Sinan looked from them to the glowing device. His voice was rough. "Rahel. She's alive. And we know where to find her."

The tent went still. Every eye fixed on him.

"Go, then—bring her back!" Oruc said, almost jubilant.

"There's more," Sinan went on, swallowing. "Doria's coming. And he's bringing King Charles, with the full force of the Holy Roman Empire." He reached into the air and plucked the astrolabe from its lazy spin. "We saw it."

Chava nodded, but she didn't lift her eyes.

The grin slid from Oruc's face. His mind turned like a tightening knot. He looked at Hizir. "It's time. Seek an audience with the Sultan's heir, Suleiman the Magnificent. Offer him our North African territories in exchange for ships, weapons, and enough men to meet the Empire head-on."

Hizir inclined his head. "Consider it done."

"I'll go with Sinan," Sayyida said, her words blurred by wine but her grin sharp. "He'll need muscle. Samson can come too."

Sinan glanced at her. "What about Chava? It's too dangerous."

"She'll stay with us," Oruc cut in, his voice leaving no room for argument. Ishak nodded, his expression granite. "We have fortifications. We'll protect her—and her friends." His eyes flicked to Achi and Tzitzi.

THE GREAT JEW PIRATE

Chava gave the smallest of nods, but her fingers stroked the astrolabe once before letting it go—as though part of her feared she'd never touch it again.

Sinan gave a short nod. Sayyida staggered toward him, waving a hand.

"So, where are we headed?"

"Venice," Sinan said. "The Jewish Ghetto."

"Sounds easy enough."

"No," Sinan replied. "It won't be."

Her brows lifted. "Why?"

"Because," he said quietly, "Andrea Doria is waiting for us there."

The words sucked the heat from the air. The laughter, the clinking, even the fiddle—everything stopped, leaving only the weight of what lay ahead.

David Nobyl

David Nobyl

38

Plague Doctor's Ambush

Rahel woke to a crash that rattled the wooden beams above her head. For a moment she lay frozen, heart drumming in her chest, then shoved the thin curtains aside and peered into the darkness. From the tenth floor of the cramped Venetian ghetto lodging, she could see little—just narrow roofs crouched together under the moonlight, smoke-like mist coiling between chimneys. The ceiling here sloped so low she could not stand fully; her knees brushed the boards as she craned for a better look.

Her eyes lingered on the twisting alleys below—not on the empty street itself, but on the way the shadows pooled unnaturally near the corners. Old habit. She'd learned to notice such things.

"Rahel," came a voice from deeper inside, hushed but firm, "get back from the window. You know it's not safe."

"I know, Hania." She pulled her head in and sat cross-legged, hugging her shins. The low, close air here was always heavy with candle smoke and the faint scent of wool. Around her, women slept in their narrow beds, breaths overlapping in the stillness.

Hania's shadow shifted closer. "What's troubling you, my dear?"

"It's nothing." The lie hung between them. Then Rahel's voice softened. "I'm grateful—more than I can say—for you taking me in. A stranger, and yet... you've treated me like your own daughter. But sometimes I feel as if my real life is still somewhere else. Out there. With Sinan."

Hania's sigh was heavy in the dark. "We are glad to have you here. But clinging to the past can be dangerous. Your husband may not be—"

"Sinan is alive," Rahel cut in, fierce certainty in her tone. "I know it."

Silence settled over them until Hania murmured, "These are treacherous days. Venice grows restless. I fear they may turn on us again."

Rahel didn't flinch at the thought—she'd imagined that scenario too many times already.

"Was it always like this?" she asked.

"Yes," Hania said. "It's no wonder your grandparents left for Spain."

"You knew them?" Rahel's voice brightened with surprise.

"I did." Hania smiled faintly, wrinkles deepening in the dimness. "They'd be proud of the woman you've become. And you know—there are still men interested in your hand."

"Have I not sent them all away already?"

"Not all. A few strays linger."

Rahel allowed herself a brief smile—just before another crash shook the building, this one loud enough to rouse the women nearest the window.

Hania's face sharpened. "Pogrom!" she barked. "They're attacking the ghetto! Quickly—take what you can carry!"

THE GREAT JEW PIRATE

The sleeping chamber erupted into frantic movement. Rahel was on her feet before the others, already scanning the room—door, window, stairwell, possible choke points. She helped the women gather their few possessions, then urged them toward the narrow stairwell.

They burst into the street—and froze. The ghetto burned. Firelight painted the brick walls in grotesque shades, and smoke clawed the air from their throats. Outside the gates, Venetian townsfolk heaved flaming bundles over the walls or clambered up ladders, eager to break inside. Iron hinges shrieked as the main gate was battered open.

Shops stood ransacked, their windows punched out, goods spilling into the street. Stone and timber smashed against shutters.

"La morte agli ebrei!" voices roared from the mob beyond the gates.

A child beside Rahel clutched her skirt, trembling. "What are they saying?"

"Back inside!" Rahel hauled her away from the crush, Hania close behind. Even in the chaos, her grip on the girl was firm, practiced.

Halfway up the stairs, she bent to the child and murmured, "They're saying 'Death to the Jews.'"

A thunderous crack split the air as part of a wall gave way, spilling rubble into the courtyard below.

"What do we do?" Hania asked.

"Fifth-floor hiding place," Rahel said without hesitation. "Go—take her."

When they were gone, Rahel turned back toward the smoke and screams, moving against the stream of people. She had no weapon. But her eyes moved the way a swordsman's might—assessing angles, gauging distance.

David Nobyl

A muffled cry drew her into a side room. At the window she saw them—neighbors she'd bought bread from, shopkeepers she'd greeted—smashing, looting, burning.

A shape vaulted in through the window: hooded, masked, its beaked face white against the dark. Rahel didn't scream. She took a single step back, her weight balanced.

"You," she said.

"The time has come," the mask rasped.

Before she could argue, a dizzy fog closed in. Her knees gave way and she collapsed.

The masked figure caught her easily, slinging her over his shoulder and stepping back through the smoke.

When Rahel woke, she was bound in the hold of a ship. A man in regal Genoese garb loomed over a battered prisoner—Andrea Doria himself.

"You thought you could challenge me with a lifeboat?" Doria sneered.

The prisoner lifted his head, bloodied but smirking. Sinan.

Rahel's heart stopped. Could it really be him?

Soldiers hauled Sinan away, and when he glanced back to wink at her, Rahel's heart jolted.

The masked figure—the same plague doctor—slipped to her side, cutting her bonds. "If you want to save our dear Sinan," he murmured, "you'll wear this disguise and follow my lead."

"Our?" she asked.

He pulled back the mask just enough for the lamplight to touch the scarred face beneath. Dr. Badoz.

Rahel's breath caught. She nodded once and took the garments.

He dropped the mask back in place. "Doria forced my service for years. But tonight is different."

THE GREAT JEW PIRATE

On the upper deck, the wind carried the tang of salt and charred pitch, but the long table between them smelled only of roast chicken, oil, and arrogance. Andrea Doria lounged at its head, tearing meat from a drumstick with a leisurely precision that made the shackles on Sinan's wrists feel heavier.

At the far end sat Leo—Sinan's Leo—hands folded, expression unreadable save for the faint curl at the corner of his mouth.

Doria dabbed the grease from his beard with a silk napkin, eyes never leaving Sinan.

"You didn't really think I wasn't watching you in Djerba, did you?"

He nodded toward the far end of the table. "Leo brought you to me. He brought me everyone—Pallache, Chava... Rahel."

Sinan's gaze snapped to Leo. The man didn't look away, didn't blink—only smiled, slow and faint.

"You're a traitor," Sinan spat.

Leo tilted his head as if studying a specimen in a jar. "You always wore that righteousness like armor. I used to admire it. Then I realized it was just arrogance wrapped in virtue. It made me sick."

The words landed harder than any blow. Sinan strained against his shackles, but Doria's voice slid between them.

"To think Sayyida's son would be such a prize ally."

Sinan froze. *Sayyida's... son?*

Doria leaned forward, savoring the silence. Piece by piece, he laid it out: the stolen children, the experiments, the Red Death toxin distilled to its purest form. King Charles' plan—not just conquest, but cleansing the earth of entire peoples.

Then, with theatrical care, he reached for his trophies: Sinan's astrolabe, its once-smooth casing scarred down the middle... and a simple black ring. The torchlight caught the Stars of David engraved on its bezel.

Sinan's breath caught. "Rahel's..."

Doria turned it between his fingers, smiling like a cat toying with a bird. "The Ring of King Solomon. Your wife wore it when I found her. You thought you were fighting for family, Sinan? No. You've been a piece on my board since before you even knew there was a game."

He set the ring down with a soft click and leaned closer, his voice deepening into something that was not entirely his own.

"More precisely..." His smile stretched too wide to be human. "...it's been me inside all along."

The name rose unbidden in Sinan's mind—one spoken only in dark corners, in whispers meant to ward it away.

The Demon of Semites.

***

Outside, clinging to the hull like barnacles, Sayyida and Samson strained to catch every word. Sayyida shushed Samson's too-loud breathing just as—*fwoom*—every torch inside snuffed out at once.

Darkness.

Then smoke—thick, acrid—rolling across the cabin like a living thing.

Shapes moved in the haze: two plague doctors, beaked masks darting through the chaos. One drew the soldiers' fire; the other dropped to one knee beside Sinan. Chains snapped open under deft hands.

"Go!" the masked rescuer barked.

THE GREAT JEW PIRATE

Sinan didn't look back. They crashed through the nearest window, hitting the deck of a waiting gondola hard enough to rattle teeth. Sayyida and Samson landed behind them in a tangle of limbs and curses.

The second plague doctor dove after them—then the crack of Doria's pistol split the night. The shot punched into his back, dropping him onto the gondola boards. Blood pooled fast.

Sayyida's return shot was instant; splinters rained from the shattered window frame as she drove the soldiers back. A glass vial arced from the smoke—shattered inside—

WHOOM.

The blast tore the cabin apart, flinging silhouettes into the firelit night.

They rowed hard, oars biting black water, until a third plague doctor waved them under a low bridge. In a blink, they'd abandoned the gondola for a waiting carriage, wheels already turning.

Inside the dim compartment, Sinan turned to the wounded plague doctor. The mask had slipped.

"...Father?" His voice cracked like dry wood.

Dr. Badoz managed a faint, real smile. "My son... you've grown so much."

Sinan clutched his hand. "I'm not losing you again."

But the old man's strength ebbed. "Please... forgive me..." The words faded—and so did the light in his eyes.

Sinan bowed over his father's body, grief racking him—until a warm hand settled on his shoulder.

Rahel. She was the other plague doctor—the one who had leapt into the fire for him without hesitation.

"I'm here," she said quietly. "We'll face this together."

A voice came from the far bench. "I'm sorry, old friend."

Sinan looked up. The third mask came away, revealing a bearded face from his boyhood.

"...Luís?"

"I go by Juan Luís Vives now," the man said, a shadow of a smile tugging at his mouth. "But to you—I'll always be Luís."

David Nobyl

39

The Grim Sultan

The Sultan's chamber was a jewel box of an empire. Silken banners draped from the rafters, mosaics coiled like frozen serpents across the walls, and a hundred candles quivered in polished brass, turning every surface to gold. It was a room designed to make a man feel small.

Hizir Barbarossa stood in its center, shoulders squared, heart rattling in his chest. This meeting—Oruc's gamble, his grand pitch to bind the Barbary fleet to the Ottoman throne—was the moment they'd been chasing for months. One wrong word, and the entire dream would crumble.

"You ready, hotshot?" Braman's voice drifted in at his side, too casual, too sour.

Hizir didn't look at him. He didn't have to. "I'd be ready faster without you breathing in my ear."

Braman smirked, already smelling faintly of raki. Hizir hated his presence here—Sayyida's little 'insurance policy,' forced on him before he'd even left port. Oruc had agreed, naturally. Sayyida wanted someone watching her interests at court; Braman was her man.

"My dear Braman," Hizir murmured, smiling with all the warmth of a scimitar's edge, "perhaps you'll learn something today. Watch closely."

The Sultan's gaze landed on him like a hawk's. He gestured for Hizir to speak.

Hizir stepped forward, letting his voice ring clear. "Great Sultan, I bring you a proposal. Grant us your ships, your soldiers, your weapons—and the Barbary Pirates will cede our North African holdings to the Ottoman Empire. Together, we can break the Spanish and secure the entire coast."

The Sultan didn't blink. His eyes weighed Hizir as if considering a cut of meat. When he finally spoke, his voice rumbled like distant thunder. "You stand before me, pirate, seeking an audacious bargain. I have heard of you—Hizir Barbarossa, who has bled and failed before Andrea Doria more than once. Why should I believe you will not fail again?"

Hizir's jaw tensed. He opened his mouth, but Braman stepped forward first—half-slouched, eyes heavy with drink, yet his words startlingly crisp.

"Great Sultan," Braman said, "you doubt him. I would too. But Hizir carries the burden of a brother's name."

Hizir shot him a warning look.

"Oruc Barbarossa," Braman went on, ignoring it, "believes in aiding all, regardless of birth or faith. Hizir... well, he's spent his life wrestling with that example."

Hizir's hands curled into fists. But Braman's tone shifted, softening. "I'll tell you something, Sultan. I am not a good man. I had a wife, children. They were taken from me. Sayyida herself pulled me out of the abyss—didn't care what I'd done, only that I could still be more than I was. That's what I ask you to see in Hizir now."

THE GREAT JEW PIRATE

The Sultan's face was carved marble, but a flicker of something passed through his eyes. He turned back to Hizir. "And what say you?"

Hizir drew himself up. "We need your fleet to stop the Spanish Armada. If we fall, the balance of the Mediterranean tips in their favor."

The Sultan's mustache twitched in amusement. "And when there are no more brothers left to fight for—what then?"

Hizir hesitated. The Sultan let the silence stretch, then waved it away. "I will give you fifty ships and fifty thousand men. In return, Algiers will fall under my direct rule. You will serve as my General there. Oruc will be Governor."

The title hit Hizir like a blow and a gift all at once. He bowed. "You honor me, Sultan."

Braman bowed, too—less gracefully—and they made their exit without further testing the Sultan's generosity.

In the corridor's cool shadow, their steps echoed on marble. Hizir muttered, "Don't think this changes anything between us."

Braman grinned sideways. "Perish the thought."

They walked on, the air between them taut, until Braman broke it with a lazy question: "Tell me, General... why is Sinan enough for Oruc, but never for you?"

Hizir's hand drifted to the hilt of his scimitar. "Because Oruc believes in helping everyone. Jews, Christians, Muslims—it makes no difference to him. I..." He exhaled. "I am not my brother."

Braman stumbled slightly. Hizir caught him by the elbow without thinking.

"You know nothing of my demons," Hizir added quietly.

Braman's eyes, half-lidded from drink, sharpened for a moment. "Then let me tell you about mine." He recounted it simply: the debt, the ransom he couldn't pay, the slaughter he watched helpless. "Every time I drink, I see them again. Don't be like me."

They reached a tall, narrow window where moonlight poured in like water. Hizir released his grip.

"Thank you, Braman," he said at last.

The cartographer smirked, though his eyes were softer now. "We Barbary pirates may be reckless, but sometimes we get it right. Just make sure, when your moment comes, you don't miss it."

***

Along the Tunisian coast that same night, the air was thick with citrus and salt. Tzitzi moved like a shadow through the brush, ears flat, eyes glinting in the moonlight.

Oruc crouched ahead, silver arm catching the faint light. Ishak trailed him, sword in hand, and between them — guarded by a ring of Barbary fighters — was Chava. They were shifting camp under cover of darkness, keeping her safe until Hizir returned with the Sultan's reinforcements.

"What's wrong with you?" Oruc asked his brother.

"I'm not a fighter," Ishak admitted.

"You are tonight." Oruc pressed a flint and striker into his palm.

They were nearly through the grove when a rustle too deliberate to be wind froze them all. The first musket shot cracked the night. The lead guard pitched forward into the sand.

"Ambush!" Oruc barked.

THE GREAT JEW PIRATE

The attackers drove hard for the center. Two men slammed into Chava, knocking the Kabbalah tome from her arms. It slid across the dirt until a heavy boot pinned it down.

"Chava!" Ishak lunged, but Oruc yanked him back just as another volley ripped through the clearing. The captors dragged her toward the ridge. Musket fire shredded the citrus leaves overhead.

A bullet grazed Tzitzi's shoulder, spinning her into the brothers. All three tumbled down the slope, crashing into the shadow of a towering whistling thorn. Above them, the chaos roared — shouting men, pounding boots, and Chava's cries fading into the dark.

Ishak shook his head, panic rising. "We can't fight them, not here—"

Oruc silenced him with a sharp gesture, then reached past him to rap his knuckles against something solid beneath the tangle of vines at the tree's base. The sound rang hollow, metallic.

"We'll make them come to us." Oruc said, eyes locked on the dark ridge above.

Ishak's brow furrowed. "A cannon? Out here?"

"Old Ottoman shipwreck. Roots grew over it. Been saving it for the right moment." Oruc's grin flashed in the moonlight. "And I'd say this qualifies."

Ishak shook his head but didn't argue. "Oruc... if something happens—"

"Nothing will happen," Oruc cut him off, but there was a softness under the steel. "Stay sharp. If I fall, you keep fighting."

Boots crunched on the sand, unhurried. Diego stepped into the moonlight with Chava bound and hooded, a pistol in one hand, rope in the other.

Before Ishak could respond, the hiss of boots in the underbrush gave way to torchlight. Diego's men emerged in a loose half-circle, muskets leveled. And at the center—Diego himself, one hand on Chava's shoulder, the other pressing a pistol to her temple. Her Kabbalah tome was clutched tight in her arms, though her knuckles were white and shaking.

"You keep making this too easy for me, Oruc," Diego called, voice slick with triumph. "First, I blow your arm off years ago. Now, I send a few false reports, and here you are — walking into my hands."

Oruc's gaze darted from Chava's eyes to Tzitzi crouched low in the brush behind him. His mind worked fast—too fast to plan, but just enough to act.

"Now," Oruc murmured.

Tzitzi burst forward in a snarling blur. Diego swore, jerking the pistol toward the movement, and Chava twisted instinctively. In that heartbeat of distraction, Oruc lunged—snatching the book from her grip and ramming it into Tzitzi's jaws mid-leap. The ocelot's teeth closed around the leather binding.

"Go!" Oruc barked, never taking his eyes from Diego. "Warn Hizir! And when the time comes—save her."

Tzitzi hesitated, eyes flicking between him and Chava, then bolted into the dark, her tail vanishing into the trees.

"No—Tzitzi!" Chava's voice cracked, but gunfire drowned it.

The first ball struck Oruc's silver arm, ringing like a temple bell. The second tore through his knee, sending him down on one leg. Still, he rose, sword in hand, teeth bared.

Diego leveled his pistol again, a thin smile on his lips. "Beg."

THE GREAT JEW PIRATE

Oruc spat blood onto the sand between them. "Ishak—now!"

The flint struck. Sparks leapt. The fuse caught, hissing toward the iron cannon buried under the tree's roots. Diego's eyes widened—then narrowed in recognition. He dove aside—

—only for no shot to come. Peering into the barrel, he laughed. "Empty. I think I'll keep it as a trophy to commemorate this moment."

Oruc's grin was feral. "Take this instead."

With a guttural roar, he ripped the silver arm from his shoulder in a spray of sparks and jammed it into the cannon's mouth.

The shot came before Ishak could strike the flint again. The ball punched through Oruc's back, tearing lung and heart in its path. His sword fell. He crumpled into Ishak's arms, the sand drinking his blood.

"It's... good, isn't it?" Oruc rasped, each breath a battle.

"Indeed, my brother," Ishak whispered, his face wet. "You always wanted an honorable death. And I—" his voice broke "—get to hold you one last time."

The second shot split the night. Ishak's body jerked, then slumped over Oruc's, their silhouettes folding together under the moon, two brothers locked in their last embrace.

***

Far across the sea, Hizir doubled over on the deck of his returning ship, a sudden, crushing weight in his chest. The Sultan's fleet surged behind him, but he felt the truth already.

David Nobyl

Two of the Barbarossa Brothers would not be there to meet him.

David Nobyl

40

Mirror to the Soul

The earth outside Venice was still damp from the night rain, smelling faintly of salt and loam. A single lantern swayed on its post, casting long shadows over the modest Jewish cemetery. Sinan stood at the fresh mound of earth, the cold wind pressing against his coat. Beside him, Rahel's hand was warm in his own. Sayyida and Samson lingered respectfully at his side, their silhouettes bowed.

They recited El Maleh Rachamim, the words rising into the winter air, followed by the Mourner's Kaddish. Sinan's voice cracked halfway through. Yet, even in the ache of loss, there was a strange comfort. For years in Djerba, he had prayed at an empty grave. Now—at last—his father lay in a real one.

When the last amen faded, Sinan turned to them. "Thank you... for being here." He pulled Rahel closer, squeezing her hand. His gaze fell on Luís. "And you—old friend. It means more than you know."

Luís smiled faintly, his wavy hair brushing his shoulders. "Dr. Badoz found me last year, during my sabbatical from the University of Leuven. He... asked for my help. Said he didn't care if he lived, so long as you and Rahel were free."

"He'd been planning for this for a long time. He stole and then slipped you the astrolabe when we were captured in Tunis the day Doria attacked," Rahel said.

Luís reached into his coat and produced a weathered envelope. Sinan's name was scrawled across it in a familiar hand. "He was certain he wouldn't survive. Told me to give you this, when the time came."

Sinan stared at the envelope, his throat tightening. He broke the seal carefully, almost fearing what lay inside.

A black ring rolled into his palm, engraved with Stars of David.

"His ring," Sinan murmured.

Rahel's eyes gleamed with recognition. "He made a copy to fool Doria a few weeks ago—slipped him herbal tonics to make him feel invincible. Won't be long before he realizes it's all a sham."

Sinan unfolded the letter. There was only one line, written in his father's steady hand.

"When you enter... go alone."

Sinan frowned. "What does that mean?"

"Could be a metaphor," Rahel offered. Then, with a sly smile, she reached into her satchel. "Or maybe it has something to do with this."

She produced the astrolabe and all three plates. "Took them from Doria during our escape. Hope you don't mind."

Sinan's breath caught. He fitted the plates into the astrolabe. At once, glowing Hebrew letters curled across its face. He mouthed each one until the final words took shape.

THE GREAT JEW PIRATE

"Rosh Hanikra," he read, wincing at his own accent. "The Green Grotto. Some legend about a guardian... I can't remember if it said golem or dybbuk."

Luís shuddered. "Don't joke about dybbuks. After what happened in the Carthage catacombs... I'm still not over it."

"So where is this Grotto?" Sinan asked.

"In the Land of Canaan. Ancient Israel."

Sinan shook his head. "No. We don't have time. Doria's invasion is about to fall on North Africa. We have to get back."

Sayyida nodded. "If we're not at sea by daybreak, my men will meet us offshore. We'll sail for Djerba. Oruc and Hizir will be waiting."

Sinan clasped Luís's shoulder. "I can't thank you enough—for this, and for years ago."

Luís's mouth curved. "We didn't part well, did we? Took me a while to understand you did it to protect me."

"I wouldn't ask you to come," Sinan said. "Just know you'll always have a place with me."

"Perhaps one day," Luís replied. "Maybe in Amsterdam. The people there... they're more accepting of us."

Sinan smiled. "Looks like you found the home you were always looking for." He glanced at Rahel. "I know I have."

They parted ways at a quiet inlet. Luís's carriage rolled back toward the city while Sinan, Rahel, Sayyida, and Samson boarded a waiting schooner. By morning, they were under sail toward Sayyida's flagship, and from there—home.

That night, the ship slept. Sinan didn't. Even with Rahel breathing steadily beside him in the hammock, a knot of unease tightened in his chest. There was Sayyida's son—how could he tell her? And the sword—was abandoning it a mistake that might cost them the war?

Unable to lie still, he slid from the hammock, narrowly avoiding a sleeping Samson, and padded to the stern. The moon hung fat and luminous over the restless sea.

He turned the ring in his hand, then fitted the plates into the astrolabe. Pressing it to his forehead, he whispered the Kaddish once more, as he had so many times at the false grave in Djerba.

Light bloomed—a green shimmer that solidified into a memory mirror, denser and sharper than any he'd seen before.

"When you enter... go alone," his father's letter echoed in his mind.

Before he could second-guess, the mirror pulled him in.

***

Rain fell in sheets, but the drops passed through him. He floated above the slick cobblestones of Valencia. A woman darted through the alleys, clutching a swaddled infant. Her breath came ragged, eyes wide with panic.

Behind her, soldiers thundered on horseback.

She rounded a corner and skidded to a halt—dead end. Stone steps rose to a worn door. She pounded. It opened to reveal a young, clean-shaven Dr. Badoz.

She stumbled inside, thrusting the child toward him in a flurry of whispers Sinan couldn't hear. Then he understood—this was his mother. And the child... was him.

A tall, hooded figure appeared on the street, flanked by soldiers. The figure pointed at the woman. Two helmets came off—Sebastian and Diego. Sebastian pressed a Toledo dagger into Dr. Badoz's hand.

THE GREAT JEW PIRATE

The woman met Dr. Badoz's gaze, laid her hands over his—and drove the blade into herself. Her body went limp in his arms, blood pooling on the steps. His scream tore through the rain, but the downpour swallowed it.

Sinan couldn't move.

"I hated myself," came a voice at his back.

He turned. Dr. Badoz stood beside him, older now, eyes heavy.

"I hated what they made me do—choosing between you and your mother. I couldn't forgive myself. Couldn't call you my son without seeing her death."

Sinan stepped forward, pulling him into a fierce embrace. "You were always my father, whether I called you uncle or not."

Badoz closed his eyes, holding him just as tightly. "And I am sorry I didn't tell you the truth sooner when there was still time."

David Nobyl

David Nobyl

41

Green Grotto

Sinan stared at his father's familiar face. "How can you be here? Is this real?"

A faint smile tugged at Dr. Badoz's lips. "Kabbalah magic is... peculiar. In this place—inside memory—death doesn't have the final word."

Sinan felt both wonder and confusion tug at him. "I don't fully understand it. Maybe I shouldn't question it. But right now... I could really use your advice."

One brow rose in that old, patient way that used to make Sinan squirm as a boy.

"I've decided not to pursue the Sword of Solomon," Sinan admitted, the words tasting heavier than he expected. "Even if it's our only chance against Doria, Diego, the Emperor. The Grotto's in the Land of Canaan—we couldn't get there and back before the invasion."

Dr. Badoz's eyes glimmered, a conspirator's light. "What if I told you, you could do both?"

Sinan blinked. "You're telling me there's a way?"

"The memory mirror," Badoz said, his tone sharpening. "It isn't only for looking backward. Our ancestors used it to cross seas. Infused with Kabbalah magic, it can take you where you need to go."

Sinan's fingers curled around the astrolabe. With a click, its face opened, and a soft violet light spilled out, swelling into a round portal that widened like the iris of an eye.

Through it, cliffs rose from an endless blue sea. Near the base, beneath the foam and crashing waves, something glowed—green as emerald flame.

"That's it," Sinan breathed. "The Green Grotto." He hesitated. "Can you come with me?"

The light in his father's eyes softened. "No, my son. I exist here, in memory. But promise me you'll remember me as more than my mistakes."

Sinan's jaw tightened. "I promise, Father."

And then he stepped through.

***

The sea closed over his head like a curtain. The water here was denser, each stroke an effort. Silver fish flashed past him. Neon octopi writhed across coral shelves like scribbles of living ink.

The green glow lured him deeper along the cliff face. His lungs ached, the burn urging him onward. A sliver of darkness appeared—an opening just wide enough for a man.

He dove up for it, fingers brushing rough stone—only to slam into a wall. Trapped.

Panic threatened to take him, but he balled his fists and struck the rock above. On the third blow, it gave way, the motion deliberate, almost welcoming. He forced himself through and broke the surface in a chamber lit from below.

THE GREAT JEW PIRATE

The Grotto's ceiling arched high, stalactites like teeth. The water glowed with an inner light, casting shadows that shifted like living things. At the far end, a cave mouth waited, dark and patient.

The air inside was cold, slick on his skin. Phosphorescent algae painted the walls in faint green. Each step echoed. Shadows stretched long and thin.

A voice drifted from the dark. "I've been expecting you."

Sinan groaned. "Everyone keeps saying that."

He raised his voice. "I heard there's a golem here guarding the Sword of Solomon. Are you the good kind or the bad kind? Because I'm in a bit of a hurry."

Footsteps approached but did not enter the light.

"Answer the riddle," the voice commanded. "I paralyze everything I touch. I am fear itself. What am I?"

Before Sinan could speak, something sliced across his chest.

"Me," said a voice he knew too well. Leo stepped into view—then his body warped into a towering, centipede-limbed monster, its tendrils snapping like whips.

Sinan's blade was in his hand before thought. He blocked, parried, ducked—but each strike was faster, more venomous than the last.

The face shifted—to Diego's sneer. "Your friends will fall. You've doomed everyone you love."

The poison in Sinan's veins throbbed cold. His knees buckled. Faces swam in his mind—Rahel broken, Sayyida dying, Samson still and silent.

Then Doria's face leaned close, whispering: "When I'm done, there won't be a soul alive to remember your people ever existed."

The horror cut deep, but in that darkness, something flared.

"No," Sinan rasped. "It's never been just me. I'm here because of my family, my people. And I won't fail them now."

The monster laughed, an inhuman sound that crawled over his skin.

A crack sounded above. Another shape scuttled into view, clinging to the stalactites—a golem, its limbs jointed wrong, its talons scraping stone. It dropped, moving with impossible speed.

Sinan let himself fall into the water. The golem followed, plunging like a stone. When it hit, its body shattered into rock. But the fragments liquefied, and a moment later the water itself rose against him, teeth closing around his leg.

His lungs screamed. His hand scraped something hard—a hilt. He tore it free and swung.

The impact drove both of them onto the rocky bank. The golem solidified again, shrieking. Sinan looked down at the weapon in his hand—an ancient, rust-caked sword. Beneath the flaking metal, blue light pulsed.

He struck again, the rust giving way to inscriptions in Hebrew and a Star of David etched into the hilt. The light burned so brightly the monsters shielded their eyes.

The centipede-thing shifted its face to look like Sayyida's. "Wait. You need to understand. I am Beelzebub. I take the faces that sway hearts. The golem is bound to me. Together, we have kept the Sword of Solomon for its true master."

Sinan's voice was flat. "And who is that?"

Rahel's face looked back at him now. "The one who fights for his people."

THE GREAT JEW PIRATE

Sinan's grip tightened. "Then I'll use it to end this war."

The centipede creature's expression darkened. "If you take it, the Demon of Semites will hunt you—drag you to the Nexus of Souls, where the stream of time itself will be turned against you. The sword will be useless there."

Sinan's gaze was steady. "I'll find a way."

David Nobyl

David Nobyl

42

Sword of Solomon

The first light of dawn spilled across Sayyida's deck, gilding the sea in gold. Near the captain's wheel, Rahel and Sayyida stood in low conversation, their silhouettes sharp against the horizon.

Sinan stepped from the memory mirror onto the wet planks, the Sword of Solomon gleaming in his fist.

Rahel broke off mid-sentence and crossed the deck, throwing her arms around him. "You're alive," she breathed, the relief in her eyes deeper than words.

Sayyida and Samson came up from below, their gazes catching on the sword's radiant edge.

"Well," Sayyida said, voice dry but not without admiration, "looks like you actually pulled it off. I do appreciate it when you bring me gifts."

Sinan's face tightened. "Then I'm afraid this one comes with bad news."

Her eyebrow arched. "Go on."

He met her gaze. "Your son—he calls himself Leo now. I thought he was my friend in Djerba, even trained him as my apprentice. All the while he was spying for Doria. He's behind the experiments on the children in Ischia... behind the Red Death toxin." His voice dropped. "I should have told you sooner."

Sayyida's eyes flickered, but her composure held. "I know."

Sinan blinked. "You... what?"

"I overheard it on Doria's ship in Venice."

"Then you know trying to 'save' him will end in nothing but ruin."

She didn't flinch. "I'm his mother. I have to try."

The conversation ended there—no victory in it for either of them. The air between them grew heavy, like the sea before a storm.

***

Djerba rose from the water like a mirage—and with it, an armada. The Ottoman fleet, conjured from Hizir's deal with the Grim Sultan, stretched to the horizon. Sleek war galleys. Towering flagships. A thousand black-and-gold banners snapping in the wind.

Sinan and Sayyida's ship had finally arrived, but Hizir was not the same as they had left him.

Inside the flagship's commander's cabin, the air was thick with hookah smoke and arak fumes.

"Hizir!" Sinan's voice cut through the haze. "The Spanish Armada is nearly here! We need to set the battle plan—now."

From the fog, Hizir's voice came slow and bitter. "Your people, is it? My brothers died for your people." A glass jug smashed across the floor, spinning to Sinan's feet—empty, but reeking of liquor strong enough to strip paint. "For Hebrews."

THE GREAT JEW PIRATE

"This is no time to drown yourself," Sinan snapped. "The Spirit of Vengeance must rise, or we all fall."

"You want the Spirit of Vengeance?" A scimitar hissed from its sheath.

Sinan ducked as steel flashed past his head. "Are you insane?"

"For the first time in my life," Hizir snarled, stepping from the smoke, eyes bloodshot, breath sour with drink, "no one holds me back. No Oruc. No Ishak. No one."

The scimitar came again, faster. Sinan caught it on the sheathed Sword of Solomon, the impact rattling his bones, a reminder that Hizir was not stumbling drunk but deadly sober beneath the fog of drink. Hizir fought like a man who had nothing left to lose.

"Stop!" Sinan shouted. "This isn't you!"

"You're unworthy!"

Sinan drew the sword. Sparks showered as steel met ancient metal. "Not worthy of life?" A parry, hard enough to splinter Hizir's blade. "Not worthy of fighting for my people?" Another blow—shards flew. "Not worthy of standing beside you and your brothers?"

The final strike shattered the scimitar to the hilt.

"What else am I unworthy of," Sinan demanded, "in your eternally disappointed eyes?"

"Oruc died for you," Hizir spat. "For people who won't remember his name. My brother is gone!"

Sinan lowered his voice. "He fought for what he believed in. For me. For my people. What do you believe in, Hizir?"

"I don't know anymore."

"Stand with me, as they did. Fight this battle with me." Sinan held out the sword.

Hizir stared at it—and turned away. "I am not Oruc. I will not fight for your people."

Sinan's jaw set. "Then you are no Barbary Pirate. Oruc and Ishak will be remembered. *You* will be remembered for nothing."

He left Hizir slumped in the smoke.

Back on Sayyida's deck, the air smelled of salt and rain.

"What did he say?" she asked from the wheel. "Did the hairy little man finally give us his navy?"

"No."

Samson grunted. "Then what's our plan?"

Rahel's voice was taut. "You mean aside from suicide?"

Sayyida grinned. "We call it 'strategically disadvantaged.' Sounds much better in the history books."

Sinan glanced toward the horizon—and froze.

The Spanish Armada filled it, one hundred and thirty galleons with thirty thousand men. The sound of drums echoed in the distance. Doria's Genoese ships formed a second wall—thirty-five more, bristling with guns. And at their heart, Diego's warship under King Sālim's banner, carrying his two-hundred elite.

Sayyida's crew? Sixty.

Rahel stared. "Strategically disadvantaged? This is strategically hopeless."

"Oh, I've won battles with worse odds," Sayyida said lightly, tightening the wheel.

Sinan studied her. "Why are you staying to fight?"

Her eyes went distant. "Asmodeus said if I enter this battle, I'll finally find my son."

"We already found him," Sinan said. "Leo."

Her jaw set. "He said I'd truly 'find' him. That's different."

THE GREAT JEW PIRATE

Before Sinan could answer, the fleets closed. Cannons primed. Oars churned. Sails bellied with wind.

"And you?" Sinan asked Samson.

"I have a score to settle with King Sālim." He pointed out the flagship where Sālim stood beside Diego.

On another deck, Doria and King Charles gleamed with medals and weapons, as if the sea itself were their parade ground.

Tzitzi hissed low in her throat.

Sinan raised the Sword of Solomon. Light spilled from it, Hebrew letters spiraling around him. Thunderheads boiled in from the west, lightning flickering in the roiling dark.

Sayyida squinted up at the clouds. "Lovely. Does it do anything useful?"

"I'm trying!" Sinan shouted over the wind. Rain came in sheets.

"Great—now we can't see who's killing us!"

Her words were swallowed by the first barrage. Diego's warship struck their starboard, Doria's galleon hammered the port. Ten cannons answered against eighty, wood splintering under the assault. Masts toppled. The deck heaved. Smoke, fire, and screams tore through the ship.

The battle had begun.

David Nobyl

David Nobyl

43

Sea of Fire

The storm seemed to pause—like the sea itself had taken a breath. For a heartbeat, the cannons fell silent.

Smoke and sawdust choked the air. Sinan pulled Rahel close, shielding her from splinters. "I told you not to come," he coughed.

"I told you," she said into his chest, voice steady despite the chaos, "we die together or not at all." Behind her, Tzitzi crouched low, tail flicking in warning.

From across the waves, Doria's voice rang out, oily and mocking. "The Great Jew Pirate! The Pirate Queen can't save you now. Hand me the Sword of Solomon before it's too late."

"I'll tell you when it's too late!" a voice bellowed—not Sinan's—and cannon fire roared to life again.

But this time, the impact came from somewhere else. The deck trembled—not from enemy hits, but from the destruction tearing through Doria's own fleet. Out of the smoke, Hizir's Ottoman galleys surged forward with blazing speed, their guns pounding the Spanish and Genoese lines.

Sinan's eyes narrowed. "The Spirit of Vengeance..."

King Sālim's shout carried over the water: "Why is he commanding the Ottoman navy?"

"That," Diego growled, "is the last Barbarossa."

Hizir didn't waste time. His ship crashed against the enemy, and he swung from a rope onto Diego's warship, cutting through Sālim's men. His boots hit the deck with a thud—and there stood Diego, one arm around a blindfolded Chava, the other gleaming silver. Oruc's arm.

Hizir froze. "You stole my brother's arm and wear it like a trophy?"

Diego smirked. "One of many. Shame I couldn't keep the real one I blasted off. His face didn't fare well either. Perhaps yours will."

"Murderer."

"You murdered my brother too—pierced Sebastian's heart clean through. I should thank you for teaching me not to leave loose ends. That's why Ishak died crawling away like a dog."

Hizir roared and lunged, knocking Chava clear.

Rahel saw her niece tumble to the deck. Ignoring Sinan's shout, she darted to the rail—Tzitzi on her heels—ready to leap to Diego's ship. Samson's massive hand caught her. "You're not the only one trying to reach that ship," he said, kneeling so she could climb onto his back.

Sayyida's voice cut through the rain. "Where is he? Tell me where!"

Samson charged. The deck shook as he launched himself across the gap, landing hard enough to make the warship list. Tzitzi sailed after him, landing gracefully but sliding with the tilt.

Sālim's guards rushed in. Samson's fists cleared them in sweeping arcs, buying Rahel and Tzitzi a path to Chava.

THE GREAT JEW PIRATE

Rahel wove through dueling blades and musket smoke until she reached her niece. "It's me," she said, yanking off the blindfold.

Chava clutched a satchel to her chest—the one she'd grabbed when Hizir struck Diego. She stuffed it under her arm and took Rahel's hand. Together they ran for the stairwell, but a Spanish soldier barred their way, sword in one hand, torch in the other.

Tzitzi leapt, knocking his sword aside. Chava swung the satchel into his face with a crack. Something inside growled. A pebble-sized head popped out—the golem Achi—and waved.

"Achi?!" Rahel gasped.

The little golem wriggled free, growing back to his full rocky size. Tzitzi purred and head-butted him, nearly knocking him over.

Up above, Hizir and Diego's fight raged. Diego's dagger sliced Hizir's tunic and into his side, the force knocking his scimitar overboard. The next throw lodged in his shoulder. Diego drew a pistol—only for Tzitzi to sink her teeth into the silver arm. She ripped it clean off and tumbled toward the stairs, dropping the prize at Chava's feet.

Below deck, Chava stuffed the arm into a barrel of nearby cannon—Diego's trophy—hidden under a sheet. She palmed Diego's fallen Toledo dagger too, ignoring Rahel's protest.

Through a porthole, they saw Sinan—now on King Charles and Doria's galleon—fighting both men at once. His crew swarmed in to help, but the Sword of Solomon alone kept Charles and Doria from overwhelming him.

Then Sinan raised the sword high. The sea heaved. A massive shadow broke the surface—the legendary

Leviathan—dragging a dozen Spanish ships beneath the waves.

Charles staggered back. Doria did not. His blade struck home, knocking Sinan off-balance.

"I know what you are, Doria!" Sinan roared. "You can burn our homes and kill our people, but you'll never break our will to fight!"

Rahel spotted Leo, cradling a glass bottle, eyes fixed on Sinan.

Doria raised something else: Sinan's astrolabe, now complete with all three plates. Black light poured from it, sweeping across the decks. Sinan was flung backward, his ring slipping free—straight into Doria's hand.

Chava and Rahel were thrown too. When Rahel scrambled to the porthole again, Doria stood holding all three Hebrew relics—the Sword, the astrolabe, and the ring.

The Sword of Solomon blackened in his grip. "We welcome you back," he cried, "Demon of Semites, Destroyer of the Hebrews!"

Shadow erupted, swallowing Doria, Charles, and Diego. From it stepped a man Rahel knew could not be there—Sebastian de Olmedo. His form flickered into Grand Inquisitor Torquemada, then blurred.

"I am born of three," the demon rasped, gesturing: *"Hate passed through blood,"*—King Charles. *"Hate for gain,"*—Doria. *"Hate forged in power,"*—Diego.

Sinan dragged himself up, sword in hand.

"Now," the demon hissed, "see the artifact's true power."

Red lightning split the sky, slamming into Sinan. His scream tore through the rain.

THE GREAT JEW PIRATE

"I was the Inquisitor," the demon snarled, "the one who made your father kill your mother—so you'd never know what it was to be a Jew."

"Why?" Sinan gasped.

"This was never about you. It was about them," he pointed—to Chava, to Rahel, to Djerba. "Only when every Jew is gone will I rest."

"You'll find no peace in genocide," Sinan spat.

"I wasn't asking. Now, Great Jew Pirate, your death—quick, or slow?"

Sinan's voice hardened. "Throw me to the sea if you want. I'd rather die free than live your slave."

The demon's grin twisted. In a blur, he lifted Sinan by the hair and drove the Sword of Solomon into his chest.

Rahel's scream cut through the thunder. Chava dropped her satchel. Tzitzi growled low, ears flat, but Chava clung to her neck.

Above, the clouds ripped open. A crimson portal bloomed in the storm, flaring like a wound in the sky.

Rahel's voice trembled. "What is that?"

Chava's answer was almost a whisper. "The Nexus of Souls... the realm between realms."

David Nobyl

David Nobyl

44

Nexus Realm

The Sword of Solomon slid through Sinan's chest with surgical precision.

No pain—just a cold, electric shiver racing through every nerve.

The Demon's face grinned as he twisted the blade, the blood-slick tip emerging from Sinan's back. With a brutal jerk, he pulled it free. Sinan's legs buckled, spilling him to his knees in a spreading crimson pool.

Then came the strangest sight—his own body, limp and still, lying before him. His hands—ghostly, translucent—reached for it.

"What... happened to me?" The words echoed hollowly in the air, as if spoken in a cavern.

Above, the Demon lifted the sword toward the heavens. The red portal split wider, spilling thunder and lightning into the world. A tornado of fire plunged into the sea, whipping the waves into a killing frenzy. Ottoman ships groaned, hulls cracking, masts splintering.

The Spanish and Genoese cheered.

Hizir and Diego's duel froze as the storm slammed into them. They clung to the rails while the wind tried to rip them from the deck. Below, Rahel wrapped her arms around Tzitzi and Chava, shielding them from the sight of Sinan's broken body. Samson clung to the rigging like an anchor in human form, tearing through a mainsail just to get a grip.

Sayyida spotted Leo—her own son—cackling as he hurled gas bombs into the gale. The wind carried his toxins across the water. She tried to shout his name, but the storm devoured her voice.

And then—Chava moved.

Ignoring Rahel's grip, she sprinted for the rail, Kabbalah tome jammed into her satchel. She vaulted onto the swaying beam between ships, dodging chunks of flying debris, and swung herself onto the enemy deck.

She dropped to her knees beside Sinan's body. "No, no, no..."

Crossbows clicked behind her. Genoese guards closed in—but Tzitzi hit them like a storm of claws and teeth, with Achi leaping from her back for extra chaos.

Chava flipped frantically through her book. "No... no—wait..."

She froze. Wisps shimmered in the air before her, barely visible.

"Sinan? Is that you?"

"I'm here!" his voice rang out in her mind, desperate.

"I can pull your soul back," she said, already reaching into her satchel for Diego's dagger, essential for the ritual. She placed it before her and began the prayer on the opened page. The words rose into the storm, and the dagger glowed red-hot, steaming in the rain.

It lifted from the deck, spinning faster and faster—then shot upward through the tornado, vanishing into the

THE GREAT JEW PIRATE

clouds before smashing down into the planks inches from Hizir and Diego.

Chava gasped. "It didn't work..." The wisps were gone. Sinan's astral form had vanished.

She bit her lip to stop it from trembling. Tzitzi pressed against her leg; Achi squeezed her finger like a child holding a parent's hand.

Then—water began to rise.

It lifted from the sea as if gravity had reversed, forming a human shape. A head, arms, shoulders—all sculpted from living ocean.

"Sinan?" she whispered. Her fingers passed through him like mist.

"You're not in your body," she said softly. "I tried to bind your soul into a weapon. But... I failed."

The water-shape tilted its head—then grinned, offering her a thumbs-up. It turned to the storm, arms rising, and the whole sea seemed to answer.

The golem of water launched skyward, colliding with the Demon's chest in a spray of foam.

The Demon's laugh cracked like thunder. "Still clinging to life? Fine—I'll end it twice." He hurled a bolt of fire and lightning, but it hissed into the water and died.

"Interesting," Sinan's watery voice said, calm as a tide. "The elements... don't always play nice together."

Before the Demon could reply, the golem's arm engulfed his mouth, crushing until the Sword of Solomon slipped free and tumbled into the sea. Sinan caught it before it sank.

"You call yourself the Demon of Semites," Sinan said, raising the sword, "but I am Sinan—Pirate of the Great Jews."

The blade blazed under the water's surface. "This sword severs soul from body... but it can also bind two together."

He drove it into the Demon's chest.

It screamed, black eyes widening as the portal above tore wider. Dybbuks and demons poured down in writhing shadows.

"You wouldn't abandon your family!" he choked.

"Never," Sinan growled. "Unless their lives depended on it."

Blue light exploded from the water golem, clashing with the Demon's red. Their souls locked together, twisting and surging higher, pulling them into the portal in a single blinding flash.

Then—Silence.

The storm eased. The sea smoothed. But the portal still churned overhead, spilling howling demons into the mortal realm.

On the galleon, Doria glanced at Sinan's body and smiled at King Charles. "Quite a spectacle."

Charles smirked. "I do enjoy the winning side."

Diego's dagger flashed again, driving Hizir back across the slick deck. Below, Rahel rummaged frantically, hunting for anything she could use.

Samson dropped from a mast, scattering Sālim's men like bowling pins. Sayyida landed on Leo's deck, cutting down Spanish soldiers as she called for her son—but Leo only laughed harder, his bombs bursting in clouds of choking green.

Through it all, Chava's gaze stayed fixed on the portal. Her voice was a whisper to Tzitzi and Achi. "I hope he's still holding on."

David Nobyl

45

Within the Void

In the mystic realm, time was no longer a river but a living thing. It glowed—flickering, shifting—stretching in both directions into eternity. Around it spiraled a vast helix of light, dotted with infinite points of entry and exit.

Wisps drifted from the helix into the surrounding void, wandering like lost fireflies.

Sinan and the demon floated in that black expanse.

"We've shed our mortal shells," the demon's voice rasped, unnervingly calm, "and stepped into the realm of souls."

A pulse of light revealed what lay beneath the Demon's stolen skin. The human mask peeled away, sloughing to nothing.

What emerged was no man—its skull elongated, teeth in a jagged crescent from ear to ear. Pupil-less eyes stared from deep sockets. There was no nose, only twin internal slits where air once passed. Its body gleamed with scales like beaten gold. Fingers—too many joints, too much reach—twirled something small.

A flickering wick.

"This flame," the demon crooned, "is your time here. You're a soul without a body. You won't last."

It tilted its head, mock-curious. "Want to know what comes next?"

"Fate," Sinan said, voice steady, "belongs to the Divine, not to demons."

The demon's grin widened. "Divinity, you say? You stand in the presence of it."

"You're no god," Sinan replied.

"Not yet," it hissed. "Look."

It gestured at the streaming lights. "That is time. Around it—the Soul Stream. Souls enter with birth, leave with death. And those drifting wisps? Lost ones. Souls denied redemption, denied a chance. Victims of your G-d's cruelty. Just like those I loved—taken by your beloved G-d."

"And yet you attack us?" Sinan's eyes narrowed.

The demon's laugh was low and bitter. "Because your Chosen People and your G-d made me."

"What are you?" Sinan asked.

"Not what—who." Its gaze sharpened. "Don't you recognize me?"

Sinan didn't answer.

"When Moses freed your people and shattered my father's empire, your G-d's plague struck me. I am Pharaoh Ramses' firstborn son."

Sinan's stomach dropped. "The one who died in the final plague…"

"Yes." The golden scales seemed to ripple with remembered pain. "I watched my family torn apart. My home destroyed."

THE GREAT JEW PIRATE

"Your home," Sinan shot back, "was built on my ancestors' backs. Whipped, beaten, enslaved to build your father's tombs."

The demon's snarl deepened. "Without His chosen people, His hold on time ends. Destroy the Jews, and I destroy your G-d."

Its clawed fingers closed around Sinan's throat, dragging him toward the silver stream.

The surface of time parted, and Sinan saw the mortal world below—Chava surrounded by soldiers, Tzitzi bristling at her side. Hizir limping below deck, arrow lodged in his thigh. Sayyida choking on her son's gas bombs as realization hollowed her eyes. Samson driving through enemy ranks while Sālim's guard aimed poison from behind. Charles and Doria's guns tearing the Ottoman fleet apart. Djerba poised for annihilation.

"You see it now," the demon whispered. "Every moment in this slice of time."

"Yes," Sinan said, his essence thinning. "And I see you'll never truly win."

"Why?"

"Because people like him—" Sinan nodded toward Hizir "—will always exist. Those who stand with us."

"That won't destroy me."

"I'm not trying to." Sinan's lips curved. "I'm keeping you here."

The demon froze.

"We're bound, you and I. A stab for a stab with the Sword of Solomon—souls tied for eternity."

"That's not possible—"

"The centipede from the Green Grotto said otherwise." Sinan winked.

The demon's roar was pure fury. "Then I'll break you, as I broke your mystics... all your Madame Miriams."

Its grip shoved Sinan's face deeper into the stream, hurtling him forward through history.

Centuries blurred.

Expulsions. Pogroms. Fires and gallows.

Then the 20th century.

1933—Nazi banners over burning books.

1935—Nuremberg Laws stripping Jews of citizenship.

1938—Kristallnacht's broken glass glittering like ice.

1939—Babi Yar, pits of corpses. Auschwitz's gas.

The years rolled into mountains of bodies, millions dead.

Sinan's soul bent under the weight until there was nothing left but ash and silence.

"You win," he whispered.

But before surrender claimed him, a light appeared—small but steady.

A young man on a ship, leaving Belarus to fight for a Jewish state. He would call himself Menachem. He would build resistance.

1948—Israel declared. Flags raised. Streets dancing with life.

Sinan's grip on the demon's wrist tightened.

He dove deeper into the stream, pulling the demon with him. Light flared around him, his form growing bright and immense. His fist shattered the demon's jaw.

"You should be mad beyond reason!" the demon screamed.

"I was," Sinan said. "But I saw what comes after. The homeland reborn. The living remembering the dead. Yad Vashem's Hall of Names. We endure."

THE GREAT JEW PIRATE

Another blow cracked the demon's ribs. "And you—" Sinan's hands tore its ribcage open "—are done."

Blue fire wrapped Sinan's hand as he plunged it into the demon's heart. The flames devoured the hatred there until the golden scales fell away.

What stood before him was a bald Egyptian boy in a linen kilt, eyes rimmed in kohl.

Sinan knelt. "Come with me. There's something I want to show you."

The boy's small hand fit into his. They stepped into the stream, traveling backward until Egypt's sun blazed above them.

Ramses wept over a linen-wrapped body. Moses stood nearby, staff lowered, sorrow in his eyes.

"This isn't you," Sinan said gently.

The boy pointed at another child in the corner—watching, silent.

"You were the second son," Sinan realized. "You saw the plague's aftermath. You saw the Red Sea swallow your father's army. You blamed us for the ruin."

The boy nodded.

"Moses grieved too," Sinan said, showing him the prophet's tears. "Pain is not yours alone. Being the Demon of Semites—it's a choice."

"Can you... ask your G-d to give my family peace? To free us from this place?" the boy whispered.

"I can pray," Sinan said. "That's all I can promise."

The boy closed his eyes. Light engulfed him, hardening into white stone that crawled up Sinan's arm. He didn't resist.

"Baruch Hashem," Sinan whispered into the dark. "Protect our people from darkness. Grant peace to those who seek it."

David Nobyl

The light claimed him fully. His form turned to stone—then dissolved into the endless brilliance of the Nexus.

David Nobyl

46

Millennia A Deux

Below deck on Diego's ship, the air reeked of gunpowder and brine. The timbers groaned under the pounding above, each blow of cannon fire rattling through the shadows. Hizir crawled through the dark, dragging his injured leg, the sound of his own breath drowned by the chaos overhead.

A click—metal drawn from a holster. Diego appeared at the top of the stairs, pistol in hand, eyes tracking the trail of blood on the planks. He descended slowly, voice oily with malice.

"Come out," he called. "Time for a reunion with your brothers. I want you on your knees, begging like they did."

Hizir smirked through the pain. "How original. But I think someone else has a message for you."

Another voice rang out from the shadows—smooth, clear, and sharp as cut glass in perfect Catalonian Spanish.

"My mother always called you a despicable murderer."

Diego's head turned. "And you are?"

"Daughter of Esther. You slaughtered her and my father before my eyes in Barcelona."

Rahel stepped into the lantern glow, hands already moving—tearing away the drape that hid Oruc's old cannon. She struck flint; sparks spat along the iron.

Diego's eyes widened in recognition. "The little girl from Montjuïc."

The barrel ignited.

The cannon roared—not with shot, but with Oruc's silver arm, loaded deep in its maw. It shot forward like a spear of vengeance, smashing into Diego's chest and hurling him through the ship's hull. The wood split with a deafening crack, seawater surging through the wound in the vessel's side.

The recoil slammed Rahel against the wall, pinning her as the tide poured in. Hizir lunged into the flood, dragging her under and out toward the light breaking through the wreckage.

***

On another ship, Leo's bomb burst among Sayyida and her guards. The Lockjaw Toxin bit fast—her lungs locked, her body heavy as lead. Her vision wavered, and through the haze came her son's face, smiling like a boy showing his mother a prize.

"This chaos, Mother—this is my purpose. I love this feeling. Why would you deny me?"

He held up a glass sphere, its liquid glowing faintly blue.

"This one's special. Cyanide. Enough to drown the world in pain." He set it before her feet, letting the cracks spider across the glass. "Time for you to join Father."

Sayyida's eyes widened in shock, but he leaned closer.

"That's right. It wasn't an accident. Not a demon. I killed him. I wanted to see the light leave his eyes."

THE GREAT JEW PIRATE

The glass began to hiss.

A shadow fell. Samson dropped from the rigging like a stone, landing with enough force to shake the deck. The shockwave sent the cyanide sphere tumbling—straight into Leo's face. It shattered, the gas igniting against his skin. His scream was high, inhuman. He flung himself into the sea, but the toxin burned too deep; by the time he hit the water, he was nothing but a blackened husk.

Samson wiped splinters from his hands. "Apologies for the delay, Captain. I gave you as much time as I could, within reason."

Sayyida coughed against the poison's grip. Samson uncorked a vial, tilting drops into her eyes—Sinan's antitoxin. The tightness in her chest eased; she drew a full breath and sagged against the railing.

"I thought the poisoned arrow…" she began.

Samson tapped his chest with a hollow clang. "Sinan's invention deflected it—straight into King Sālim's neck."

A thin smile crossed her lips. "So I should call you King now."

He bowed slightly. "To me, you'll always be my Queen and Captain." His voice softened. "I never cared for the boy, but I know you fought to protect him. I'm sorry for your loss."

Her gaze drifted to the sea. "I lost him years ago. The night he killed my husband, he became my demon. Thank you for giving me time to see it—and for saving my life."

***

They reached the rail together just as Hizir surfaced, Rahel clinging to him. Samson hauled her up; Sayyida pulled Hizir in after.

"Is she—?" Samson began.

"She's alive," Hizir said, catching his breath. "Didn't think Sinan would appreciate me leaving her trapped under a cannon. Especially after she fired one at Diego for me."

Rahel stirred, groggy but conscious. Sayyida's sharp gaze fell to Hizir's bleeding leg.

"You're wounded."

"Impressive deduction, my queen," Hizir said with a crooked smile. "But I'll manage."

She unwound the silk sash from her hair and bound his thigh with quick, sure hands. "And Sinan?"

Samson's eyes shifted toward the bow. Chava and Tzitzi stood over Sinan's still body, Achi pacing in frantic little circles. The others followed him onto the splintered deck of Doria's ruined ship. Charles and Doria were gone, their surviving men fleeing without a backward glance.

The air above was thick with fleeing shadows—demons ripped from their hosts, spiraling toward the closing portal. Even Asmodeus knelt before Sayyida; her silent nod was enough to send him willingly into the vanishing rift. Crimson lightning faded. The sea stilled. Sunlight cut through the ragged clouds.

Sinan's eyes opened. His breath came slow but steady. Rahel fell to her knees beside him, clutching his hand.

"You're alive," she whispered. Tears streaked her salt-crusted cheeks. Chava let out a breath she'd been holding, and Achi waddled in an uneven victory lap.

Sinan's smile was faint but warm. "We either die together or not at all, right?"

Chava's brow furrowed. "But... how did you come back?"

David Nobyl

47

Sunset Sonata

Several weeks after the battle, Hizir gathered the survivors for one last duty—farewell to Oruc and Ishak.

The beach of Djerba was painted in the molten gold and rose of sunset. Waves whispered against the shore, their rhythm almost mournful. The gathered crowd—pirates, townsfolk, allies from distant seas—held flickering candles and wreaths woven with bright flowers.

Sinan walked beside Rahel, her arm linked in his. Ahead, Hizir limped slightly, his recovery slowed by an injured leg and Sinan's constant ribbing—payback for the torrent of insults Hizir had thrown during Sinan's own convalescence. Sayyida and Samson followed behind, the giant's shadow stretching far across the sand.

At the water's edge, Hizir stepped forward alone, the sea foaming at his boots. He kissed two wreaths—one tulips, one roses—then let the tide take them.

"My brother Oruc always wanted a burial at sea," he said, voice carrying easily over the hush. "And Ishak... he only ever wanted to be by Oruc's side. Let the currents carry them to their next great voyage—together, as they've always been."

Sinan and Rahel placed their own wreath—white and blue blossoms, braided tight—into the surf. One by one, the others followed. The sea accepted them all without question.

***

That night, the main plaza of Djerba glowed with lanterns and the smell of roasting lamb. The feast was loud, messy, and joyful—the kind of celebration that happens only when survival itself feels like a miracle.

"So," Sinan said between mouthfuls, "what now?"

"What now?" Hizir scoffed. "Now we walk the paths we've chosen."

Sayyida leaned forward, smirking. "And what path is that for the esteemed General Hizir Barbarossa?"

Hizir raised his cup in salute. "To follow in Oruc and Ishak's steps—protect those who can't protect themselves, regardless of creed. And to temper justice with reason, as Ishak would have wanted. Yes, I just said that. And you, Queen Sayyida?"

"It's time I take the throne of Morocco seriously," she said. Then to Samson: "And since you've dethroned Sālim, I'll teach you a few things before you start ruling Djidjelli."

"I'm sure he'd appreciate it," came a voice from the end of the table. Braman, nursing a drink, grinned.

Sinan blinked. "Where have you been?"

"Right here," Braman huffed. "Way to notice the little guy."

"I swear I didn't see him," Sinan murmured to Rahel, who only shrugged.

THE GREAT JEW PIRATE

Samson cleared his throat. "I've learned much from you all. I'd be honored to keep learning."

Sayyida nodded, then fixed her gaze on Sinan. "About the Nexus Realm. You still haven't told us what you saw there."

A lilting voice answered before he could. "Yes, do tell."

Chava appeared with Rabbi Pallache at her side—and to Sinan's astonishment, Madame Miriam herself. Achi leapt into Miriam's lap, earning a delighted cackle. Tzitzi draped herself behind Pallache like a furry sea serpent.

"Madame Miriam?" Sinan said.

"What, I can't visit my students? You defeat the Demon of Semites and don't even send a letter? Outrageous!"

"Given how often he's been knocked out, I'm surprised he remembers any of us," Hizir muttered.

"There have been a lot of concussions," Samson added. "Might be worth a check-up."

Sinan lifted his hands. "I'm just glad we're all together."

Braman raised his cup. "Now, about the Nexus Realm—"

"Yes, and how you got back healed," Hizir cut in.

"Let him speak," Sayyida said firmly.

Hizir leaned forward, arms uncrossed. Chava nodded along.

Sinan smiled. "The Sword of Solomon—it can separate soul from body, temporarily. That's how I came back whole."

"So we can do it again?" Hizir's eyes lit.

"No. The sword vanished."

Miriam nodded grimly. "King Solomon made it so—it appears only when those who truly need it seek it."

Rahel squeezed Sinan's hand. "What did you see?"

He hesitated, then: "The Demon threw me into the Stream of Time. I saw everything—the past, the future. Most of it's already fading, but one memory won't leave me: Jerusalem. We never left. No matter where we lived, our souls always returned home."

Miriam's eyes shone. Rahel's filled with tears. "My parents... would be overjoyed."

"They are," Sinan said softly. "I saw them. And your sister. They're together, at peace."

Rahel looked skyward, lips moving in a silent prayer.

"And Oruc and Ishak?" Hizir asked quietly.

"They were worried you might lose your way. But you didn't. They'd be so proud."

Hizir swallowed hard. "You think so?"

"I know so."

Miriam exhaled. "Baruch Hashem."

"One day," Sinan said, "we'll have a home again. A Jewish homeland. It might not be in our lifetimes, but it will come."

"The hope your people carry," Hizir said, "is the anchor that holds you."

Chava tugged Sinan's sleeve. "And the Demon? Gone?"

"This one is at peace," Sinan said.

Miriam's voice turned solemn. "But such demons return when fed by hatred."

Rahel gave a small, determined smile. "Then may the sword appear again when needed."

Sayyida's gaze sharpened. "And Doria? Charles?"

"They'll be back. And we'll be ready."

"We?" Hizir said.

"You think I'll leave all the pirating to you?" Sinan grinned.

THE GREAT JEW PIRATE

Hizir studied him, then nodded. "Commander it is then. Sinan Reis."

"Wait, seriously?"

"You've escaped the Inquisition, fought demons, trained under a Kabbalah master, stolen a magic sword, and survived lightning—twice. Why wouldn't I make you my commander?"

Sayyida laughed. "You have my blessing, too. Morocco would be honored to be guarded by the Great Jewish Pirate."

David Nobyl

David Nobyl

48

Epilogue

Many years later, history would again bear witness to Captain Hizir Barbarossa and Commander Sinan Reis. Together, they would break the power of Charles V, Holy Roman Emperor, sweeping his warships from the waves. Their greatest triumph would come at Preveza in 1538, where Andrea Doria's proud fleet would splinter under their guns.

Barbarossa would go on to rule Algiers as Governor under the Ottoman Sultan, still steering the fate of empires. Sinan, though, would turn his prow toward quieter waters. With Rahel and their children, he would trade the roar of cannon for the laughter of family, learning to value the warmth of a shared meal over the spoils of battle.

Sayyida al-Hurra would return to Morocco, her reign unbroken, her name whispered with both reverence and caution in the courts of kings. Samson remained at her side as the quiet shield of Djidjelli. Braman, Chava, Tzitzi, and even the ever-faithful Achi carried their own legends to distant ports, each adding new threads to the tapestry of the Great Jewish Pirate's crew.

His final resting place would remain unknown. Some would whisper he died at sea, wrapped in sailcloth and given to the deep. Others would swear he made Aliyah, vanishing into the hills of the Holy Land to end his days in the shadow of Jerusalem's stones.

As for Doria and Charles, they would surface again—older, diminished, but unrepentant—only to find the seas less kind to those who once thought themselves untouchable.

What was certain was that Sinan's name did not sink with him. Around firelit tables and under the low beams of dockside taverns, sailors would tell of the Great Jewish Pirate who defied kings, demons, and death itself. Those tales would light a spark in the hearts of a new generation of Jews, urging them to stand, to fight, to claim their own freedom.

In Morocco, a boy named Isaac Pallache would grow up on those stories. Born in 1550, he would become the Rabbi Pirate, a man who built a haven for his people in Amsterdam and called it New Jerusalem.

Centuries later, in 1898, Theodor Herzl would set foot in the land Sinan had dreamed of. He would come not as a conqueror, but as a planter of seeds—the spiritual father of a state that did not yet exist.

And then, on May 14, 1948, the seed would break the earth. The State of Israel would be declared. A homeland reborn. The long exile ended.

Perhaps, somewhere beyond the veil, Sinan Reis would stand on a sunlit deck, watching the flag of Israel rise over Jerusalem, the wind tugging at his coat. And perhaps he

THE GREAT JEW PIRATE

would smile—knowing the course he had glimpsed in the Stream of Time had, at last, found its shore.

David Nobyl

Historical Figures Reference Guide

Sinan Reis ("Sinan the Jew," d. 1546) — A Sephardic Jew expelled from Spain, Sinan settled in Ottoman lands and became one of their most skilled corsair captains. Ottoman naval chronicles and European dispatches alike name him as a commander under Hayreddin (Hizir) Barbarossa. At the **Battle of Preveza (1538)**, Sinan's tactics were credited with securing the Ottoman victory over Andrea Doria. His life is evidenced by both Ottoman records and Spanish/Italian accounts that feared him as "the Great Jew Pirate."

Sayyida al-Hurra (Lalla Aicha bint Ali ibn Rashid al-Alami, c. 1485–1561) — Daughter of the governor of Chefchaouen, she became ruler of Tétouan after her husband's death. Known locally as **Hakimat Tétouan** (*Governor of Tétouan*) and across the Mediterranean as **Sayyida al-Hurra** (*the Free Lady*), she allied with the

Barbarossa brothers to lead corsair raids against Portugal and Spain in the 1520s–1540s.

Portuguese archives record her naval campaigns, while Moroccan chronicles confirm her long rule. In 1541 she married Sultan Ahmed al-Wattasi, forcing him to come to Tétouan rather than relinquishing her own power. She ruled until 1542, and is remembered as the last Muslim woman in history to hold the title *al-Hurra*.

Hizir Barbarossa (Hayreddin Pasha, c. 1478–1546) — Born on Lesbos to a Muslim father and a Greek Christian mother, Hizir rose from corsair beginnings to become **Kapudan Pasha (Grand Admiral)** of the Ottoman Navy.

After his brother Oruc's death in 1518, he was appointed Beylerbey of Algiers and later commanded Ottoman fleets across the Mediterranean. He is most famous for his decisive victory at **Preveza (1538)**. His tomb in Istanbul remains one of the city's landmarks, confirming his celebrated place in Ottoman history.

Oruc Barbarossa (c. 1474–1518) — The eldest of the Barbarossa brothers, Oruc appears in Spanish and Genoese records as a feared corsair around 1505. In 1516 he seized Algiers in the name of the Ottoman Sultan, establishing a power base for the family. He was killed in **Tlemcen (1518)** fighting Spanish forces, an event documented in Spanish chronicles and Ottoman reports. His death elevated Hizir to supreme command.

Ishak Barbarossa (fl. early 1500s) — The least known of the brothers, Ishak is mentioned in Ottoman tax registers and North African chronicles as managing family affairs while his brothers raided. Though overshadowed historically, his existence is confirmed through Ottoman administrative documents.

Admiral Andrea Doria (1466–1560) — A Genoese admiral and statesman whose career is extensively documented in Genoese archives and Spanish correspondence. First appearing as a mercenary captain in the 1500s, he entered service under Charles V and commanded Habsburg fleets against the Ottomans. Defeated at **Preveza (1538)** by Barbarossa and Sinan, his rivalry with the Ottomans defined Mediterranean naval warfare. His palace in Genoa still stands as a tangible legacy.

Luís (Juan Luis Vives, c. 1493–1540) — A Spanish humanist and philosopher of converso origin, often called *"the father of modern psychology."* Born in Valencia, his family fell victim to the Inquisition — his father was executed and his mother's remains were later exhumed and burned. Vives fled Spain, studying in Paris and later teaching in Bruges and Leuven.

His writings on memory, learning, and the human mind (*De Anima et Vita*, 1538) laid the groundwork for psychology and educational theory. Extensively documented in his own published works and European university records, his life reflects both the brilliance and the peril of converso intellectuals in the 16th century.

Dr. Lorenzo Badoz (fl. late 15th–early 16th c.) — Cited by historical sources as a Jewish physician in the service of Queen Isabella I. He is described as part of Isabella's inner circle, attending to the births of her children. While direct archival evidence is limited and later sources vary in detail, his name is associated with the broader historical pattern of Jewish and converso doctors serving in royal courts despite growing Inquisitorial suspicion.

Doctor Torralva (Antonio de Torralva, c. 1480–1531) — A Spanish physician documented in Inquisition trial records. He was accused of necromancy and trafficking with demons, offering historians a rare window into how medicine, superstition, and heresy intersected in early 16th-century Spain.

Church of Santa María la Blanca (Toledo) — Originally built as a synagogue in 1180, its transformation into a church in 1411 underlines Spain's shifting religious landscape. Surviving records and the building itself bear witness to the cultural erasure of Spain's Jewish communities.

Don Diego de Córdoba (1463–1518) — 2nd Marquis of Comares, a Spanish nobleman and general during the Italian Wars. His campaigns are documented in dispatches from the **Battle of Ravenna (1512)** and the wars in Navarre. He also served as governor of Oran in North Africa, appearing in Spanish military records.

Sebastián de Olmedo (fl. 1480s–1490s) — A chronicler whose writings survive in Inquisition histories. He famously described Tomás de Torquemada as "the hammer of heretics," giving historians one of the earliest pro-Inquisition accounts.

Diego de Deza (1444–1523) — Dominican friar and theologian, disciple of Torquemada, and **Inquisitor General (1498–1507)**. His leadership is preserved in inquisitorial decrees and royal correspondence. He also tutored Prince Juan, the son of Ferdinand and Isabella.

Emperor Charles V (1500–1558) — King of Spain (as Charles I) from 1516 and Holy Roman Emperor from 1519. Vast amounts of correspondence, treaties, and decrees document his reign, which spanned Spain, the Netherlands, Austria, Italy, and the Americas. He struggled against the Protestant Reformation and the Ottoman Empire. In 1556 he abdicated, retiring to the Monastery of Yuste, where he died in 1558.

King Ferdinand II of Aragon (1452–1516) and Queen Isabella I of Castile (1451–1504) — The Catholic Monarchs, whose marriage in 1469 united Castile and Aragon into a single Spain. Papal bulls and royal decrees confirm their reign, during which they completed the **Reconquista (1492)**, sponsored **Columbus's voyages (1492-1504)**, and issued the **Alhambra Decree (1492)** expelling Jews. Isabella died in 1504; Ferdinand ruled until 1516. Their tombs in Granada remain a physical record of their legacy.

Princess Catherine of Aragon (1485–1536) — Youngest daughter of Ferdinand and Isabella, she married Henry VIII of England in 1509 and served as Queen of England until their annulment in 1533. Royal marriage contracts, diplomatic letters, and English state papers document her piety, learning, and political influence.

Joanna of Castile, "Juana la Loca" (1479–1555) — Daughter of Ferdinand and Isabella, married to Philip the Handsome of Burgundy. She inherited Castile but was declared unfit to rule due to alleged madness, possibly severe depression or psychosis. Her confinement at Tordesillas for nearly 50 years is confirmed in royal records and chroniclers' reports.

King Salim al-Tum of Djidjelli (fl. early 1500s) — Mentioned in Spanish expedition records around 1514–1515 as the local Berber ruler of Jijel (Djidjelli), modern Algeria, though little else is known.

Sultan Suleiman the Magnificent (1494–1566) — Ottoman Sultan from 1520 to 1566, under whom the empire reached its height. Extensively documented in European diplomatic reports, and architectural legacies, his reign encompassed Sinan and Barbarossa's greatest campaigns.

Graphic Novel Preview

David Nobyl

THE DRIFTER

VOLUME 1

MEDITERRANEAN SEA. DECEMBER, 1515.

MOONLIGHT CARESSED THE TURBULENT WATERS. AND THROUGH THE FOG SAILED THE PIRATE QUEEN.

Character

Design

Adult

Sinan — Child / Adult

Braman

Deception

Oruç Reis

Hizir Barbarossa

Ishak Reis

Young Sinan

SAMSON

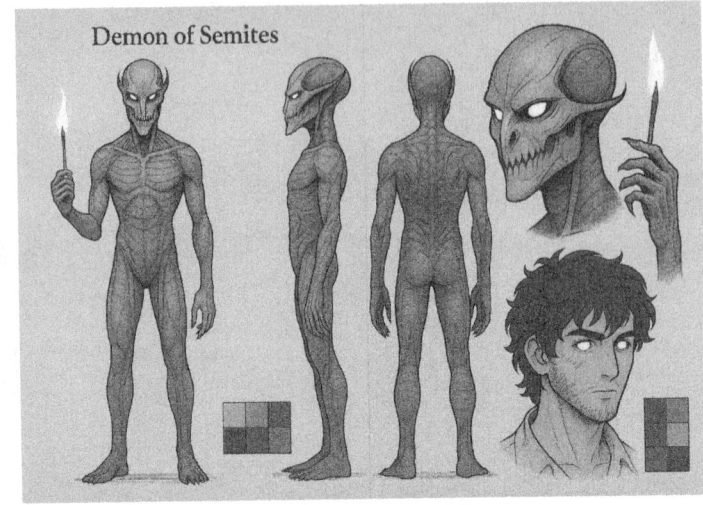

Made in United States
North Haven, CT
17 October 2025

80947317R00246